**Tor books by
Elizabeth Fackler**

Backtrail*
Billy the Kid*
Blood Kin

*forthcoming

BLOOD KIN

ELIZABETH FACKLER

TOR

A TOM DOHERTY ASSOCIATES BOOK
NEW YORK

TO BUD SONKA

This is a work of fiction. All the characters and events portrayed in this book are fictitious, and any resemblance to real people or events is purely coincidental.

BLOOD KIN

Copyright © 1991 by Elizabeth Fackler

Reprinted by arrangement with M. Evans and Co., Inc.

Cover art by Maren
Typesetting by AeroType, Inc.

A Tor Book
Published by Tom Doherty Associates, Inc.
175 Fifth Avenue
New York, N.Y. 10010

Tor® is a registered trademark of Tom Doherty Associates, Inc.

ISBN: 0-812-53338-0
Library of Congress Catalog Card Number: 91-31908

First Tor edition: October 1993

Printed in the United States of America

0 9 8 7 6 5 4 3 2 1

DECEMBER 1880

1

She was sixteen and lost in the desert. A rattler had spooked her horse and she'd been thrown, scrambling away from the snake only to watch her horse disappear. She was alone with no food or water, no blanket though it was winter and cold. All she had was a loaded .45 pistol stuck in her belt and whatever gumption she could summon.

She walked the rest of the day, heading northwest toward the mountains. At night she nearly froze, huddled in a crevice in the bank of an arroyo. Her jacket was suede and cut the wind but gave little warmth. She wore a shirt and trousers over high Apache moccasins because she'd dressed herself as a boy in her attempt to run away, hoping to cross the wilderness unmolested. She had even cut her hair, cropped it off so short at the back of her neck it barely showed beneath the floppy brim of her hat.

In the morning she saw the smoke from a campfire farther up the arroyo. Carefully she edged closer until she could see around a bend. A man hunkered near the flames a hundred yards away, sideways to her and drinking from a metal cup. Behind him, his sorrel horse shone like blood in the rising sun. She pulled her pistol from her belt and spun the cylinder so the hammer would fall on a live shell, then watched as the man stood up and doused the fire with the remnants of his coffee. She stifled her hunger for the coffee as she waited for him to turn his back.

He was a tall man, wearing a gunbelt fully loaded with cartridges that caught light as he moved. She saw a rifle in his saddle scabbard as he shook the pot out then enclosed it in a buckskin bag. It was a small pot but still he had to work to cram it into his saddlebags and she crept closer, holding her gun in both hands. She raised it, pointed at his back, and cocked it with her thumbs.

He heard the noise and looked over his shoulder, his eyes gray in the morning light.

"Put your hands up and move away from the horse," she said, as mean as she could.

He raised his hands halfway, laughing softly as he turned around. "Who the devil are you?" he asked.

"Never mind about me," she retorted. "You should be thinking of yourself."

"I am," he said. "What do you want?"

"Your horse."

"You're gonna have to kill me to take it."

"That wouldn't bother me none," she said, squinting in an effort to look mean. "Move away from it now."

She saw him look behind her for anyone else, then he looked at her pistol again and took a few steps away from the horse. She moved closer, holding the gun tight in her hands. "Step back further than that," she said.

"Maybe we can work out a compromise," he said.

"I'm not interested," she replied, scowling again. "Move away from it!" she ordered, struggling to keep her voice low so he wouldn't guess she was a girl.

"You gonna leave me afoot a hundred miles from nowhere?" he asked, taking a few more steps away.

"You'll make out," she said, sidling up next to the horse. She untied the reins from the protruding roots of the scrubby palo verde tree growing on the bank. The sorrel snorted as she threw the far rein across its withers, not taking her eyes from the man.

"You gonna leave me some water?" he asked.

"Maybe. If you back off a little more," she said. When he did, she said, "I don't like doing this, mister. But you can see it's one or the other of us."

"Doesn't have to be," he suggested. "The horse can carry us both."

"You're probably not going my way," she said.

"Why don't we talk about it and find out?"

"Where're you going?"

"El Paso."

"That's where I'm coming from, and not keen on going back."

"Well, I'd rather ride to where you're going than walk to El Paso," he said.

She liked the humor in his voice, but it also told her he wasn't much afraid of her gun, so she shook her head. "Can't risk it," she said, throwing a glance at the stirrup. It was way too long and she'd have to scramble to gain her seat. She hesitated, anticipating her approach, then jumped to grab the horn and pull herself up.

In the instant her back was turned, he covered the distance fast, took hold of her coat and hauled her to the ground, kicking the .45 so the gun flew across the sand. She fought with flailing fists but in five seconds she was beat, pinned beneath his weight and gasping for breath.

He laughed down at her for a minute, half crouching to keep his full weight off her chest. Visions of rape flashed through her mind but he stood up, retrieved her .45, opened and spun the cylinder so the hammer rested on a dead shell, then stuck the gun in his belt, not even bothering to draw his own. She looked at him fearfully a moment, then leapt up and ran. When she had almost gained the turn of the arroyo she heard him shout, "I'll still give you a ride."

She stopped and stared back at him. There was no hint of lust on his face and she thought he hadn't seen she was a girl. Maybe she could keep on fooling him long enough to get out of the desert. "Still going to El Paso?" she asked.

"Yeah. Can drop you in Mesilla, though."

She considered, then asked, "Why would you give me a ride after what I did?"

"Hate to see man or boy either one left afoot in the desert," he said.

She didn't let herself smile as she edged closer. "Will you give me my gun back?"

"When we get there."

"All right," she said.

"All right," he laughed, turning to his horse, swinging on and looking down at her.

She picked up her hat and brushed the sand off, then tugged it tight onto her head again, still eyeing him suspiciously. He held his hand down and she took it, feeling his strength as he easily lifted her up behind him. "What's your name?" he asked, turning the horse up the arroyo.

"What's it to you?" she sassed.

"Not a damn thing," he said.

2

They camped that night in another arroyo much like the one in the morning. The soil was gray caliche, the terrain a rough, rolling desert of rocks and gullies cut by flash floods. This late in the year, half the plants were dead, the rest cactus that wouldn't burn anyway. He gathered the hollow stalks of ocotillo and crumbled sticks from beneath creosote bushes, keeping an eye on her to make sure she didn't make a move on his horse. She watched him a while, then pitched in until they had enough to build a fire.

He scooped out a pit in the sand, piled the kindling carefully, then struck a match and watched the splinters catch as he hunkered close to the flames. She studied his face, the strong line of his jaw and his cheeks stubbled with whiskers, his mouth that during the day had often worn a smile which rarely touched his eyes, as gray as gunmetal. His hair was light brown and straight, falling to cover his coat collar turned up against the wind, his clothes expensive and clean, his boots fine quality, his spurs with small rowels, so she knew he didn't control his horse through violence. There was a roughness about him, though, that made her keep her distance, a coldness in his eyes, even when he laughed, that intrigued her.

Slowly he added more wood to the fire until a healthy blaze rewarded them with heat. Cautiously she moved to squat on the other side and hold her hands close to the flames. She caught him looking at her hands and she pulled them back, thrusting them into the pockets of her jacket.

He dug into his saddlebags and pulled out a hunk of cheese and a couple of oat cakes. Dividing the food, he took his share from the bandanna and pushed the rest over to her. She was so hungry she bolted it down, then looked up to see he'd barely started on his.

"I'm Seth Strummar," he said, handing over the canteen as he munched on an oat cake. "I don't care what your name is but if we're gonna travel together, it'd be nice to have a handle to put to you."

"Joe," she said.

He nodded, taking his canteen back and washing down the last of the meager meal. "You're welcome to share my blanket," he said.

"I'm all right by the fire," she answered, not looking at him.

"Suit yourself," he said, standing up and shaking out his bedroll. "If you change your mind in the middle of the night, you best holler. Anyone who comes on to me when I'm sleeping, I'm apt to shoot him."

She watched as he rolled himself in his blanket, keeping his rifle and both sixguns close to his body.

She thought he must be an outlaw to say something like that. No one else would live so wary as to anticipate shooting someone who came onto them while they were asleep. She added more stalks to the fire, watching him lying still in the warmth of his blanket. The wind was icy and she added all of the wood that was left, but the fire died fast and she shivered in the cold. She looked at him again wrapped in his blanket and she wanted to be warm more than anything right then.

She stood up and cautiously approached him. "Mr. Strummar?"

His eyes opened and she saw the barrel of his sixgun catch light from the coals of the fire. He looked at her shivering a few feet away, then slid over in his blanket. She dived under the shelter, trembling violently. He turned his back and she let herself nestle up against his warmth, shaking so badly she was afraid her bones were jabbing him and he would complain. But he said nothing and after a while she fell asleep.

In the morning, she woke up alone and struggled to remember where she was. She looked around and saw him standing a few yards away pissing into the sand. She stared at his pecker, never having seen one before though she'd heard plenty about the hurt they could inflict on a woman. He looked over and saw her watching and their eyes held as he finished and closed his pants. When he came back toward her, she huddled deeper into the bed in fear of him.

"You best move if you're coming," he said, flipping the blanket off, picking up his saddle and carrying them over to his horse. She got up and walked way down the arroyo to where it turned, then squatted beyond its protection as she pissed. When she came back around the bend he was already on his horse and she ran, afraid he'd leave her behind. He held his hand down to lift her up behind him, and they started off on their second day together.

After a mile or so, he asked, "You get in trouble in El Paso?"

"I got out of it," she replied.

"I can see that," he said. "You run off from your folks?"

"No," she lied, afraid he'd make her go back.

"Don't you have any?"

"Guess not," she said.

He turned around and looked at her, studying her face so long she was afraid he'd figured it out. But all he said was, "You're not big on conversation, are you?"

"Just because you gave me a ride doesn't mean I owe you anything," she retorted.

"No, I reckon not," he said, facing forward again.

After a minute she asked, "What're you going to El Paso for?"

"Going to do a job," he said.

"What kind of job?"

"Illegal kind."

She snorted delicately. "Figures," she said.

"What makes you say that?"

"Anyone who'd piss in plain sight of a stranger isn't exactly a high class gentleman."

Again he turned around and looked at her. "That unusual where you come from?"

"I never saw it before."

"Then you must not have been in El Paso long," he said.

"Why? Do they do it on the streets?"

"They do in most of México, and El Paso's mostly Mexican."

"I thought it was Texas," she sassed.

"Doesn't sound to me like you've ever been there," he said.

She kept quiet.

"I don't care where you've been, what you've done, or even who you are," he said, "so there's no need to lie to me."

Again, she was silent.

He sighed. "I don't suppose you have any money."

"You thinking of robbing me?"

"As I remember, you started off trying to rob me."

"That was a mistake," she said, knowing he was an outlaw now.

"Yeah, it was," he said. "I'm glad you see it that way."

"If I'd gotten away with the horse, I'd see it differently, though, wouldn't I?"

"You might. Until I caught up with you."

"Are you Geronimo's head tracker or something?" she scoffed.

"Something," he said.

She wondered who he was, then asked, "Have you ever been in El Paso before?"

"Yeah."

"Ever hear of a man named Jade Devery?"

"No. Who is he?"

"Nobody," she said.

He shook his head. "Gonna stop at a place up here for some food. That's the only reason I was asking about money."

"I sure am hungry," she replied with enthusiasm.

"Well, as small as you are, don't figure you'll eat much."

"Does that mean you'll feed me?"

"Reckon."

"Why would you do that?"

"We're traveling together, ain't we?" he said.

When he reined up in front of a station on the Butterfield Road, she slid off over the rump of the horse so he could swing down. Inside the low, smoky room, she saw several men look their direction with a wariness in their eyes that made her wonder again who she was traveling with. His name meant nothing to her, but her stepfather had kept her so cloistered she didn't hear much gossip. She followed Seth to a table in the corner where he took a chair with his back to the wall. She ordered what he did, watching him watch the other men in the room, even after the food arrived and he was eating. Though she'd been starving when they sat down, she couldn't finish the huge bowl of chile beans and pushed it away half-full.

There was a light of fun in his eyes when he looked at her. "You done?" he asked.

She nodded, watching him pull her bowl in front of him and finish what she'd left. She thought he ate neatly for an outlaw, using his spoon with precision and taking his time, though she couldn't see how he could digest anything in comfort since everyone in the room was watching him carefully from the corners of their eyes. She caught them looking at her too, and she almost laughed that they'd be so wary of a girl just because she was with him.

Seth paid for their meal with gold coin and she wondered where he'd got it, if he'd killed for it. He met her eyes as they walked back outside into the sunshine. "You sure got big eyes, Joe," he laughed. "Makes me think you've never seen the world before."

She didn't answer, afraid of betraying herself. He swung onto his horse and held his hand down again. As she let him lift her up behind him she caught herself wishing he wasn't going to El Paso so she could stay with him longer. She knew that was dangerous, though. Sooner or later he'd figure out she was a girl and, since he was an outlaw, he'd rape her as easily as not. She liked him and the idea wasn't totally abhorrent to her, but she didn't want to lose her cherry for nothing. Without virtue, life would be an upstream battle just to amount to anything more than a whore totally dependent on men's generosity. She intended to make her own way in the world. As much as she was beginning to like Seth, she decided she had to part company with him at her first opportunity.

His thoughts were moving along the same line. There was something intriguing about the urchin riding behind him, but he was going to El Paso to kill a man and didn't need any green kid along to foul him up. When he left the Butterfield Road he headed north again, intending to drop Joe off at a friend's place.

3

Half a day's ride north of Mesilla was the vineyard of
Ramon Gutierrez, an old outlaw pal of Seth's who'd
retired. On their last job together Ramon had taken a
bullet in his thigh that had come from close enough
range to go on through the saddle and kill his horse.
Seth had killed the attacker and kept the others at
bay while Allister went back and picked Ramon up
and they'd made good their escape, hightailing it out
of town with the bank's money.

But Ramon was superstitious and he'd taken it for
an omen. When they'd split the spoils in their cabin
the next night, he told Seth and Allister he was
pulling out. He was ten years older than Allister who
was that much older than Seth and he'd had enough,
he said, adding a dire warning that times were chang-
ing and they should do the same if they wanted to live
much longer. They'd both laughed at him but now

Allister was dead and Seth still alive only because he'd quit robbing banks.

They'd kept a woman at the cabin, a good cook who provided other services without being picky who asked, and Ramon had taken Esperanza with him when he'd ridden out of Texas. Now he cultivated his small vineyard alongside the Rio Grande. The vines were dead-looking in the middle of winter, but come spring they'd leaf up and he would age a decent red wine from the small sweet grapes. His home was a flat-roofed adobe surrounded by a wall. Seth reined up outside and hollered.

Ramon was thick around the middle, his beard grizzled with his fifty years. He opened the gate cautiously, then laughed. "Hey, Seth. It's been a long time."

Seth swung his leg over his horse's neck and slid down, extending his hand. "Good to see you, Ramon."

"Sí, compadre, come on in." He opened the gate wide, eyeing the boy sitting behind the saddle as Seth led his sorrel inside.

"This here's Joe," he said, nodding for the kid to get down.

He slid off over the horse's rump and didn't extend his hand to Ramon, who grimaced. "You get yourself an apprentice, Seth?" he asked.

"No, he tried to steal my horse yesterday. After he figured out that wasn't gonna happen, he accepted a ride."

Ramon grinned. "Steal a horse from Seth Strummar, that's funny, no?"

"I thought so," Seth smiled.

The kid looked sullen.

"Cheer up, Joe," Ramon said. "If you had stole his horse, you'd be dead now."

"I'd be halfway to Silver City," the kid retorted.

"Maybe," Ramon nodded. "In a grave in the desert." He laughed again. "I'm glad you stopped to see me, Seth. It gets lonely out here."

"Ain't you still got Esperanza?"

"Ah, the old cow. You think she's company?"

"Warm in bed," he smiled.

"Wait 'til you see her. She's bigger'n me now. Go on into Rosalinda's room. She ain't here no more."

"Thanks," Seth said, watching him lead the sorrel away. He turned to one of the doors along the portal, opened it and went on in. The room was small, with the same patchwork quilt on the bed and a full jug on the bureau. He dropped his gear, poured water into the bowl, then took off his coat and rolled up his shirtsleeves to wash. In the mirror, he saw Joe eyeing his rifle beside his saddlebags on the bed. "You wouldn't make trouble for my friends, would you?" he asked, not turning around.

Joe met his eyes in the mirror and said, "I don't want to be here."

"Go ahead and leave then," Seth said, dunking his face in the water and scrubbing the dust off. When he looked up from the towel, the kid was watching him. "Ain't you ever seen a man wash up, either?" Seth laughed.

"No," the kid said.

"What kind of place was it you lived, if men didn't piss nor wash?"

The kid shrugged.

"Raised by women, were you?" he asked, thinking that explained his shyness about his body.

"What's it to you?" Joe retorted.

Seth unbuckled his gunbelt and hung it across the back of the chair, lay the .45 on the seat out of the kid's reach, then pulled his shirttails out, unbuttoned the shirt, took it off and tossed it to cover the sixgun. "Someone's gonna knock that chip off your shoulder real hard if you don't straighten up," he said.

"You, maybe?" Joe scoffed.

"Maybe."

"I'd like to see you try."

"Would you?" he smiled.

The kid took a step back and Seth laughed. He moved to his saddlebags and pulled out his clean shirt, shook it loose and put it on. "Least you can wash," he said, reaching for his gunbelt again, "even if you ain't got a change of clothes."

"Maybe I'd like to do it in private."

"That's too bad. I ain't leaving you alone with the guns and I don't feel like toting them to the kitchen."

"I don't need to wash," Joe said.

Seth shrugged. "Let's go then." He opened the door and waited for Joe to go out first. Under the roof of the portal was a key and Seth turned the lock before pocketing it, then led the kid across the courtyard to the kitchen.

A rotund woman with a pretty face and thick black hair woven into a sleek bun at the back of her neck turned at his entrance. "Ay, Seth!" she laughed, coming close to give him a hug. She looked up at him with a saucy grin. "I thought you'd be dead by now."

"Thanks, Esperanza," he smiled, leaning down to give her a quick kiss. "It's good to see you, too."

"Who's this?" she asked, looking at the kid.

"Name's Joe," Seth said. "This is Esperanza." The kid didn't nod or smile, and Seth said, "He ain't real friendly."

"He looks like a girl," Esperanza said softly. "Such a pretty thing, no?"

Seth laughed, watching the kid blush, then hung his hat on a hook by the door and sat down at the table. "Ain't it getting close to Christmas?" he asked.

"Yesterday," Esperanza said, bringing a jug of wine and two glasses to the table. "You missed it."

"Not entirely," he smiled. "I got Joe, here. Guess he's a present from St. Nick."

Esperanza's laugh boomed through the room. "You must've been bad or he would've left you a woman."

"Like you said, he's pretty enough to pass."

Joe stood up and walked outside again. They both stared at the closing door, then looked at each other. "Touchy, ain't he?" Esperanza said.

"Figure he's been mistook for a girl more'n once," Seth said, pouring himself some wine. "And not in ways he liked, either."

Ramon came in. "That little sprout you brought is heading for the stable."

"Sonofabitch," Seth said, getting up and going after him. He found the kid already leading the sorrel out of the stall. Stopping in the door, Seth said, "That horse means a lot to me."

Joe whirled around, searching for paths of escape.

"Why don't you let him get some rest," Seth said. "He's carried your extra hundred pounds for two days now."

Joe did as told, then tried to walk out as if nothing had happened. Seth grabbed the kid's coat and threw him against the wall, watching him slide to the floor holding his head. "You try it again and I won't be so gentle."

Joe looked up at him, blinking back tears.

"What'd you expect me to do?" Seth asked. "Wish you better luck next time?"

"It isn't fair!" Joe cried. "All I need is a horse."

"Maybe if you work for Ramon, he'll pay you with one in a while."

"Doing what?"

"You'll have to ask him."

The kid stood up, brushed the straw off his clothes, and muttered, "Shoveling shit and forking hay."

"That's how men build up muscles. Seems to me you could use a few."

"All I need is my gun back," Joe retorted.

"You can't have that, either," Seth said, jerking his head for the kid to move toward the house.

They walked back into the kitchen, Esperanza and Ramon smirking at the kid. Joe walked sullenly over to the table and sat down. Seth picked up his glass of wine and stood leaning against the door, sipping it. "Pretty good, Ramon," he said. "This last year's harvest?"

"No, three years old," he answered. "Is my best."

He smiled, appreciating the compliment. "Tastes good after all the rotgut whiskey I've been drinking."

"So where you been, Seth?" Esperanza asked, patting tortillas at the stove.

"Tascosa," he shrugged. "Albuquerque, Dodge City. Around."

"Still looking for Pilger?" Ramon asked.

He nodded. "Heard he was in El Paso."

"Sí," Ramon answered. "Been there about six months now."

"What do you want with him?" Esperanza asked.

"I'm gonna kill him," Seth said, watching the kid's blue eyes turn toward him.

"I'll say a rosary for his soul," Esperanza laughed. "That way you won't spend so many days in purgatory for doing it."

Seth laughed, too. "What makes you think I ain't going to hell?"

"No one goes to hell for killing a pimp," she answered.

"Is that what he is?"

"Sí, him and his partner Jade Devery."

Seth refilled his glass with the red wine, watching the kid. "Looks like we got something in common," he said.

"Why are you gonna kill Pilger?" Joe asked.

"He led the mob that lynched my brother," he answered, watching the blue eyes flare with shock.

"I heard about that," Esperanza said sorrowfully. "Happened in Austin, didn't it? Ten years ago?"

He nodded, still watching the kid. "Back in May of 'seventy," he said. "Pilger's prob'ly feeling real safe about now."

"He's a fool if he feels safe long as you're alive," Esperanza said carrying bowls of chile verde con pollo and frijoles to the table. "Sit down and eat, Seth," she said with compassion, turning back for the stack of warm tortillas.

It was dark by the time they finished. The kid stood up and started for the door without any word of thanks. "Where you going?" Seth asked.

"To the outhouse," Joe answered defiantly.

"You go near the stable and I'll tan your hide."

"Huh," the kid said, walking out.

Seth looked back at Ramon, shaking his head. "He's a little short on manners."

"What're you gonna do with him?" Ramon asked.

"I was hoping to leave him here."

"We don't want him," Esperanza said quickly. "He's trouble and nothing else."

"Reckon you're right," he said.

Esperanza stacked the dirty dishes in the sink and came back to the table with a deck of well-worn cards. "I'll tell your fortune, Seth, eh?"

He laughed, pouring himself more wine. "Don't give me any bad news."

"Why not?" she asked, shuffling the cards with a light touch. "Would you rather ride into it blind?"

"Maybe your telling me will make it happen," he teased.

She shook her head. "The cards only reveal, they are not the cause. Will you cut the deck?"

He gave her a playful smile as he reached out and divided it into two stacks. She rejoined them, then took four cards off the top and laid them on the table in the form of a cross.

A horse whinnied and he stood up. "Sonofabitch," he said, walking out and crossing the yard fast. He found the kid in the stable again, this time with a black mare already saddled. "You're a little slow on the uptake," Seth said, walking toward him.

Joe leapt into the saddle and yanked the horse around, kicking it hard. Seth grabbed the bridle as the mare ran past, jerking the horse to a stop and hauling the kid onto the floor. He stood towering over him. "I oughta beat the shit out of you."

"What's stopping you?" Joe taunted.

"Maybe I feel sorry for anybody so stupid," he said. "Now get up and put that horse back."

Slowly the kid stood up, walked over and caught the reins, then cast a quick look out the door.

"You try it and I'll shoot you," Seth said.

"Maybe you'd miss," the kid said.

"Maybe."

"You don't understand," Joe argued. "I gotta get to Silver City."

"Why?"

"None of your business."

"Then it ain't my concern either, is it?"

"What if I could tell you something that'd make it easy to get at Pilger?"

"What of it?"

"Would you trade me a horse for the information?"

"No."

Joe watched him, maneuvering for an angle. "El Paso's got a marshal now. I've met him and he's a lot meaner'n you are."

"Unsaddle that horse or I'll show you how wrong you are," Seth replied.

The kid had to think about it, but finally he led the mare back to the stall and pulled the saddle and bridle off. He could barely carry the saddle over to the rack and Seth wondered how he'd managed to heft it onto the horse's back in the few minutes he'd been alone. The kid had gumption, he had to give him that.

"What do you think I should do with you, Joe?"

"You should've left me on the desert," came the sullen reply. "At least I was closer to Silver."

"You would've died out there without any water."

"What's it to you?" the kid cried in exasperation.

Seth looked at him with pity, wondering if his life had been so hard that the human compassion of not leaving someone to die of thirst was foreign to him. "Let's go back to the house," he said gently. "And while we're walking across the yard, you try and think of the words to thank my friends for the supper you ate."

"They didn't do it for me," the kid sassed.

"That's right. They did it for me, but you got the nourishment."

Ramon was still at the table, Esperanza at the sink washing the dishes. They both watched them coming back into the kitchen. Seth looked at the kid.

"Thanks for supper," Joe said.

"You're welcome," Esperanza said.

"Sit down," Seth told him, watching him take the same chair he had before, then sitting down himself, filling his glass with more wine and smiling at Ramon.

Ramon laughed. "You want to truss him up tonight, Seth? Leave him outside, maybe, teach him to appreciate kindness?"

"No, I'll keep him with me," he said. "I think we understand each other now."

But he knew he was overestimating his cut of the kid. When they went back to the room, he locked the door, then stood watching him build a fire in the hearth. "Maybe I should tie you up," he said.

"Who cares?" the kid said, not looking at him.

"I don't. If you want to spend the night on the floor with your hands tied to your feet, won't put a crick in my back."

Joe stood up and faced him. "Do I have another choice?"

"You can sleep in the bed with me."

"I'd rather sleep on the floor."

"Then I'll have to tie you up or you might try to get at the horses again and I don't relish chasing you in my underwear."

"You sleep in your underwear?"

Seth looked at him with pity. "I ain't gonna fuck you," he said. "Boys ain't my pleasure."

The kid turned around and hunkered in front of the fire. Seth undressed then put all the guns under his side of the bed and faced him. "Get in," he said.

Joe moved slowly to obey, sitting on the edge to take his moccasins off, then sliding under the blankets fully clothed. Seth shook his head, blew out the lamp and climbed in to lay flat on his back, a foot of space between them. "Why is it you're so ornery all the time?" he asked.

"Just defending myself," Joe answered defiantly.

"You mean this is all an act and you're really a sweet kid?"

Receiving no answer, Seth sighed, then turned his back and went to sleep.

In the middle of the night he awoke to hear Joe crying. The kid was still asleep, moaning and whimpering, thrashing his legs. One of his knees came up and jabbed Seth's side and he caught and held it, a skinny leg, all bone and not much else. The kid flailed out at him and Seth had to dodge his fists, then grabbed them and pinned them down on both sides of his head. Quickly the blue eyes opened, their color bright even in the dim light of the dying fire. He glared at Seth holding him down.

"You were having a nightmare," he said, letting loose and moving away again.

After a few minutes, Joe said softly, "I'm a lot of trouble to you, aren't I."

"Yeah, you are," he answered.

"Why do you bother?"

"Maybe I figure you were a Christmas present and I should make do."

For the first time since they'd met, the boy laughed, a feminine sound. "Guess your luck isn't any better than mine."

"We'll have to work on improving it," he said. "Go back to sleep."

Again there was a pause. "Seth?"

"Yeah?"

"Thanks for being so patient with me."

"You're welcome," Seth smiled.

4

In the morning, he left the kid asleep and took all the guns to the kitchen with him. Esperanza watched him laying the rifle and .45 on the table. "How's Joe?" she asked.

"Still in bed," he said. "Is the coffee hot?"

She nodded. "That boy is trouble, Seth. You should leave him behind."

"You already said you didn't want him here," he said, finding a cup and filling it with the fragrant dark brew.

She laid a slab of bacon into the pan where it sizzled with a quiet hissing sound. "You never asked what I saw in the cards last night," she said, not looking at him.

He carried his coffee to the window and looked out, knowing she would tell him whether he wanted to hear it or not.

"I saw deception in front of you," she said. "Something withheld that will bring danger."

He shrugged. "The world's full of deception."

"There was more. Death is riding behind you," she said, concentrating on flattening the bacon with a long fork. It sizzled and crackled in the heat. "He is so close you will feel the ice of his breath whisper in your ear."

He laughed. "Well, as long as he's behind me, can't see that it matters much."

"Joe rides behind you," she said, meeting his eyes now.

"You think he's death?" he scoffed.

She nodded, her eyes solemn.

"He's just a smart aleck kid," he said, watching her as he sipped his coffee.

"You think death is a big strong hombre? Or a pretty señorita maybe, flirting behind her fan?"

"Maybe it's a fat, old whore cooking in a kitchen," he smiled.

"I'm a fat, old whore, all right. That doesn't mean I'm wrong."

Seth wasn't superstitious but he still didn't like hearing a premonition of his death. He looked at the bright sky above the adobe wall and consoled himself that the day would be clear and dry for traveling. Joe came out of their room and walked across the yard to the outhouse. Seth watched him, thinking if he let his hair grow and put on a dress he'd pass for a girl well enough to fool just about anybody. Then it dawned on him that maybe he was. It would explain his shyness to piss in front of him or even undress enough to wash. And how weak he'd been when they'd tussled, even a hundred pound boy should have more strength than that.

Joe came out of the outhouse and looked longingly at the stable, and Seth waited to see if he'd try for a horse again. But the kid came on toward the house and pushed through the door into the kitchen. Seth looked for some of the softness left over from the gratitude of the night before but it was gone, the blue eyes as sassy and defiant as ever. He watched him cross to the table, assessing his gait in the light of his suspicion. The kid was limber and so lean it was hard to tell. He couldn't detect any swell of breasts under his shirt or bulge in his pants either one, but then the clothes were so baggy they could have been deliberate camouflage.

When Ramon came in, Seth asked if he had an extra horse he could part with. Ramon shook his head. "Just have the black mare. Rosalinda took the bay when she left."

"Where'd she go?" he asked.

"El Paso," he smiled. "You gonna look her up when you get there?"

"Think she'll be glad to see me?"

"After she puts a knife in your back," Esperanza warned.

Seth laughed. "Always was partial to women with a lot of spit," he said, looking at the kid.

The blue eyes met his without betraying an ounce of emotion.

"Sit down," Esperanza said. "At least you can eat before you leave."

When he led his saddled sorrel out of the barn, the kid was waiting by the hitching rail. Ramon was there, too, and Esperanza stood beside him, her arms folded across her voluminous breasts. Seth bent low to kiss her cheek. "Thanks," he smiled, but she didn't smile back. He shook hands with Ramon.

"Buena suerte," his friend said. "Come back when you've finished your business."

"I'll do that," Seth said.

He swung into his saddle and held a hand down for the kid. The small hand grasped his and the lithe body leapt on behind, the chest brushing against his back for a moment. Seth still couldn't feel any breasts beneath the buckskin jacket and he thought maybe he was making the same mistake others had, seeing femininity where there wasn't any. He didn't feel any cold breath of death on his ears either, though. He smiled at Ramon as he opened the gate, then turned his sorrel out of the yard, loping across the desert to catch the road following the river south.

All morning he tried to think of a question that would broach the subject of Joe's sex but nothing presented itself that wouldn't have been an insult if he was wrong. When they stopped at noon he almost walked off to piss in private but didn't trust Joe alone with the horse. Anyway, he figured, it wasn't something the kid hadn't seen before. And taken exception to, he remembered. He did turn his back when he unbuttoned his pants, then when he was done and had turned around again, the kid was out of sight. When he returned, his shirttails were half out so he'd dropped his drawers to do his business, but that in itself didn't prove anything. Seth took the bag of food Esperanza had given him and walked over to the riverbank to eat, letting the horse graze on the stubby winter grass behind him. After a minute, the kid came over and sat down nearby. Seth wrapped a tortilla around a hunk of cheese and handed it over, watching the kid eat.

"You have a problem?" the kid asked, seeing how he watched him.

"Maybe," Seth said.

"Me, you mean."

He nodded.

"When we get to Mesilla, I'll go my own way."

"Where you gonna get a horse?"

"I'll steal one."

"Hope you're better at it than last time."

"Never mind about me. I'm not your concern."

"No," Seth agreed. "You're not."

"On the other hand," the kid said, "I know the man you're looking to kill. Maybe I could help you out."

He wondered about Joe's life, if he knew both the marshal and the town's leading pimp. But all he said was, "Why would you?"

"In trade for a horse."

"Maybe I could buy you one," he said. "Wouldn't take much to carry you."

"Just as long as it gets me to Silver."

"What're you gonna do when you get there?"

The kid was silent.

"I admire a man can keep his mouth shut," Seth smiled. "Or a woman, either one."

The kid looked away, then after a minute looked back and asked, "You gonna find Rosalinda when you get there?"

"Prob'ly."

"You eager to have a knife in your back?"

He laughed. "Rosalinda might try to kill me, but she wouldn't try real hard."

"You're pretty sure of yourself, aren't you?" the kid teased.

"Women tend to like having me around," he smiled.

A soft flickering of agreement shone in the blue eyes and Seth figured he'd pinned the kid right. But if Joe felt safe passing herself off as a boy, Seth could give her that. He leaned back in the sun, pulling his hat low over his eyes and watching her from beneath it. She stared at the river a moment, then stood up and walked over to the water, knelt down and washed her face. Then she sat down crosslegged and held her head in her hands. Seth wondered what she was fighting and what she thought was waiting for her in Silver City. He told himself that when they got to Mesilla he should buy her a scrub horse and send her on her way.

They camped that night outside the pueblo. He could hear the guitars playing in the cantinas and had a thirst for some whiskey, but he didn't want to take Joe into a saloon or leave her alone with his horse, either one. So he shook his blanket out in the sand and went to bed feeling discontent.

She sat down a few feet in front of him. "Aren't we gonna have any supper?"

"We'll get breakfast in the morning," he said. She didn't move and he added, "I wish I had an extra blanket to give you, but I only got the one."

"You shared it before," she said softly.

"Yeah," he sighed, "and I'll do it again."

She came over and lifted the edge then slid in, closer to him than before. Seth tried to identify something feminine in her scent but there was only a sweaty smell coming off her dirty clothes.

"How come you to be traveling alone?" he asked.

"I'm not," came the hopeful reply. "I'm traveling with you."

He had to concede he was trapped in the truth of that. "I generally get something for my trouble," he said.

"You're welcome to anything I have," she whispered.

He rolled onto his side and pulled her closer, sliding his hand up under her coat and feeling the small breasts through her shirt. He smiled in the darkness. "Joe's a funny name for a girl."

"It's Johanna," she said, her voice coming ragged as he fondled her breasts beneath the soft cotton.

He unbuckled the belt holding up her trousers, not needing to unbutton them because they were so big he could easily slide his hand down against her skin. She was trembling. He felt her silken growth of hair as he nudged her legs apart then slid his finger inside until it bunted up against her hymen. "Shit," he said, pulling his hand out and turning his back.

"Don't you like girls, either," she taunted, though her voice nearly broke against tears.

"Not virgins," he muttered.

"Why not?"

"I don't like blood on my blanket," he said. "It draws bugs."

She was quiet a minute, then said, "We could do it in the dirt."

He rolled over and stared at her, barely able to make out the glimmer of her eyes in the dark. "Is that what you want?"

She was silent.

"If it isn't, why would you say such a thing?"

"Someone's gonna do it sooner or later," she sassed. "Might as well get it over with."

"That's a real sweet invitation," he said.

"I'm not sweet," she retorted.

"I noticed."

She was quiet again, then said, "I'm not sleepy. What are we gonna do, just lay here thinking about it all night?"

"You thinking about it, Johanna?" he smiled.

"I'll trade you," she said. "You can do it in the sand if you promise to buy me a horse."

"Maybe I'd do it and not keep my promise."

"I'd kill you then."

He laughed. "You are the most contrary kid I've run across. Why don't you just answer some questions and maybe I'll buy you a horse."

"What kind of questions?"

"Who's Jade Devery?"

"My stepfather."

"Why'd you run away from him?"

"Because I don't like him."

"A little short on details, but I'll accept it. What's in Silver City?"

She was silent.

"Two short answers don't add up to a horse," he said.

"My virginity ought to be worth a horse," she retorted.

"Yeah, but if I take it I'll pay hell getting rid of you."

"You think I'll fall in love with you or something?"

"Something," he said.

"So what? You can just get on your horse and ride away."

"I could've done that from the start."

"Why didn't you?"

"Maybe I felt sorry for you," he said.

"Big, bad Seth Strummar with the soft heart," she mocked.

"You're asking for it."

"You gonna beat me up? You can't rape me since I already offered my favors."

"Is that what you call what you offered me?"

"No, a goddamned curse!" she yelled.

"Damn straight," he said, turning his back again. But he had to work at not taking her up on her offer, whatever either one of them called it.

5

While she still slept wrapped in his blanket against the chill of dawn, Seth took her .45 from his saddle-bag and emptied all but one bullet from the chambers. He stuck the gun in his belt, then built a small fire from fallen ocotillo and managed to keep the flames going long enough to brew a pot of coffee. He was sipping the first cup, hunkered over the already dying coals, when she woke up.

Her eyes were so blue they were like pieces of reflected sky. Quiet as a mouse she rose from the blanket and walked away from the camp to do her morning business. By the time she returned, he had his sorrel saddled.

"Coffee's hot," he said.

She moved to squat by the coals and fill his cup. "Thought we were gonna get breakfast in town," she said.

"We are in a bit. First I want to find something out."

"What?" She watched him suspiciously over the rim of the cup.

"If I give your gun back, are you gonna shoot me?"

She looked at the .45 in his belt, then met his eyes again. "No," she said.

"Good. Let's see if you can hit anything." He extended the gun butt first toward her.

She set the cup down and stood up, accepting the pistol then popping the cylinder out and checking the chambers. Her eyes were indignant when she looked at him. "You took my bullets!" she accused.

"I'll give them back when I'm sure you won't shoot me."

"I could shoot you right now with just the one," she retorted.

"Yeah, but even if you hit me, I'd kill you before I was on the ground."

"Not if I hit you square between the eyes," she said.

"Want to try and find out?" he smiled.

"No," she said.

"Good. Try and hit the orange fluff on that Spanish Bayonet over there. Think you can do it?"

She spread her legs for balance, raised the heavy pistol with both hands, then sighted down the barrel quickly and pulled the trigger. The big gun boomed in the silence and Seth looked through the smoke and saw the dried blossom blown away.

"That's damn good, Johanna."

"You're surprised, aren't you?"

"Yeah, I am. But maybe it was luck." He tossed her another bullet, watched her slide it in without hesitation and cock the gun.

"Now what?"

"You choose."

She smiled mischievously, as if she might shoot him after all, then turned and scouted out the countryside. "How about that ocotillo way over yonder?"

"Kind of small, but if you think . . ."

The gun boomed again and half the ocotillo branch was gone.

"Goddamn," Seth whispered, impressed not only with her accuracy but her speed.

She laughed. "I've been practicing," she said.

"It shows," he nodded approvingly. "Come here."

He walked down to the riverbank then turned to watch her approach, the .45 stuck in her belt now. The gun helped her look like a boy and he intended to aid the illusion along a little. When she was beside him he took a handful of mud and smeared it on her face. She tried to back off but he held her with his hand on her shoulder, rubbing the dirt in to saturate her pores.

"You look more like a boy now," he said.

"Afraid you'll be tempted again?" she smirked.

He looked down at her standing there so saucy in front of him, feeling desire even then to find the femininity beneath the filthy clothes. "What makes you think I was tempted?" he smiled.

"You wanted me last night. I don't know why you didn't do it."

"A person can't go through life always giving in to their inclinations," he said with measured control. "You get a little older, you'll understand that."

"So you did want me!" she crowed.

He laughed. "Let's go eat," he said, walking back to the camp, dumping the coffee and putting the small pot in his saddlebag, then swinging onto the horse. He held his hand down and she leapt up behind him, snuggling close with her arms around his waist. "That's no way for a boy to ride," he said, not looking at her as he clucked the horse forward. She let go and he could feel the coolness on his back that came with the loss of her warmth, missing it already and knowing he'd made the right decision to send her on alone.

They rode into the plaza of Mesilla, past the San Albino church and the flat-roofed adobe homes ringing the plaza. He reined up in front of a cafe and she slid off the back so he could swing down. The restaurant had only one table open and they sat across from each other, enduring the scrutiny of the other customers who looked offended that anyone so filthy would eat inside. But the guns both of them wore squelched any comments. The waitress came over and asked, "What'll it be, boys?" and Seth smiled at the dirty-faced urchin across from him. They both ordered ham and eggs, then drank more coffee while waiting for their food.

Seth watched the other people in the cafe and couldn't tell that any of them suspected his companion was a girl. If they had they would have stared harder, still being discreet because of his presence, but such an ill-kept girl in trousers would have caused a commotion at least behind their eyes. The people only glanced their way, however, and Seth thought she had a chance to make it to Silver City on her own.

When they'd finished their breakfast, he paid for the meal and they walked out to his sorrel and led it across the plaza. He'd seen a livery on the way in and noted the corral held a scruffy pony, too small for any man. When he saw the hostler forking hay over the fence, Seth stopped and looked down at Johanna. "You think you could get along with that pony?"

"Kind of small," she said.

"So are you," he laughed. "Keep your mouth shut and let me do the talking."

He approached the hostler, who hadn't failed to notice them standing there. "You got any horses for sale?" Seth asked.

"Yeah," the man said, eyeing his sorrel. "Ya lookin' fer a trade?"

"No, a mount for the boy."

The hostler turned around and studied the horses in the corral. "Sell ya that dark bay geldin' fer eighty," he said.

"Too much horse for him," Seth said.

"It is not," Johanna piped up.

"I told you to keep quiet," he warned.

The hostler smiled. "Well, if it's a gentle horse you're wantin', how 'bout that gray mare fer sixty-five. She's got a smooth gait on 'er."

"Too much money," he said.

"Aw, Seth," Johanna complained. "You're gonna put me on a burro before you're done."

"I told you to keep your mouth shut," he said again.

"I could come down a bit," the hostler said.

"What about that bay pony?"

"He's got a mean streak. Not sure the boy could handle 'im."

"How mean?"

"He's been mistreated. Will bite when ya come close, then buck when yer on. Run off and leave ya in the dirt if ya lose your seat. I'll let ya have 'im for twenty and glad to see 'im go."

Seth frowned. "I don't know. Is there anyone else around here sells horses?"

The hostler sniffed loudly. "Let ya have the mare fer sixty, but I ain't makin' no money on 'er."

"I'll give you fifty if you throw in an outfit."

"Jesus, mister, I'd be bleedin' all over the yard if'n I did that."

"Don't need nothing fancy."

The man squirmed his face around a minute. "Got an Apache saddle I could let go, reckon. And a bridle that's been mended once or twice, but it's strong."

"Throw in a nosebag and three days' grain and you got a deal."

"Won't be makin' no profit a'tall," the man scoffed.

"Gold coin, American."

The hostler's eyes lit up. "Reckon that'll be all right," he finally said.

"What do you think, Joe? That gray mare good enough for you?"

"Yeah!" she laughed, sounding feminine again.

The hostler looked at her hard.

"Saddle it up," Seth said. "We're in a hurry."

The man climbed the fence into the corral and Seth walked back to his sorrel. He dug into his saddlebags for the two bullets he had left for her .45 and handed them over, watching her slide them into the chambers. Then he took a Gold Eagle from his pocket and gave it to her.

"That's sixty dollars I've spent on you," he said. "You be sure and make it to Silver in one piece."

"You mean you're letting me go?" she asked with surprise.

"You can make it back to Ramon's tonight. You were so sour they won't be glad to see you but if you tell them I said so, they'll put you up. Try to be nice, though. It's my welcome you're wearing out when you're sour, remember that."

She was staring down at the gold coin as if she didn't believe it was real. He halfway expected her to bite it.

"He's got a .45 and will sell you some more ammo. Don't spend all that on bullets, though, or you'll go hungry."

When she looked up, tears glimmered on her lashes. "How can I ever thank you, Seth?"

"By promising you won't try to steal nothing from nobody, ever again. And don't cry. Boys don't, you know."

She nodded, blinking back her tears. One fell anyway and glistened in the sunlight on her cheek. She wiped it off with her sleeve, leaving a streak that looked like warpaint. "I promise," she said.

He smiled, lifting her hand and dropping the fifty dollars in beside the Gold Eagle. "Don't forget the grain," he warned. "You won't find much forage on the desert and you'll make better time if your horse is well fed." Then he turned around and swung onto his sorrel.

"Aren't you gonna kiss me goodbye?" she whispered.

"Now, wouldn't that look peculiar?" he laughed, holding down his hand, almost wishing she was going to leap up behind him again. But she shook with her tiny one, keeping both moccasined feet firmly planted in the dust. "Hope you find what you expect in Silver," he smiled.

"I will," she promised. "Good luck, Seth."

He nodded and turned his sorrel away, kicked it into a lope heading south and didn't look back. If he pushed it, he could be in El Paso by dark and sleep with Rosalinda that night.

6

El Paso was a squat, adobe town with a tenderloin district bigger than the respectable part. The stark desert mountains towered on either side of the famous pass, east and west, with the river a broad expanse bordered by bosques. In the light of the rising moon, the Rio Grande was as silvery as its reputation, though Seth knew that come daylight it would be the color of mud, which it mostly was in the dead of winter.

The streets were wide, hard-packed caliche, crowded with all breed of men. The railroad was due to arrive early next year and entrepreneurs of every moral degree had flocked to the town in hopes of making easy money. Along with them had come the ladies of the night and south Utah Street was lined with bawdy houses, degenerating into cribs as they approached the border. In one of them, hopefully the better class, Rosalinda probably worked. She might have changed her name, though, and he hadn't seen her in over two years so she could have changed her hair color, too. He tied up in front of the Ruby Saloon and went in for a whiskey.

The last thing he wanted was to announce his presence but a man turned as he came through the door and shouted loud enough for the people on the street to hear, "Seth Strummar! I'll be goddamned!"

Heads turned down the long, narrow room and he could tell that some of them recognized his name. The man was coming forward with his hand outstretched as if Seth would be glad to see him, but he wouldn't have been, even if he'd known him. He stared at the stranger's face, keeping his own hand loose by his gun. "Don't think I know you," he muttered.

"George Cullin," the annoying man boomed. "Don't you remember me? I was a friend of your brother's."

Seth shook his head. "I don't have a brother."

Cullin's face fell into mock sorrow as his hand dropped back by his leg. "Was a shame, what happened," he murmured softly. "No man deserved it less, that's for damn sure. Why don't you let me buy you a drink? For old times' sake?"

"I don't remember any old times with you. Thanks anyway." He moved away, feeling the man's eyes on his back. When he turned around at the bar, Cullin was gone. Straight to Pilger, if Seth had taken his cut right. Any man that would shout his name across a crowded barroom wasn't a friend and wouldn't likely waste time taking the news of his arrival to the man in town who would care most and be pleased least. Seth ordered a whiskey and sipped it, studying the room.

Nothing but hardcases filled the saloon. No city-slicker dapper gents in suits and bowlers for the

Ruby. These men all sported guns and looked mean enough to be adept at using them. He saw a burly, red-headed man coming toward him, the first repercussion of his welcome.

"Howdy," the man drawled with a nasal Midwestern twang.

"Evenin'," Seth said, watching him as he finished the whiskey.

"Let me buy ya another," the man said.

"Why?"

The smile spread real slow, revealing long horse teeth. "Maybe ya don't recognize me. Red McDowell."

Seth shrugged.

"Ya never heard of me?"

He shook his head.

Red laughed. "Well, I heard of you. What brings ya to El Paso?"

"Just minding my own business," Seth said.

The man's ugly laughter thundered through the crowded room, turning heads again. Seth cursed beneath his breath.

"How's that?" Red asked. "I didn't catch what ya said."

"I said I don't know you and don't care to."

Red's smile wavered. "If Allister was here, he'd tell ya I'm square."

"Allister's dead."

"Was a corker how he died, wasn't it? I heard tell ya hung the woman what killed him."

"You hear a lot of stories when you live in the gutter," Seth said.

The smile was gone now. "You're a mean sonofabitch, ain't ya."

Seth looked at his empty glass with regret, wishing he'd started looking for Rosalinda and not come into the Ruby. But there was no help for it now. "You got a problem with that?" he asked.

"Uh-uh. Least I won't in a minute," Red said, backing away, his hand poised by the sixgun on his hip.

"I got no quarrel with you," Seth said in a low voice, but the saloon quieted down.

"I jus' can't stand a man who ain't friendly," Red laughed. "I come over and offer to buy ya a drink and ya insult me. Seems you're in need of a lesson in manners."

"You gonna give it to me?"

Red nodded, taking a few more steps away.

"You're gonna be dead if you don't back off more'n that."

"Allister told me you was better'n him," Red smirked. "I'm better'n Allister was in his prime and I been waitin' a long while to find out how good ya really are."

The room was silent now, all eyes pinned on the two men facing each other like cocks in a pit. Seth was sick of this kind of challenge. It didn't accomplish anything but make him unwelcome when it was over, and he'd hoped to lie quiet until he'd done what he came for, but that hope was already gone. "I don't want this fight," he said loud enough for everyone to hear. "If you back off, I'll forget I ever saw you."

"Like ya forgot ya ever heard of me? I know Allister told ya of me so that was a lie, and I figure what ya jus' said is, too."

Seth waited. It seemed like a hundred times he'd faced a man like this and as many times walked away. One day he wouldn't but this wasn't it, he felt confident of that. The seconds ticked by, audible from the clock on the wall.

"Why don'cha draw?" Red sneered.

"Got no reason to kill you," Seth said.

Red smiled with derision. "I saw your brother hang. Know what his last words were?"

"Nothing your tongue could spit out."

"He cursed ya. Said, 'Goddamn Seth's soul to hell.' Then someone slapped the horse and he was kickin' thin air." Red grinned. "The rope didn't break his neck and he strangled. Was an awful sight."

Seth could feel his hand's desire, but he held it back.

"Takes a lot to rile ya, don't it?" Red laughed.

"More'n your lies."

"Ya callin' me a liar?"

"Three times now."

The big freckled hand reached for his gun. Seth drew and fired square into the ugly scowling forehead. Red fell with a thud, his gun clattering to the floor.

Seth let his gaze flit around the room for any back action, then holstered his gun and flipped a coin on the bar to pay for his drink. It rattled in the silence as he met the barkeep's eyes. "Tell the law I'm in the Central Hotel. You saw I didn't want it."

The barkeep nodded and Seth walked back out to his horse, who nickered when he came close. He swung on and trotted to the south side of the plaza, left his sorrel at the Exchange Corral because he knew they fed their animals well, then walked over to the little plaza at the head of El Paso Street.

The Central Hotel was an ancient building of two-foot-thick adobe ringed by an arched colonnade. The rooms were small and dark, opening off a center courtyard that was barren with dust, and usually half of them were empty because the structure was decrepit and poorly maintained. This night, however,

Seth was told he was lucky to get a room as the desk clerk crowed about the railroad crowding the town with new business.

Seth wasn't happy to see the railroad pushing so far west, knowing it brought a loss of freedom for men like him who lived without the comforts and complications of kinship. He felt melancholy as he found his room along the front, locked the door and walked over to the window to stand looking through its dusty panes as he reloaded his gun.

El Paso Street was a wide avenue leading to the border and crowded with every breed of riffraff in the Southwest, every one of whom would know soon, if they didn't already, that he was in town. Including Pilger, who would sweat his guts out at the news. But first there was the law to deal with.

His name was on half a dozen wanted posters still valid in Texas, carrying a substantial reward for his body, dead or alive. Johanna had told him El Paso finally got itself a lawman and Seth wondered if whoever it was would have the balls to try and collect. It didn't take him long to find out. Half an hour after he'd closed the door, he opened it again to a man with a big silver shield on his coat.

"Seth Strummar?" the man behind the badge asked.

He nodded.

"I'm George Campbell, town marshal here. Mind if I come in for a minute?"

"A minute," Seth said, stepping aside to let him pass.

The man came in and closed the door. "I come alone, hope you appreciate that."

Seth waited.

"Red McDowell was killed in the Ruby Saloon a short bit ago. I talked to the barkeep and he said you killed him fair, that McDowell picked the fight and drew first. I don't guess you got anything to add?"

He shook his head.

"You know any reason why McDowell would challenge you?"

"No."

"You're a wanted man in Texas. I guess you know that."

"This is El Paso," he said.

"Still Texas."

"So?"

Campbell walked across to the window and looked toward México. "This is a loose town, lot comes down that another community wouldn't tolerate. I ain't a gunman, neither, so there's some that say I'm not the right man to be marshal here. They want to hire someone like you and maybe they're right." He turned around and faced him. "But for the time bein', I got the job. It would make things easier on me if you'd just ride on."

"I will, when I've done what I've come for."

"And what's that?"

"I'm looking for a friend of mine."

"Who?"

"Rosalinda Sisquieros. You know her?"

Campbell shrugged. "Lot of women workin' Utah Street. Is she that kind?"

"Reckon."

"There's a Rosalinda works at Annie Walker's. Think the last name's Montoya, but most of 'em change their names." He studied Seth a minute. "I can let you slide for now. But any more killin' and I'm gonna have to do something. You can appreciate I don't hanker to tangle with you, but I will if I have to, and I won't do it alone. You get my drift?"

He nodded.

"So you look up your friend and don't dawdle. Then maybe we can all greet the new year in good health." He moved to the door, opened it and turned at the threshold. "I heard about what happened to your brother, and I want you to know it was a damn shame and not fair in anyone's book. But more killin' won't bring him back. You understand that, don'cha?"

"Yeah, I do."

Campbell nodded. "Hope I don't have to come lookin' for you again."

He closed the door and Seth listened to the lawman's boots crossing the hard-packed dirt of the courtyard. Then he picked up his hat and went in search of Annie Walker's bordello.

7

He found the bawdy house on the corner of an alley and Utah Street, a respectable-looking edifice with a wide front veranda empty in the chill of the winter evening. The parlor was decorated for Christmas with piñon boughs stuck on the walls sporting naked angels with halos. A dark, corpulent woman with thick makeup camouflaging her age didn't add to the cheer. She laboriously gained her feet and was about to yell up the stairs for the girls when Seth stopped her.

"I'm looking for Rosalinda," he said.

"She's feelin' poorly," she cooed. "Won't one of the other girls do?"

He shook his head. "Tell her Seth Strummar's asking to see her."

The black eyes flashed more of their whites and he knew she'd heard of the killing already. "I'll tell her," she answered sharply, "but I'll be surprised if she sees ya."

He just smiled, knowing she was wrong. After a few minutes she came back down the stairs, her face pinched with disdain. "Cost ya ten bucks," she said ungraciously.

He dug the coin out of his pocket and tossed it to her.

She examined it carefully, then said, "Third room on the right."

Brushing past the unpleasant woman, Seth wondered why Rosalinda always worked for such ugly madams. He climbed to the second story and pushed through her door without knocking.

She was sitting in a pink kimono, in front of her dressing table, watching him in the mirror as she stuck a pin into the auburn hair piled on top of her head. She sat stock still a minute, then snarled, "You low-crawling, slimy-gutted, sonofabitch."

"Nice to see you, too, Linda," he smiled, shutting the door.

"How'd you find me?"

"Town marshal said you were here," he answered, dropping his hat on her bed then sitting down beside it, leaning back on his elbows as he watched her.

"I don't have to ask why you was speaking to him." When she turned around on her stool to face him he saw she'd been crying. "That was my fiancé you killed."

"You tell him about me?"

"I may have mentioned your name, with nothing good connected to it."

"That explains why he came on so strong. Wasn't anything I wanted."

"Why'd you have to come back just when I had something good going?"

"Seems to me I did you a favor. Being wife to a shitface like him wouldn't have gained you much."

She threw a jar of face cream at him but he ducked. "I wish I was a man," she cried. "I'd kill you myself."

He laughed, standing up and pulling her to her feet, holding her close though she squirmed to escape him. "I'm glad you ain't, Linda," he smiled. "We wouldn't have nearly as much fun."

"You always did have a rough idea of fun," she said, finally standing still.

He leaned to kiss her but she turned her head away. "I been gone more'n two years," he laughed. "Ain't you got a warmer welcome than that?"

"You said you'd be gone a month!" she retorted.

"I told you not to wait."

"Fucked me like I was the Virgin Mother then said you wouldn't be back. It's not my fault I believed your actions more'n your words."

He kissed her then, feeling her warm to him again. "You didn't really love that red skunk, did you?"

"No," she pouted.

"Let's go to dinner, then. I'm starved."

"Will you take me to the best in town?"

"Okay," he laughed. "But don't expect a tip later, I'm near broke."

"Spent it all on another woman, no doubt."

"Put your dress on," he smiled, letting loose of her and walking over to the window, looking out on the back yard and the saddled horses of the house's clientele.

She sat in front of the mirror, patting powder over the effect of her tears. "What are you gonna do when you get old, Seth? Find a whore to support you?"

"You offering?" he asked, watching her.

She stood up and untied her kimono then tossed it on the bed beside his hat. She wore a corset over her shimmy. "Not unless you marry me, and you ain't gonna do that, are you?"

"No."

She laughed bitterly, crossing to her chiffonnier. "Think I'll wear my red dress in commemoration of my near widowhood." She pulled the tight-skirted frock over her head and turned her back for him to hook her up, then said, "Goddamn, Seth, if you'd waited two more days to ride into town, I *would* be a widow. And Red fought in the War, I'd have a pension."

"Wasn't my fault," he said, connecting the row of tiny hooks and eyes. "You shouldn't have told him about me and he wouldn't have picked a fight."

She was quiet as he worked his way up the back of her dress, then said softly, "I've missed you, Seth."

He snorted, closing the last hook. "Couldn't have missed me much if you were gonna marry Red McDowell."

"Maybe I was trying to get over a broken heart," she said, turning to face him.

She was lovely in the elegant gown, her breasts half-revealed over the satin bodice shimmering like fresh blood. He traced the voluptuous curves with his fingertips. "Reckon there's a heart in there some-where," he smiled. "Let's go eat."

Annie Walker stared at them so incredulously as they came down the stairs that Seth had to laugh.

"He's an old friend," Rosalinda explained.

"Huh!" Annie said, letting her gaze slide down his body, stopping just a second on his gun, then meeting his eyes again. "Seems like a dangerous one to me."

"Those are the best kind," she laughed. "I'll be back later. Or will I?" she asked, looking at him.

He shook his head.

"I'll be back tomorrow, Annie," she laughed again. "Seth's gonna help me get over my loss."

"He didn't pay for an all-nighter," the madam said.

"I'm in mourning," Rosalinda protested. "I ain't working tonight."

"You lay under a man, you're workin'," she warned.

Seth took a Double Eagle from his pocket and tossed it to the fat woman. "You satisfied?"

Her smile was friendly all of a sudden. "Come back anytime, Mr. Strummar."

He opened the door and guided Rosalinda out. "Goddamned vulture," he muttered on the veranda.

She laughed. "Just looking out for herself and her girls."

"Ain't an old friend got a right to take you to dinner?"

"Not if he's a man, which you are," she smiled.

"How much is this restaurant gonna cost?"

"Are you really that broke, Seth?" she asked, solicitous now.

"I only got about a hundred dollars on me," he admitted.

"Dinner won't be more'n that," she said.

"It better be a damn sight less," he said.

Later, as she lay all sweaty in his bed in the Central Hotel, she watched him cross the room half-naked to fetch the bottle and she felt an unpleasant suspicion that his being in El Paso had nothing to do with her. Despite the fact that he'd just returned, she felt she'd lost him. Softly she said, "You've changed, Seth."

"How do you mean?" he asked, handing her a drink.

She dropped her lashes coyly, hiding her confusion. "Was a time I'd be sore all over right now."

He just smiled, half-filling his own glass then carrying it over to the window and looking out as he sipped it. The street was still crowded with revelers, though it was well past midnight. "You know a man by the name of Travis Pilger?" he asked.

"Yes," she said coldly, her suspicion confirmed.

"Know where he does business?"

"Annie Walker's Bordello and the Rio Bravo Dance Hall."

He turned around fast. "He owns you?"

"Please, Seth," she said, punching the pillows then sitting up to lean against them. "I work for the man, is all. Besides, Jade Devery owns the brothel. Pilger's just his manager. He's a full partner with Devery in the North Pass Saloon, though."

"Do you know Devery?"

"Jade's a regular caller of mine."

"What's he like?"

"Like you used to be," she smiled, "hard on his women."

"Know his daughter?"

"She's his stepdaughter," she answered with a sharp edge, "and a little young for you, isn't she?"

"Never met her. How old is she?"

"Sixteen," she answered, watching him carefully. "Why are you interested?"

"He's partner to Pilger, is all."

"And what's Pilger to you?"

"An old connection from Austin. You know where Devery lives?"

"Sure. He's got the biggest house on Montana Street. The one with the gables on the roof."

He came back and stood over the bed, smiling

down at her. "Your hair looks pretty falling over your breasts like that."

"Why, thank you, Seth," she answered with surprise. "You're short on praise. Long on questions, though, among other things."

He laughed, dropping his trousers and sliding under the blankets beside her again.

8

In the early light of dawn, Seth woke up to someone knocking. He pulled his pants on and carried his gun when he crossed the room to open the door. Johanna stood there, wearing a modest, peach-colored frock with a high neck.

"Mornin', Joe," he smiled, pleased to see her though he knew he shouldn't be. "Thought you'd be in Silver City by now."

She looked past him at the woman asleep in his bed. "Is that Rosalinda?"

He nodded.

"Can I talk to you?" she asked, her voice trembling with need.

He saw the hurt in her eyes and knew she'd come for help. "Wait for me on the side veranda," he said, closing the door.

As he finished dressing, he asked himself how far he'd be willing to go for her. He'd gotten himself in

trouble before trying to help young girls, delayed his
purpose of finding Pilger and nearly lost himself in
the quagmire of need that women liked to throw in
his path. Rosalinda had pulled him out of the last
mess, and then he'd abandoned her because she'd
become just as much of a trap. She appeared to be
soundly asleep now, and he admired her beauty but
it also triggered a warning inside him. As before, she
stood in opposition to the young girl of virtue, and it
made him feel weary to be facing it all again. He
buckled on his gunbelt and walked out, across the
still-shadowed courtyard and through the narrow,
arched passage to the veranda, blindingly bright.

Johanna was sitting on a rawhide settee, staring
down the road toward México. She looked up at him
and they both smiled warily.

"What're you doing back in El Paso?" he asked,
sitting down beside her with a foot of emptiness
between them.

"Jade's gunman caught me just north of Mesilla,"
she answered.

He could see the answer in her eyes but he asked
anyway, "Did he hurt you?"

She nodded, watching him. "He raped me," she
said.

He winced, touching her hair where it was cropped
off so short at the back of her neck. "You tell Devery
he did it?"

She nodded again, a tear falling on her cheek. "He
says I have to marry the man."

Seth looked down the street to the river and Paso del
Norte sprawling up the hill on the other side, telling
himself the girl's problems were none of his own.

She said, "I wish I was a boy. I'd run away and
become an outlaw."

He laughed gently, meeting her eyes again. "You think that's an easy life?"

"Couldn't be worse than marrying a man I hate," she said. "I'm not gonna do it. He can't make me, can he, Seth? I mean, no preacher'll marry a girl screaming that she doesn't want to do it."

Her blue eyes were begging for help and he figured the least he could do was advise her to the best of his knowledge. "Judges can marry people, and I ain't heard of one yet that can't be bought off."

She stared at him in desperation, then leaned forward with a sob and buried her face in her lap as she cried. If he touched her now he was in, he knew that, but he reached out anyway and lifted her against his chest, holding her close. Finally she was quiet and sat up away from him, reaching into the pocket of her skirt for a handkerchief, drying her eyes and blowing her nose, then giving him a brave smile that tore at his heart.

"Sorry," she said softly. "I just want to get away from him but every time I try he catches me and brings me back. He punishes me in ways I'd be too ashamed to tell anyone, and he says terrible things about my mother. She was a fine lady from a good family. When my grandfather found out she'd married Jade, he changed his will so everything would come to me instead of her. It's only 'cause of my inheritance that Jade hangs onto me so hard."

"Is your grandfather still alive?" he asked, thinking the old man might be an easy out.

"No. I haven't any family. All the money's in a bank somewhere."

"You don't even know where?"

She shook her head. "I know the lawyer's name. He's in San Antonio." She smiled mischievously, looking for the first time like the kid he'd known as Joe. "That's where Pilger went," she said.

"You know that for sure?"

She nodded. "I heard him and Jade talking, that's how I knew where you were."

"How'd they find out?"

"I told you I know the marshal," she smiled. "He's a friend of theirs and he told them."

Seth stood up and walked over to the edge of the veranda, watching a man tack a notice on a tree at the corner. San Antonio was crawling with Rangers, and unlike the law in El Paso, they wouldn't let him slide if they got their hands on him. But there was only one thing he wanted yet to do and that was kill the man responsible for lynching his brother. He turned around and looked at the girl, knowing he should send her away but asking instead, "You got any proof of who you are?"

"I have my baptismal certificate and a letter from my grandfather," she answered, her eyes shining with hope.

He hesitated, then sighed. "Looks like I'm going to San Antone. If you want to ride along, I'll take you."

"You mean it?" she whispered.

He nodded. "If we left at noon, how long do you think it would take Devery to discover you were gone?"

"Joaquín would cover for me. He could say he sent me on an errand and Jade probably wouldn't ask again. He's giving a party tonight and I don't think he'd check on me until tomorrow."

"Who's Joaquín?"

"A kid who works for us."

"And he'd risk making Devery mad?"

"He's Mexican," she laughed, "and not afraid of anything. He's the one who helped me run away to Silver City. I told him I had kin there who'd take me in but it was a lie. I just saw it on a map and thought it sounded pretty. It was Joaquín's idea that I dress like a boy and he's the one taught me to shoot. We're always pulling things over on Jade."

"Why don't you ask Joaquín to take you to San Antone?"

She looked away. "He has another love," she said.

"But otherwise you would?"

She looked up to meet his eyes and he caught himself thinking hers were the same blue as the desert sky at dusk. "It's you I want," she whispered.

"Why?" he scoffed, not liking the response her words evoked in him.

"I've never met anyone like you, Seth. You're strong and gentle at the same time. You came here to kill a man yet didn't take your pleasure from me because I was a virgin, even though I offered it and you wanted to. You bought me a horse after I tried to steal yours! How many men would've done that? And your friends, Esperanza and Ramon, they'd do anything for you. So would I."

"When we get to San Antone," he warned, "I'll take you to that lawyer and we'll part company."

She smiled, standing up and coming close. "I'll have the whole way there to please you."

He laughed despite himself. "I'm a dangerous man, do you understand that? You won't be safe traveling with me."

"I can pull my own," she laughed. "I'm a good shot, remember?"

He nodded. "You'll find shooting at lawmen a little different than cactus."

"I'll be good cover for you, though. I mean, no one will expect you to be traveling with a kid."

"Least of all me," he said.

She touched the front of his shirt, smiling up with her deep blue eyes. "We could go to México after. My grandfather was a wealthy man and whatever money's there, it's gotta be a lot or Jade wouldn't hold onto me so hard. We could get married and live in a grand hacienda. Doesn't that sound fine, Seth?"

He touched her cheek, soft and fresh with youth. "More'n I deserve," he said. "You go home and pack all the things you mentioned that prove who you are. Then meet me at the end of Montana Street at noon."

"I'll be there," she said, standing on tiptoe and kissing him quickly. Then she ran from the portal and down the street.

He stood watching her disappear from sight, telling himself he was a fool, but sometimes it was the fool who had the last laugh. He had to stop himself from yelling after her to be careful.

9

Earl Mawson had been a Texas Ranger half his life. He'd ridden under McNelly on the gulf end of the Rio Bravo in '75 when the illustrious captain had defied orders from Washington and invaded México to retrieve stolen cattle. Recently he'd ridden into México again under the leadership of George Baylor to route the renegade Apaches with Victorio. The war chief had been killed and the Rangers had returned to their garrison in Isleta, ten miles downriver from El Paso, only to ride out almost immediately in pursuit of the remnant of the band into the Guadalupes. Mawson hadn't gone on that foray, and when he heard Seth Strummar was back in Texas, he was glad he wasn't off chasing Indians.

The various bounties offered for the outlaw's capture amounted to two thousand dollars but Mawson wasn't interested in the money. He saw Strummar as a scourge on decent people and a defiler of the name

Texan, and Mawson meant to stop him. He'd capture and take him back to Austin for trial if he thought he had a reasonable chance of achieving that end, but he didn't expect it to happen that way.

In his years under McNelly, Mawson had learned that kindness and mercy weren't concepts desperados understood. He considered himself a reasonably good man. If the circumstances warranted leniency, he wasn't above letting criminals off on the promise of good behavior. Those were young bucks not yet set in their ways, though. Seasoned killers were another breed altogether.

Seth Strummar was a seasoned killer in anybody's book. No one knew for certain how many men had died from his gun, but the estimates ranged as high as two dozen and a woman was included in that tally. The story was she'd killed Ben Allister and Strummar had taken his vengeance for the death of his partner, but Mawson figured the man just had a hunger for blood. He'd been in Austin when the Rangers spotted Strummar and Allister and attempted to arrest them. Rather than negotiate to any degree, Strummar had opened fire and the Ranger he'd killed had been a friend of Mawson's.

In misspent retaliation, the citizens of Austin had lynched the outlaw's brother, and it curdled in Mawson's stomach every time he thought about it. Not so much the miscarriage of justice, which was pathetic enough, but that any man would let his kid brother take his grief. To Mawson's way of thinking the outlaw was solely responsible for the lynching. If he hadn't killed a Ranger on the streets of their city, his family would have been spared the horror of watching their innocent son strung up for his brother's crimes.

At thirty-seven, Earl Mawson stood well over six feet tall and weighed nearly two hundred and fifty pounds. He rode a huge bay gelding and habitually wore a bandolero of ammunition across his chest, carried a Colt .45 in his holster, and in his saddle scabbard the Springfield needle gun he'd been issued under McNelly. As soon as he heard Strummar was in El Paso, he rode in and called at the office of the town marshal, who wasn't happy to see the Ranger darken his door.

Campbell didn't move from where he sat with his feet on his desk, sipping his morning cup of coffee. "What'cha doin' here, Mawson?" he asked by way of greeting.

"I could ask ya the same thing," he replied gruffly, lowering his bulk into the opposite chair without invitation. "I heard tell Seth Strummar killed a man in the Ruby yesterday afternoon."

"Was a fair fight," Campbell frowned. "Whole barroom full of witnesses."

"So ya din't arrest him?"

Campbell shook his head.

"Don't matter that there's half a dozen outstandin' warrants agin him?"

"What happens in the rest of Texas ain't my concern."

"When a wanted man rides into your jurisdiction, it sure as shit is your concern."

"Look, Mawson, this town don't pay me a salary. All I get is a percentage of the fines I collect and I don't feel inclined to risk my life to arrest a man that's not threatenin' me."

"Two thousand dollars on his head and wouldn't be no percentage, ya'd get it all."

"I'd be dead and you goddamn well know it."

Mawson hacked up a gob of phlegm and spit it into the cuspidor in the corner. "How 'bout if I go with ya?"

Campbell knew he had to do it but he didn't like being pushed. He also knew even as rough a man as Earl Mawson was stretching his luck to think he could just walk up to Strummar and slap handcuffs on him. "He won't let us take him alive, you know that."

"So?" the big man said.

"My deputy's drunk and won't be worth a chigger on a dog. You got anyone else to go with us?"

"If ya'd quit stallin', we could catch him still in bed," Mawson said, standing up.

"Prob'ly sleeps with a pistol in his hand," Campbell muttered, standing too and shifting the gunbelt on his hips. "Let's go. I know which room he's in at the Central Hotel."

He pulled his hat low over his eyes as they walked into the cold sun of the last day of the year. He figured he'd let Mawson go in first, then when the shooting was over, he'd tiptoe in and see which one was still alive. They walked up the street and entered the lobby of the hotel. The desk clerk watched them approach with apprehension. "Strummar still here?" Campbell asked.

"Far as I know," the clerk answered, watching Mawson pull his gun and check the chambers.

"He alone?" Mawson asked.

The clerk shook his head. "Took a woman into his room last night."

Campbell said, "You go in shootin', Mawson, and you're apt to kill the woman, too."

"Any bitch with him won't be no loss to the world," he answered. "Let's go."

As they entered the bright courtyard, Campbell drew his gun just to make it look good, but he meant to stay clear of the door as long as he could. When they came to the room, Mawson took a deep breath, kicked the door open and jumped in with his gun cocked and ready.

Campbell heard a woman scream and then silence. He edged around the corner of the doorjamb and saw Rosalinda Montoya standing stark naked against the far wall. No one else was there.

"Jesus Christ," she laughed, pulling the blanket off the bed and wrapping it around herself.

"Where's Strummar?" Mawson barked.

"He was here when I went to sleep," she smiled.

Mawson took a few quick strides across the room and slapped her hard enough to knock her down. "Where'd he go?" he snarled.

She looked up, holding a hand to her face. "He didn't say," she retorted.

"You jus' slept right through his leavin'?"

"I heard him open the door and say hello to someone named Joe."

"That's a big help," Mawson grumbled.

Campbell turned around and saw the desk clerk edging toward them. "He gone?" the clerk whispered.

"Looks like it," Campbell smiled, not hiding his relief.

Mawson came back outside and the clerk took a step away from the anger on his face. "Ya see anyone come through the lobby this mornin', anyone ask Strummar's room number, anyone ya know carries the name Joe?"

The clerk shook his head. "Was a girl."

"Who was she?"

He shrugged. "Never seen her before. Little girl, sixteen maybe, had her hair cropped off short."

"She leave with Strummar?"

He shook his head again. "I didn't see him leave, like I told you before. She was with him half an hour maybe, then I saw her running down the street."

"Runnin'?"

"Yeah. She was smiling, too. I thought to myself it was odd such a little girl come away from a man like that smiling so happy."

Mawson glared at Rosalinda, who didn't look the least bit happy. Then he shouldered his way past Campbell and lumbered back through the lobby to the street.

At almost the same instant, Jade Devery walked out of his house and crossed the yard to the stable. Joaquín stood up from where he'd been cleaning the wheels of the carriage and watched him approach. Devery was a tall, well-built man with a handsome face that won many innocent girls to his purpose, and a dandy in his dress, sporting a Prince Albert coat over striped trousers this morning, his high white Stetson decorated with a sprig of holly for the season. He stood puffing on his black cheroot as he perused the gray mare Johanna had brought home. "What do you think of this little mare, Joaquín?" he asked.

"She's a good horse," he answered cautiously. "Gentle and strong."

"You know where Johanna got it?"

He shook his head.

"A gunman bought it for her. She resisted telling me, but over the years I've learned how to make women talk. Would you like to know how?"

"No," Joaquín said.

Devery laughed. "I rig up a tube between a pair of bellows and a tub of water, then I pump the water up their ass. It always works."

Joaquín looked away.

"Works on boys, too," Devery said, puffing on his cigar. "Cantankerous boys who don't mind their boss. You know who I'm talking about?"

"No, señor," he answered.

"Well, you think about it, and about your insides all swollen about to burst, and then next time she taps on that window and wants you to let her out, you think about it again." When the kid gave no answer, Devery said, "I didn't hear you, son."

"I am not your son," Joaquín answered.

"But you understand what I'm saying, don't you?"

"Sí, señor."

He nodded, puffing blue clouds of smoke above his head. "She's in the tub now, emptying out. In fifteen minutes I want you to bring the runabout around to the front. Think you can manage that?"

"Sí, señor," he said again.

Devery laughed. "You hate me, don't you, Joaquín?"

"I feel sorry for you," he answered.

Devery slapped him. The hand was out of the pocket so fast that Joaquín didn't see it coming and it knocked him down. "I don't need a little spic greaser feeling sorry for me," Devery said in a mild tone. "I gave you a job because I felt a fondness for your mother. But you've cancelled out that sentiment, and if you cross me one more time in the slightest degree, I'll make you regret you were born."

Joaquín picked himself up, keeping his distance. "Where are you taking Johanna?"

The smile spread slowly around the skinny black cigar clamped in the strong, white teeth. "When you were teaching her to shoot, I noticed the two of you were fond of each other and I got the idea to marry her to you. But I've since changed my mind. You don't understand the concept of cooperation, so you'll die a poor man. Maybe a young one, too. Now that she's lost her cherry there's any number of uses I can make of her. I thought I'd give her the tour today and see if she has a preference."

He sucked on his cheroot, watching the kid. "I'm giving you one more chance, Joaquín. If you let me down, you'll find yourself dumped on the other side of the river worse off than when you came across." He waited, then smiled. "Aren't you going to ask what it is I want you to do?"

Joaquín wanted to spit in his face, to punch him in the smiling teeth, but he knew he would die if he did either of those things and Johanna would be friendless. "What is it, señor, that you wish from me?"

"A man by the name of Seth Strummar is going to call today asking for her. I want you to send him to the Rio Bravo as if you were letting a secret out, as if I didn't want him to know where she is and won't be expecting him. If you fail me, I'll kill you. Do you understand?"

He nodded.

"Good. Harness that gray mare to the runabout. Let's see if Mr. Strummar has any taste in horseflesh."

Devery turned around and walked away, confident his stableboy wouldn't hurt him. The pitchfork was right there and Joaquín knew he could have thrown it in Devery's back and killed him with an especially painful method, but murder was against God's commandments and Joaquín had ambitions to become a priest. He would have quit his job months ago and applied to the Franciscans, but he reasoned he couldn't begin his vocation in the act of abandoning an innocent child to the mercy of the Devil. So he waited, tending the man's horses and carriages, keeping his barn clean and tidy, biding his time until the daughter would marry and free herself and him, too.

He saw her when he led the runabout to the front of the house then stood holding the head of the gray mare as Devery and Johanna came out and climbed in. Johanna wouldn't look at him but Joaquín could see she'd been hurt. Rage curdled in his heart when he watched the devil man lift the whip and crack it on the little mare's back. The buggy lurched out of the yard and west on Montana Street toward the tenderloin.

When Joaquín returned to his room in the stable he stood a moment staring at the daguerreotype of his mother. The portrait had been made when she was Johanna's age, before the disease ravaged her beauty. She had worked for Jade Devery in his México City brothel until she'd been incapacitated by syphilis and had to quit. Although Joaquín was only ten, he had supported her, doing odd jobs. They had lived in near destitution for the six years it took her to die. By then her face was crusted with sores and her body gave off an odor of decay. Joaquín had held the travesty of his mother in his arms as she died, then he had bowed his head and sobbed with the relief of surrendering her suffering to Christ. Almost her last words had been aimed at convincing him to travel north to El Paso and ask Devery for work. He had resisted the advice for over a year, but when the priests turned him down because he was illiterate and without assets to contribute to the Order, he finally came to understand that only in the United States could he better himself.

He didn't like being around brothels, though, and had asked Devery to put him to work doing anything else. So he kept the man's horses and during the time he'd been in charge of Devery's stable, he and

Johanna had grown close. Their friendship began when he asked her to teach him to read, and her cheerful praise of his quickness had helped him regain the confidence in his abilities the priests had nearly destroyed. When she noticed his skill with a gun and asked him to teach her in return, he had agreed though he felt uncomfortable giving her lessons in such a masculine skill.

As they worked in the yard, he found it necessary to put his arms around her to show her how to hold and aim the weapon, and many times their fingers touched handling the bullets. Although he considered himself a virgin, he had grown up in a brothel and knew too well the things that happened between a man and a woman. Sometimes he thought Johanna was much too free with her affection. He knew she was innocent and forgave her the liberties she took with touching him, but he worried how she'd do with a man who didn't look on her as a sister.

More than once he'd seen Devery watching her with lust. Joaquín had also been called into the room where Devery lay with his whores, and he'd seen that violence was necessary to the devil man's pleasure. He worried that one day Johanna would provoke her stepfather's wrath strongly enough that his sexual greed would break through the limitations of parental punishment. Now that he'd been told the method of that punishment, he knew everything Devery did with a woman was degrading, and also that Johanna was no longer exempt from his appetites. His greatest fear was that someday Devery would put her to work in his brothel, and from what the devil man had said, Joaquín thought that day had come.

He turned away from the portrait of his mother, lifted his gunbelt off the hook on the wall and strapped it on, intending to do what he must to prevent Johanna from being destroyed as his mother had been. He loaded the gun then dropped it back into the holster, meeting his eyes in the small mirror over the bureau. Joaquín was alone in the world but he had come to feel Johanna was kin, and though he knew murder was against God's laws, any man would act in defense of his family. Wearing his weapon, he went back outside to wait for the gunman, Seth Strummar.

Johanna followed her stepfather up the back stairs into the high class bordello on Utah Street. An ugly fat woman sat over the kitchen table, her small mean eyes assessing her as they came in.

"She's kind of skinny, ain't she, Jade?" the woman snickered.

He laughed. "This is my daughter. Johanna, this is Annie Walker. She works for us." Then to the woman who was suddenly scowling, "I'm giving her a tour of the family business. Someday, if she's smart, it'll belong to her."

Annie's eyes were cold with jealousy. "Come into the parlor, then," she said.

They followed the corpulent woman into a room gaudy with red velvet furniture and colorful paintings of nude women in various postures of display. Devery led Johanna over to one in which the woman sat on the edge of a rumpled bed smoking a cigarette. "This is my favorite," he murmured softly. "You know why?"

She shook her head.

He slid his hand around her waist and smiled as he watched her. "I like to think about the uses I could put that cigarette to."

Johanna tried to pull away but Devery held her close, then smiled at Annie. "Tell Rosalinda to come down."

"She ain't here," Annie said, a note of triumph in her voice.

"Where is she?"

"Went out last night with an old friend."

Johanna watched the muscles in her stepfather's jaw clench with anger. "Did you catch his name?" he asked between his teeth.

Annie nodded. "Seth Strummar."

Johanna saw his scowl change to an evil smile. Just then, at the worst possible moment for herself, Rosalinda walked through the front door. She frowned at her boss's daughter, then she smiled but it didn't touch her eyes. Johanna remembered seeing her asleep in Seth's bed a few hours before, and she thought if she hadn't gone to his room and asked for help, Rosalinda might still be there.

Softly, Devery asked, "Did you enjoy yourself, Rosie?"

She shook her head. "My fiancé was killed last night. I needed some time alone."

"Is that what you call servicing Strummar?"

Rosalinda looked at Annie's mean smile and her face lost its prettiness with fear. "He's an old friend, Jade," she pleaded.

He let loose of Johanna and took a cheroot out of his pocket. Annie picked up a box of matches from off the mantle and lit his cigar but he didn't bother to thank her. He stood puffing up great clouds of smoke as he watched Rosalinda with a cruel smile.

"He didn't take anything from you," she argued. "Annie got her cut."

"I'm glad to hear it," he said, taking his cigar from his mouth and looking for an ashtray. Annie held a crystal bowl up and he knocked his ash in without any recognition of the service. "But it seems he's pushed his way into more of my life than I care for. My daughter's a new friend of his, and my favorite whore an old one. I don't think I like having him around."

He reached out and took hold of Johanna's arm, impelling her toward Rosalinda. "Take my daughter upstairs and put her in a dress you think he'll like. If you fight me in the least degree, I'll send you to work in the Rio Bravo tonight. Would you like that?"

"No," she said.

"Do it, then."

"Come on," she said brusquely, turning away to climb the stairs. She walked into her room, then watched Johanna come in. "Close the door," she said.

Johanna did, then faced her again.

"Seth told me he didn't know you. Apparently he lied." When she made no reply, Rosalinda laughed harshly. "It wouldn't be the first time. Has he fucked you?"

"No," she answered, surprised at the bald question.

The woman's gaze slid down her body then met her eyes again. "I don't think you could handle him, honey. He's what they call well-endowed."

"He must like you," Johanna said, trying to be friends, "since he went to all the trouble to find you."

"What do you know about it?"

"I was with him at Ramon's."

Rosalinda laughed without joy. "You're lucky he didn't leave you there. It's a hellhole to get out of. How did you meet him?"

"I tried to steal his horse."

This time her laughter was wicked with delight. "He stopped you, did he?" Johanna nodded without answering and Rosalinda frowned. "But he didn't fuck you?"

"He started to then discovered I was a virgin."

She moved across the room to open the wooden shutters and stare out the window. "I wonder what woman turned him around," she murmured to herself.

Johanna thought about that a minute, then asked, "You mean there was a time he would have?"

"Oh, yes," she said, facing her angrily. "With pleasure." Again she let her eyes peruse Johanna's body, then sighed. "I have an old dress I've been meaning to alter to the new style. Maybe it'll do." She walked across to the chiffonnier and lifted out a bright satin of canary yellow. "What do you think?" she asked, holding the gown against her body. It clashed painfully with the blood red of the dress she was wearing.

"It's pretty," Johanna said cautiously, noting the risqué bodice.

"Think Seth will like it?"

She shook her head. "Not on me."

"That's what Jade wants, isn't it?"

"What do you mean?"

"To make him mad. But Seth isn't one to be carried away by his emotions."

"Have you known him long?"

"Three years or a hundred, take your pick. Do you have any idea what Jade has in mind?"

She shook her head.

"Whatever it is, it won't be pretty."

"Will you help Seth?"

Rosalinda studied her coldly. "Should I?"

"He likes you enough to have looked you up his first night in town."

"Did I catch a note of jealousy?" she mocked. "Many a girl has fallen in love with Seth Strummar. Don't think you're the first, or the last."

"Has he ever fallen in love back?"

"Not that I know of," she said. "Take off that schoolgirl frock and let's get you dressed like a whore. Who knows? You may be the one to catch him."

The yellow dress fell from a low neckline to drape in shimmering folds across her bosom, cinched in tight at the waist with a voluminous full skirt. Rosalinda reached in roughly and stuffed silk stockings down the front, pulling Johanna's breasts up so the material cut them just above the nipples. "The skirt is out of fashion," she smiled, standing back and surveying the effect, "but all Seth will see are your tits falling out."

Johanna studied herself in the mirror, thinking she looked ridiculous in the tart's gown with her short-cropped hair.

"Yes, the hair's unfortunate but nothing we can do about that, is there?" Rosalinda said, walking across and opening the door.

"Aren't you coming?" Johanna asked.

She shook her head. "Not unless Jade orders me to and he's gonna have to say it twice. I've seen Seth when he's crossed. The man is deadly." Her smile gave Johanna the shivers. "But don't tell Jade I said that. Nothing would please me more than to have Seth kill him."

Johanna walked down the stairs alone, watching Devery smiling up at her. "What did I tell you, Annie? Put a nice girl in a harlot's gown and you've got yourself a whore."

Annie laughed. "That's about all the bosom she's got, just what you see hangin' out there."

"I know all about her bosom," he smiled, and Annie laughed again.

Johanna followed her stepfather outside and let him hand her into the buggy, then they drove down the street and into the back yard of the Rio Bravo. He opened the door with a key and led her through a storeroom and into the cavernous dance hall, empty and stinking of stale whiskey and smoke. Beau Olwell came out of a side room and she shrank away from the man who had raped her. Both men watched her fear with ribald humor.

"Seth Strummar may be paying us a call in a bit," Devery told Olwell. "Let him in and then follow him upstairs with your gun ready."

"You want me to kill him, Jade?" he asked with a grin.

"When I give the word," he said. Then he took hold of Johanna and pulled her roughly across the dance floor and up the stairs, down a hall with a wide, wooden bench on one side, then through another door and into a room with a brass bed in the middle. The mattress was bare and attached to each of the four posts were steel shackles gleaming in the morning light. Devery held her arm, forcing her to follow him across to a wall decorated with a collection of whips.

"Look at them, Johanna," he said in a soft voice. "Which would you rather have used on you?"

"None of them," she said.

He chuckled. "That isn't one of your choices. Of course, we're just practicing. But if you were the girl assigned to be the entertainment in this room and a man gave you a choice, which would you choose?"

"I wouldn't," she said again.

"I'm trying to help you," he said, smiling as if it were true. He lifted a whip made of three leather thongs with knots tied every few inches. "How about this? Does it look kinder than the others?"

"No," she said.

"You're right. It's one of the worst." He put it back and took a horsetail switch and ran it through his hands, smiling at her. "How about this one? Would you like to feel it laid across your breasts?"

She shook her head.

"It would be a wise choice, though," he said. "It doesn't leave any scars." He put it back and lifted a quirt down. "Now this is the most cruel. There's a shaft of steel inside the leather binding and it gouges deep. There's a lot of blood when this one is used."

She turned away with a whimper.

"Not anything you care to contemplate, is it?"

"No," she said.

"It's the choice you're making by refusing to marry Beau," he smiled.

"I hate him!" she cried in desperation.

"He suits me," he answered. "Come out here a minute." He took her arm and led her back to the hall. Stopping by the bench, he flicked his handkerchief over the surface then sat down, pulling her onto his lap. "You know what happens here?"

She shook her head.

"Men pay a dollar to bring a girl up here. She sits on his lap, not quite like you are. She sits astride and the man has his pants open and he pokes her while they're sitting here. The girls who work downstairs bring ten or fifteen men up here every night. Does that sound like something you'd prefer over marrying Beau?"

She shook her head, not looking at him.

"This is the family business, Johanna. It's what your grandfather did in México, I would think you'd have more of a taste for something so deep in your blood."

"You're lying," she said.

"No I'm not," he replied. "I've told you before how your mother fell in love with a musician who played guitar during parties at the villa. She surrendered her virtue and your grandfather couldn't forgive her, not so much for doing it but for choosing a poor man. After you were born he put her to work in his bordello. That's where I met her. It was quite touching, watching her former lover serenade us while she serviced another man's lust. Made the experience more piquant." He laughed softly at the memory. "So you can see that I'd merely be continuing a family tradition. Of course, your mother worked in a house similar to Annie's and I'd start you there. I just wanted to show you the alternatives if you disobey me again." He watched her face. "Now how do you feel about marrying Beau?"

"He turns my stomach," she said, biting her lip against crying.

10

It was half past noon when Joaquín saw the American ride into the yard. He rode a flashy sorrel and kept his hand loose by his gun while his gaze scanned the grounds in unceasing vigilance. Joaquín walked out to greet him. The man swung down, then stood watching him approach.

"Buenos días," Joaquín said, stopping a few feet away.

"My name's Seth Strummar. I'm looking for Joaquín," the man said. He had gray eyes, cold as gunmetal.

"I am Joaquín Ascarate."

"Are you the only Joaquín that works here?"

"Sí, señor."

"Johanna told me you were her friend."

"I am."

"I was supposed to meet her half an hour ago but she didn't show. Do you know where she is?"

Now that the moment had come to betray Devery, Joaquín hesitated. There was little kindness in the eyes of the man who stood before him and he wasn't sure Johanna would be better off under his control, but he couldn't send him blindly into a trap. Unsure of what to do, he asked softly, "Are you the one who bought her the mare?"

"Yes," he said.

"May I ask why you did that?"

"She needed a horse."

"Many people need a horse, señor."

A warmth of regard flickered in the cold gray eyes and it made Joaquín feel better.

"If she changed her mind about meeting me," the gunman said. "I only need to hear it from her and I'll be on my way."

"I will tell if you take me with you," he answered.

The man flicked his gaze to the pistol Joaquín wore. "Johanna told me you taught her to use a gun. You did a good job."

"Gracias," he said carefully.

"You ever shoot at a man?"

"I am not a killer, señor."

"Then maybe you'd better let me go alone," he smiled.

"That is what Devery wants."

"He tell you that?"

"Sí. He punished Johanna this morning and I feel badly for her, but I'm not sure she will be better off with you."

The man smiled again. "You're a smart kid, Joaquín. I can see why she chose you for a friend. I'm her friend too, and I won't hurt her."

"If I tell you where they are, what will you do?"

"Reckon I'm gonna take her away from him."

Joaquín marveled at the simple declaration, as if the gunman had no doubt of his success. "He won't be alone," he said. "I know the building and think you should take me with you."

The gray eyes assessed him, then finally the man said, "All right. You got a horse?"

"Sí, I will get it."

Seth watched the kid walk back into the stable, thinking he probably wouldn't be much help if it came to a shootout but his knowledge of the building would be an asset. That Devery had punished Johanna meant it hadn't been her idea not to show up as they'd arranged, and Seth didn't feel he could just ride off and leave her after promising to help. When he'd gotten her away from Devery, maybe he could send her to San Antonio with Joaquín. Despite her professed desire, he didn't figure she deserved the danger of riding with an outlaw. His own desire was secondary to his sense of survival: any man who let himself care about someone else more than himself was a sitting duck for any man who didn't.

Joaquín came out of the stable on a bay gelding that looked older than he was. Seth smiled at the kid and together they trotted out of the yard and up Montana Street, turning south on Utah into the bowels of the tenderloin. They rode past Annie Walker's bordello, still shut up tight so early in the afternoon, and on south another two blocks. The Rio Bravo Dance Hall was quiet and apparently empty, but in the back yard Seth saw the gray mare hitched to a buggy and tethered to a corner pillar of the porch.

"Over here," Joaquín said, nudging his bay into a lean-to that would obscure the horses from above.

Seth tied his sorrel next to the bay and looked up at the huge, clapboard building. "How many doors?" he asked.

"This one, the one in front, and another on each side," Joaquín answered. "They will all be locked now, the side ones always are. There's a watchman inside. He should be alone so early in the day."

"Does Devery wear a gun?"

"Sí. In a shoulder holster. I have a plan, señor, if you will listen."

"I'm listening," he said, studying the windows. There was no escape from the top floor, so they'd have to come back down the stairs if that's where Devery was.

"I know the watchman. When I knock he will open the door, then I will ask him to come look at the harness. I will tell him someone has cut it. He will be eager to carry the news to Devery and while he's looking at the harness, you can hit him on the head."

"Why can't you?"

"He's a big man, señor."

"That's a good plan, Joaquín," Seth smiled. "I'll wait here."

"Bueno," he said, not moving. He looked at the man with the cold gray eyes standing beside him. "The watchman is named Beau Olwell. He raped Johanna. Did she tell you this?"

"She told me it happened."

Joaquín nodded. "Hit him hard, señor. We don't want him following us inside."

"He won't," Seth smiled.

Joaquín repressed a shiver. "Will you kill him?" he whispered.

"You just get him outside and let me take care of the rest," he answered.

"That's a good plan, too," Joaquín said. He squared his shoulders and crossed the yard, climbed the three steps and knocked on the door.

After a minute, Olwell opened it with a frown. "Whaddaya want?" he growled.

"Excuse me for disturbing you, Señor Olwell," Joaquín placated. "I think someone has cut the harness on Señor Devery's buggy. It looks to me like someone wishes him to have an accident."

Olwell looked over at the gray mare tethered a dozen yards away. "Cut it? You sure?"

"Come look for yourself, señor," Joaquín said, stepping aside.

Olwell pulled the door closed and crossed the space.

"It's the belly strap," Joaquín called. "One strong pull and the harness will come undone."

Olwell leaned down. "I don't see nothin'," he complained.

"Is hard to see. Whoever did it was smart." He saw Seth come out from the lean-to, his bowie knife flashing in the sunlight. With horrid fascination, Joaquín watched him lift Olwell's head by clamping his left hand over the man's mouth. The knife gleamed in his right and then disappeared as he plunged it deep into the throat, severing the artery. Blood spurted out in front of him, drenching the ground beneath the mare, making her snort and pull at her tether. Seth dragged the body out of sight around the corner of the building then bent to clean his blade on the dead man's clothes. He stood up resheathing his knife as he watched Joaquín. Then, incredibly, he smiled. "One down," he said.

Joaquín's stomach was queasy but he couldn't help admiring Seth's efficiency. In less than a minute of silence, he had killed a man. In another, he was beside Joaquín and they were walking into the building.

They were in a back foyer, whiskey kegs lining the wall. From above the dance floor, they heard voices and Seth drew his gun, standing beside the door and looking around from a protected angle. He couldn't see anyone, but the voices were coming from the top of the stairs. "Let's wait and see if they come down soon," he whispered to Joaquín.

"What if they don't?" he whispered back.

"Then we'll go up," he answered, not looking at him but watching the stairs.

After a moment, Devery came into view on the balcony. "Beau?" he yelled into the darkness of the foyer. "Who're you talking to?"

Joaquín glanced at Seth, but he still wasn't looking at him.

"Beau!" Devery yelled, his voice angry now. Then he scowled and Seth knew he suspected something amiss. Devery turned out of sight again and after a minute a door closed.

"You go on up," Seth said softly. "Tell him the same story about the harness."

"He won't believe it," Joaquín said.

Seth figured that meant Devery knew the kid was against him. "He'll listen, though," he said. "That'll give me a chance to get within range."

Joaquín walked across the empty dance floor, up the stairs, then disappeared. Softly Seth followed him. Crouching low to keep his head from coming into view before he could fire, he climbed the stairs and came out in the long, broad hall. A door was open, letting sunlight fall across the stained floor, and he heard Joaquín speaking inside.

"Señor Olwell is outside now looking at it," the kid finished.

"If you're lying, Joaquín," Devery said, "I'll have your hide."

Carefully, Seth eased toward the door. A board creaked beneath his weight and again Devery yelled, "Beau?"

Seth stepped into the door, his gun cocked.

Devery was quick. He grabbed Johanna and held her in front of him, pulling his own gun in the same motion and cocking it against her temple. "Mr. Strummar, no doubt," he grinned. "What a surprise."

"Help me, Seth!" she cried, squirming in the man's grasp.

Seth cast his gaze quickly around the room to make sure they were alone. "You always hide behind women, Devery?" he mocked.

"When I think it prudent," he answered with an amused smile.

"All I want is the girl. Turn her loose and I'll let you live."

"That's generous of you, but she's my daughter."

"I am not!" she objected, continuing to squirm though he held a gun to her head.

Devery laughed. "Why don't you relieve Mr. Strummar of his gun, Joaquín?" he suggested lightly.

"No, señor," he answered, drawing his pistol. "I have my own."

Devery's facade of humor fell from his face. "I'll kill her if either of you makes another move."

Johanna wasn't fighting anymore. Her eyes were pleading, her mouth closed in a tight line of fear.

"Looks like we have us a standoff," Devery smiled. "If you shoot me, I'll pull the trigger. Then this will all be for nothing."

"You'll still be dead," Seth said.

Devery took a step toward the closed side door. "What did you do with Beau? Knock him out? He's likely to wake up any minute now and he has a bad temper."

"I cut his throat."

Devery's eyes hardened as he realized what breed of man he was facing. Not the two-bit outlaw Pilger had described, but a man who could dispatch someone as tough as Olwell without even getting his clothes dirty. He regretted his own handling of the situation, thinking he should have befriended the man who stood opposed to him, endeavored to bring him into his organization by offering what he intended to give Beau, since Strummar obviously had a taste for the girl. Devery didn't see Johanna's leg rise beneath the yellow skirt but he felt her foot kick hard at his knee and instinctively he let go. She almost toppled with him as he fell but at the last instant kept her feet. He raised his gun and fired through the flying skirt of her dress.

Seth felt heat tear into his side as he pulled the trigger, hesitating only long enough for Johanna to lurch halfway out of the line of fire. Devery twisted, dropping his gun and clutching his shoulder, blood spurting through his fingers. Seth thought it was a damn poor shot and he'd need another before he was done, but Johanna was running half-crouched toward him, blocking his line of fire again. Then he saw Joaquín raise his gun over Devery's head and crack him hard with the barrel.

Johanna sprang into Seth's arms. He yanked her aside with his left and was about to fire again when Joaquín came between him and Devery. "Get the fuck out of the way," Seth demanded.

"Let's go," Joaquín said, standing between them. "He's out, we have no need to kill him."

"Come on, Seth," Johanna pleaded. "You're hurt."

He glanced down at the blood soaking his shirt just below his ribs, looked back up and saw Devery's hand groping for his gun on the floor. With a growl of impatience Seth reached out with his gunhand and knocked Joaquín aside. Devery had his gun now and Seth watched him pull the trigger just as he fired too. He felt a new heat tear into his shoulder at the same instant Devery's brains splattered onto the wall behind him.

Johanna cried out and clung to Seth. He looked at her yellow dress soaking blood from his wounds, then turned and headed back down the stairs. Joaquín was in front of them, running to open the door, disappearing in the bright sunlight outside. By the time he and Johanna got there, the kid was holding the horses ready and Seth holstered his gun and reached for the saddlehorn, feeling the blood hot down his side and his head woozy as he gained his seat. He held a hand down for Johanna and felt a wrench of pain as his arm took her weight. She leapt nimbly up behind, her yellow skirt brilliant in the sunlight, and then he slumped forward and lost the reins. Her arms came around and caught them just before they fell, the sorrel spun and Seth's vision whirled with it.

He heard the hoofs clattering on the hard caliche, voices of men yelling, close at first, then left behind. Joaquín was ahead of them, leading the way. Seth groped for the reins but his hands were numb, he couldn't feel them at all and knew he'd been hit bad. He struggled for control but the best he could do was think about the strong, swift legs of his sorrel carrying him to safety. He looked down at the blood soaking his side, a lot of blood seeping from the two wounds in an inexorable flow, and he concentrated on Johanna's hands on the reins and the sound of the sorrel's hooves, the bay's almost lost in the pounding of his pulse.

The next thing he saw was the bosque, tules growing thick, snagging at the yellow satin of Johanna's dress, then mud sucking under the horses' hooves. He struggled for consciousness, lost it, regained it as they skittered across the river, heard the splashing and felt his legs wet and cold. Then the horses clambered up the other side and Seth held on. The pain came then in surging gashes, tearing at his side and shoulder, throbbing with the ebb of blood, draining him of volition. He would have fallen if not for the girl's thin arms on either side of him, and suddenly he remembered Esperanza saying Johanna was death sitting behind him on the horse.

11

Earl Mawson stood staring down at Olwell's corpse, noting the clean way his throat had been cut and knowing only a man with a lot of practice could have achieved it. He turned around and met the eyes of George Campbell. "Ya still say this ain't your concern?" he mocked.

"We don't have any proof Strummar did this," the marshal argued.

"Ya sayin' it's a coincidence that within twenty-four hours of his ridin' into town three men die violent deaths?"

Campbell shrugged. "Lot of gunmen in El Paso."

"Ya ever try to cut a man's throat?" the Ranger asked angrily. "It ain't easy and no common gunman did this. Ya got a real killer in your jurisdiction. If ya'd arrested him when ya should've, least Devery and Olwell'd still be alive."

Campbell just turned away, thinking maybe that was true but he'd be dead if he'd tried to arrest Strummar. That prospect may not bother Mawson but it bothered the hell out of him.

The Ranger spit onto the ground right in front of Olwell's dead eyes. "Think I'll go see that whore," he muttered. "Ya comin'?"

Campbell shook his head. "I got work to do here."

Mawson snorted. "Clean up his dirt? That what ya think your job is?" But he didn't wait for an answer, he stomped out of the yard and up Utah Street to Annie Walker's bordello.

It was still early in the afternoon and the door was locked. He pounded on it hard enough to rattle the glass and would have kicked it down if Annie hadn't run to open it.

"Which room is Rosalinda Montoya in?" he barked.

"Third on the right, top of the stairs," she answered, cowering away from the angry man.

He took the stairs two at a time and pushed through the door without knocking. She whirled around in front of her chiffonnier, wearing only a shimmy and her auburn hair loose down her back. Mawson slammed the door behind him and glared at her.

"What do you want?" she whispered.

"Your lover," he said.

"Which one?" she laughed, but her eyes were scared.

"Same one I was askin' for this mornin'."

"I haven't seen him," she said, pulling a wrapper from a hanger and putting it on.

"He's killed two more men in the meantime," Mawson said. "Jade Devery and Beau Olwell. Cut one of 'em's throat and splattered the other's brains across a wall." He saw her eyes warm with pleasure and he strode across the room and slapped her backwards until she fell on the bed. Towering over her, he snarled, "Ya got any idea where he is now?"

"No," she moaned, curled into a ball on the quilt.

"I figure an outlaw's whore ain't no better'n he is," Mawson said. "And I ain't above hurtin' a woman to catch a killer, so mebbe ya oughta think a little harder."

"I don't know!" she cried. "I hadn't seen him for two years."

"Ya don't know any friends nearby that might hide him out?"

She thought of Ramon's vineyard north of Mesilla but she hid her eyes and held her tongue.

He grabbed the front of her wrapper and half-lifted her off the bed. "I asked ya a question!"

"No!" she cried.

He threw her back down. "Texas is offerin' two thousand dollars for his capture. I'll give ya all of it if ya help me."

"Why should I believe that?" she scoffed.

"I ain't int'rested in the money," he answered, thinking he'd found a crack in her loyalty.

"I suppose you just want to bring him to justice!" she jeered.

"That's right, Rosie," he said, solemn with conviction. "Strummar's a killer and he's gotta be stopped. I'm the man to do it."

She stood up and tried to brush past him, but he caught hold of her again and pulled her close. "I'm gonna catch him, so ya might as well get something for yourself out of it."

She studied his mean face, thinking it might be justice if she collected the reward on Seth after all they'd been through, but she'd have to be damn careful doing it. To the Ranger's hard, cold eyes, she said, "You're wasting your time."

But he'd noted her hesitation. "Why are ya protectin' him?"

"I'm not," she said. "I don't know where he is."

He let her loose and watched her walk across to her dressing table, admiring the way her body moved and thinking Strummar had good taste in whores. "Let me ask ya something else, then," he said, meeting her eyes in the mirror. "He was seen ridin' out of town with a woman in a yeller dress sittin' on the back of his horse. Ya know who she might be?" Her eyes narrowed with jealousy and Mawson smiled inside but it didn't show on his face.

"Johanna Devery," she spit out.

"Ya sure about that?"

She turned on her stool to face him. "I gave her the dress myself."

"Why would ya?"

"Her father asked me to, real nice."

"Why?"

"He was laying a trap for Seth, using Johanna as bait."

Now the smile spread across Mawson's mouth. "Ya jus' gave me evidence it was Strummar what killed him. Since ya've gone that far, don't ya wanta collect the two thousand dollars?"

"My life won't be worth jackshit if I help you and you know it."

"I'll protect ya."

She snorted with ridicule. "Like Devery protected Johanna?"

"I ain't no fool, Rosie, and I won't get caught in any trap I lay myself."

He could see her assessing him behind her eyes. Then she smiled sweetly. "How long would it take for the money to come through?"

He grinned. "I'd pay it myself out of my own savin's. How's that sound?"

"Too bad I don't have the information you want," she shrugged.

He laughed. "Well, think on it, Rosie. I'll be roomin' in the Central Hotel if ya remember something helpful."

He walked out, back down the stairs, through the empty parlor and out the front door to the street. He didn't know whether Rosie had been honest with him or not, but the jealousy in her eyes at mention of the girl in the yellow dress had been real. He had a hunch she'd betray Strummar if she felt safe. Mawson retrieved his horse, then rode the ten miles downriver to the garrison at Isleta to enlist the help of his favorite Apache scout.

His name was Tcha-nol-haye but Mawson couldn't get his tongue around that mouthful and called him simply Cha. The Indian was twenty-five years old and had spent his youth fighting under the great Apache chiefs. He was married now and had three children and it was for their welfare that he had surrendered and agreed to scout for his people's enemies. His family was safe and well-fed in the small village near Tejoe where he visited twice a year. The rest of the time he spent with the Rangers based in Isleta, combing the desert and mountains for the war chiefs who refused to surrender. His heart was with the fighters he sought to defeat, but he had made his decision for the survival of his family and he did his work honestly and well.

Cha stood five feet, eight inches tall, weighed one hundred and thirty pounds, and rode a scruffy mustang that looked almost like a pony beside Mawson's mount. But scrawny as they were, Cha knew he and his mustang could outlast the Ranger and his huge horse with ease, and he felt contempt for the enormous amounts of food and water the white eyes required. Despite his contempt, he bore a grudging respect for the Ranger, who was tough and could take the punishment the desert dealt any man who tried to live off the scarce resources beneath the pitiless sun. He had also fought with Mawson and knew him to be fearless. But as he listened now to what he was asking, most of all Cha knew he'd prefer tracking a bad white eyes over betraying his own people.

They rode into El Paso and Mawson showed him the bodies of Devery and Olwell where they'd been moved to the back room of an undertaker's parlor. Devery had been shot and there was nothing in that to give any indication of the man who'd held the gun. Olwell was a different matter. The Apache crouched on the floor to examine the wound closely, being careful not to touch the corpse and asking his Power for protection against the ghost. He noted the one clean stroke into the exactly fatal point of attack, and that the blade had been removed along the same path it had entered. Also the lack of bruises anywhere else on the man's throat and face meant his death had occurred too quickly for him to fight it. When he stood up, Cha smiled in anticipation of an opponent worthy of his skills.

The trail started in the dusty yard behind a bordello and led onto a well-traveled road. By the time he got there, a lot of horses had passed since the two whose hooves dug up the caliche in their haste. He walked the road to the tules along the river, saw where the tracks crossed, then stood up and shrugged at Mawson. "South," he said. "To México."

"Could ya pick 'em up on the other side?"

Again Cha shrugged. "Many horsemen ride this road. I could find tracks, but not say whose they were."

"Nothin' special about his a'tall?"

Cha shook his head. "Only that they were in a hurry."

"Let's go on over and see what we find," the Ranger said.

Cha knew they were breaking the law by doing that and he met the Ranger's eyes.

"Yeah, I know. But we're not gonna do nothin', least not yet. I jus' wanta know if ya can follow him."

So they waded across the wide, muddy stream and saw where the horses came out. Cha knelt and studied the ground carefully, touched the wet sand and raised his fingers to his nose. "Blood," he said, looking up at Mawson. "One of them was wounded."

Mawson smiled. "Which way from here, Cha?"

He followed the deep-dug hoofprints to where they were lost beneath the tracks of a herd of goats that had traveled the road since. He stood up and shrugged again.

"Dammit, Cha," Mawson growled. "Can't ya tell me nothin'?"

"Goats are from the Christian devil," the Apache smiled.

"Don't give me none of that superstition crap," Mawson retorted. "Jus' do your job."

Cha walked away, thinking Apaches enjoyed laughing at their enemies, but Mawson didn't have any appreciation of a joke. He went first one way on the road, then the other, seeing that the goats had obliterated any traces of the running horses, so he returned to the Ranger and shook his head.

Mawson stared across the vast expanse of desert leading south to the Sierra Madre. To the west there was nothing but badlands. To the east the road skirted the Texas border with a sprinkling of villages, but it was unlikely they'd seek haven there since Isleta sat right across the river. Mawson knew Strummar wasn't stupid and he didn't think the outlaw would hole up so close to a garrison of Rangers. "Okay," he grunted. "We'll wait."

They walked back to town and he settled Cha into a stable where the hostler was hungry enough to have an Apache on the premises, then he went to the Central Hotel and took a room. He figured if Strummar was traveling with Devery's daughter, sooner or later she'd come back to claim her father's property. Even if she came alone, he felt confident he could make her say where they'd been and then Cha could find their trail. But from the look in Rosalinda's eyes when he'd asked about the girl in the yellow dress, he had a hunch she wouldn't come alone.

12

An old woman in a black rebozo carrying a basket red with apples polished to catch the light. Her long, bony finger reached out to touch Seth's heart and he slapped her with defiance. She didn't reel away from him, though. She came closer and smiled, her ugly face suddenly as comforting as a warm bed on a cold night. A bed with a woman laughing her invitation, the darkness between her legs inviting him in, the moisture glimmering like silver. A long shiny tendril undulated through the air to touch him with its sticky warmth, bind him and pull him closer.

Again he slapped the old woman, but she only laughed with a siren sound that came in waves, loud and soft between the thunder of galloping hooves. He struggled against the dark swamping over him, the heat of his own blood welcoming him back into the passage from which he'd come. Numbly he reached for the knife at his belt, had it in his grasp and heard the old woman's laughter, soft and forgiving, as he thrust the blade deep into the red walls all around him. He took the knife in both hands and slashed at her laughter, husky with deception, sweet with succulence, though she offered death.

Blood rained on his head and he sucked hard to catch air in his lungs but all he breathed was blood, coagulating in his throat. He sank into softness, a bed he thought, and he lashed out at the knife coming close, in her hands now. Then a man's voice, distant and foreign. "Bullets out," she said, not the old woman, someone else, someone he trusted not to deceive him, and he buried his face in her breasts as the blade cut deep, her tears hot with pain. He groped and caught cold rods of metal as the tip of the knife probed the flesh of his side, hearing his name murmured over and over as a promise of succor that he wanted but couldn't find. The blade moved to his shoulder and he lurched again, then the knife was gone and he was alone in a swamp of blood sucking him down into sleep.

A dim flicker of consciousness made him struggle for air. He could taste it but couldn't suck enough into his lungs, and he tried to sit up to get closer to the sky but the old woman's hands held him down. They were scaly, rough and dry like the rope as he eased it over Oriana's blonde hair, her laughter mocking him as she twisted in the noose, then Jeremiah taking her place, crying for Seth to save him. Esther crying, a long ceaseless wail of supplication. "Stay with Angel," he told her. Choirs of angels singing carols, the boy with wolf eyes drawing a gun from beneath his robe, smiling and pulling the trigger and killing the eyes he'd come from, then Esther's face coalescing from the smoke. "Esther," he mourned.

The old woman answered him, smiling through broken slimy teeth as she murmured, "It's easy, Seth. You'll like it." But he knew it as deception. All he wanted was his gun to shoot the old woman, to blast her evil smile into kingdom come, but his gun wasn't there.

Kingdom come echoing in his father's voice, kingdom come in the rhythms of a long supple switch, a belt, a strap of harness leather raising welts on the flesh of his son, then raising his hands dripping with blood as he led his congregation in prayer for love among the brethren. A Mexican kid asking that he take him along. "May I ask, señor, why you did that?" Bettina cleaning the welts on his back saying, "Hung her, Mr. Strummar? A woman with petticoats and all?" Esperanza's cards forming a cross on the table. "Deception before you," she said, "death riding behind." "Help me, Seth," a young girl cried, her eyes as blue as the sky, and the Mexican kid saying, "We have no need to kill him." Knocking the kid aside and the gun echoing in the silence of his brother's mouth as he twisted in the noose of a black, starless night.

A deep, dreamless blackness that comforted with nothingness. Then the feminine voice of compassion cooing his name over and over, like the thudding of hooves on hard ground, the knelling of a bell muffled in the distance. Yellow satin stained with blood, his cock hard, the voice saying, "It's too soon, Seth," but the cunt wet, with blood or come? He couldn't tell. It was small, his cock surging with life, throbbing as she surrounded him, then the come dripping and a soft, silken laughter from the mouth of a girl. He reached for her but his hand closed on nothing and he fell into darkness again.

Finally the darkness was pierced by red light coming hazily into focus. He saw he was in a small room of raw adobe, a red ristra of chiles on the wall, sunlight shining through a burlap bag over the window, red letters spelling out "Frijoles del Castile," "el mejor del mundo." He looked at his gun above his head, reached for it and felt the pain down his side, but not so bad he couldn't stand it for the cold comfort of the weapon. He checked the chambers, saw the three live shells, the dead one under the hammer and two others dead. Spent where? Into whose flesh? He couldn't remember, spun the cylinder so he had a hot one ready and cocked the gun with his thumb, feeling alive as the hammer eased into the notch, putting death in his hands again where it belonged. The door opened and he raised the gun, the trigger like a clit throbbing for attention.

A girl in a yellow dress smiling at him, sunlight flooding in behind her.

"Mornin'," he said, trying to remember who she was, then remembering.

"It's afternoon," she laughed, crossing to kneel beside the bed, taking the gun from his hand and sliding it back in the holster. "It's right there if you need it, but you're safe here."

"Where am I?"

"Zaragoza," she said. "With friends of Joaquín."

The name tumbled through his memory until he matched it with a face, the kid who'd been smart not to trust him. "Is he here?"

"Yes, outside. Do you want me to call him?"

He shook his head, the effort taking more energy than he could have imagined. "How long have I been here?"

"Three weeks. How are you feeling?"

"Lousy," he said.

She laughed. "Better though. It's good to see you, Seth."

He raised himself on his elbows, feeling the pain stab his shoulder. He threw the covers off and saw himself naked except for the bandages, rusty with dried blood, one around his middle just below his ribs, the other on his shoulder, stiff. Left side, he thought. Not my gunhand. He smiled at the girl. "My horse?" he asked.

"In the stable," she answered.

"Keep him inside," he said. "Anyone who knows me . . . "

"Will recognize the horse," she smiled. "You've told me."

"Have I?"

She nodded. "And asked those questions a dozen times."

"What questions?"

"Where am I? Is he here? Where's my horse? How long have I been here? The answer to the last one had to change as the days passed."

"Three weeks?" he asked, lying back again.

"You'll be all right in a little more time."

He looked at her yellow dress stained with his blood, her tiny hands, remembering them on the reins, then over the campfire in the desert, before Ramon's, when he'd thought she was a boy. He raised his gaze to her small breasts barely showing above the line of yellow cloth, then met her eyes. "Did we make love?"

"Yes," she smiled. "I tried to stop you but you were determined."

"Too bad I missed it," he said, trying to remember. "Did I hit you?"

"No," she said.

"I remember hitting someone."

"The doctor," she smiled again. "When he came at you with the knife to take the bullets out."

He studied her delicate face, the short-cropped hair curling wispily around her ears now, grown since he'd seen it last. "Did I call you Esther?"

She nodded.

"Thought I saw her, guess it was you. Thought I saw my brother, and my father praying for his congregation."

"Your father was a preacher?"

"Does that surprise you?"

"Nothing about you would surprise me."

He struggled to remember their connection, then remembered. "Is Devery dead?"

"Yes. We read of it in the newspaper. I kept it, if you want to read it later."

"Did it mention my name?"

"No," she said. "Just your red horse and my yellow dress. People saw us riding out of town."

"El Paso," he said.

She nodded.

He tried to get up but couldn't gather enough strength.

"Wait a while," she said. "You lost a lot of blood."

"Have to buy you a new dress," he smiled.

"When we get some money."

"What happened to what I had?"

"Joaquín's friends are taking a risk, keeping us. The money made them feel better."

"You gave them all of it?"

She nodded. "Joaquín's working to pay for our food."

"He's a good friend."

"I know how to pick men," she answered.

Her face wavered until she was lost in the darkness again.

When he opened his eyes, he saw the fire in the hearth, Johanna in a chair before it, Joaquín standing by the window. Two people who had saved him at great risk to themselves. They could have dumped him off the horse and ridden on, free. But they hadn't. Slowly he sat up, feeling his head spin, the floor cold under his feet. "Where are my clothes?" he asked.

Both of them whirled around to face him. Johanna was coming toward him, but he looked at Joaquín. "Thanks," he said.

The kid smiled. "No problem," he said.

Seth laughed. "Prob'ly the biggest lie you ever told."

"Maybe," Joaquín said.

"Don't get up now," Johanna said. "It's nearly bedtime."

"I'm awake," he said.

"Are you hungry?"

"Thirsty."

She crossed the room, poured a dipper full of water into an earthen mug, and brought it to him. He took it with his left and saw how his hand shook as he drank. "I want to get up," he said. "Where's my pants?"

She brought him his clothes, tugged his socks onto his feet, then his trousers, letting him lean on her while he closed them. She helped him into his boots and pulled his shirt up his arms, buttoned it for him and tucked it in. He reached for his gunbelt.

"You're safe here," she said.

He buckled it on anyway. "Want to see my horse," he said. "Will you help me, Joaquín?"

The kid crossed the room and let him lean on his shoulder as they left the girl behind. Joaquín was smaller than he was, his body wiry and tight but strong, taking more of his weight than he did. Seth thought of the times he'd tussled with Johanna and how weak she'd been and he marveled at his stupidity for ever thinking she was a boy. The night air was cool, refreshing in his lungs after so many days in the smoky room. He looked up at the stars in the black sky. "Almost lost it that time, didn't I," he said.

"Yes," Joaquín smiled.

His horse nickered as he came into its stall, moving through darkness until Joaquín lit a lantern. He leaned on the glistening red neck as he rubbed the sorrel's nose, then turned to lean on the horse's back as he looked at the kid watching him. "I owe you, Joaquín."

"I have lost nothing," he said.

"You lost your job," Seth smiled.

"I wanted to go anyway, but not to leave the girl. She'll be all right now with you."

Seth wondered what that meant, what he wanted it to mean. He looked at the kid and asked hopefully, "Do you love her?"

Joaquín shook his head. "My mother worked for Devery in México. Maybe it was growing up in a brothel, but I have felt no interest in women that way, wishing only to serve God."

He remembered Johanna saying Joaquín had another love, and he knew now she'd meant not a woman but the Church. The glow of devotion on his face made Seth wonder if his father had ever looked like that. In his youth maybe, before he married and spawned a son who became a killer. "You aiming to be a priest?" he asked.

Joaquín looked away. "Once I thought so. Not now."

"What changed your mind?"

The dark eyes turned to him, hopeful of finding understanding. "It was my fault you were so badly wounded. I held you back from shooting Devery the last time and you were nearly killed instead. Priests do nothing if not preach mercy, but in such a case mercy was a mistake. Then, too, I watched you kill Olwell and felt only a sickness in my stomach and admiration for your method. A priest would have felt sorrow."

Seth smiled with regret. "And you still say you haven't lost anything?"

"The world is a strange place," Joaquín answered. "There is need of all good men, even those who live by the gun."

"You think I'm a good man?"

He nodded. "Otherwise God would not have saved you."

"Maybe God didn't have anything to do with it."

"The Devil would not have helped you. Devery was his servant."

"Maybe the Devil didn't have anything to do with it, either. You're the one who helped me. You and Johanna."

"An innocent girl and a man wishing to serve God," Joaquín smiled.

Seth studied him a moment, amused at the answer. Then he asked, "What will you do now?"

"I would be proud to ride with you."

"I'm a poor substitute for religion," he laughed.

"In one afternoon you taught me more about how to live as a man than I learned in all the hours on my knees in church. Since I am a man, it is God who made me so and He will not be displeased if I act like one."

"There're other ways to live as a man than the one I've chosen."

"But none so bold," Joaquín smiled.

"Sometimes a bold life is also short."

"I would rather live a short life standing on my feet than a long one on my knees."

"That's what I decided," Seth smiled.

"Then we will be buen compadres, no?"

"Seems to me, we already are."

13

Across the river from the small Mexican village of Zaragoza lay the town of Isleta, headquarters for a garrison of Texas Rangers. Seth knew of the tenacity of their commander, but the last he'd heard, Baylor had ridden north into the Guadalupes chasing the remnants of Victorio's renegade Apaches. Seth had been in Zaragoza a month, time enough for people to talk and for the talk to drift across the river. Time enough, too, for Baylor to return and be scouting new prey, though the Rangers couldn't legally come onto foreign soil for the purpose of arresting an outlaw. A treaty with México allowed them to pursue Apaches into Chihuahua, however, and Seth knew they could pick him off without too much trouble if they caught wind he was there.

He'd been back on his feet a week now, and he and Johanna spent their days in games of nonsense and their nights in the gentler rhythms of passion. Her body was small and easily wounded but he was still recuperating so it wasn't hard to restrain himself from enjoying the more rambunctious coupling he usually shared with whores. He even found he liked the tenderness of their lovemaking and occasionally caught himself wondering if he couldn't become accustomed to it as the staple of his amorous activities. He scoffed when those thoughts entered his mind, however, telling himself that when his energy was back to snuff, he'd be hungry for the stronger passions that bordered on violence. He'd learned to temper his drive in the last few years and no longer beat women, but his normal tastes were still a far cry from gentleness.

Yet with Johanna he enjoyed being gentle. He liked seeing the warmth in her eyes when he caressed her desire into a fire that smoldered as cozily as coals in a hearth. And he liked to tease her during the day until fury flashed in her blue eyes for just the second it took her to realize he was playing. Then the anger would be replaced by a childish delight in the trick he'd played, and he found the delight satisfying in the same way he'd once found the anger stimulating. With other women, he'd roused their anger then dragged them into bed to see what challenges he could taunt from their rage. With Johanna, he did it to see her face flash with joy when she caught onto his game, and the joy challenged him with a contest more intricately enticing than the violence had.

Maybe it was just because he was older, with years of violence under his belt. Maybe it was simply time for a change, a new year that should have started fresh with his vengeance behind him. He'd been diverted from his purpose by rescuing her, but it seemed that he had the reward without achieving the deed. Sometimes he wished they could stop time and stay in Zaragoza forever, caught in a frivolous limbo between the violence of his past and its resumption when he entered the world again.

He recognized his feelings for her as a sweetness he didn't deserve, a tenderness of regard he wanted to sequester away from the reality of who he was. In his past he had loved only one other woman as deeply and he had abandoned her rather than inflict the weight of his crimes on her life. He felt comfortable with that decision, knowing Esther was better off without him, but his loneliness hadn't receded in the light of his sacrifice. For nearly ten years he had ridden with his partner, Ben Allister, and after his death Seth had stayed alone, not wanting to lose someone again. Since his life was such that all could be lost in the whistle of a bullet, he kept himself detached.

Johanna's lighthearted gaiety made him ache to own it for himself. He reasoned that maybe her youth could reclaim some of what every man was promised on the threshold of life, the love of a good woman, a value he had abandoned when he became an outlaw. In Zaragoza it was easy to let their love grow, but he knew that once they were back in the world it would be altogether different. He was different, lolling in the comfort of his recovery, in the sweetness of her solicitude. Her love was like the sun shining through the bare branches of the cottonwood outside their window, resplendent now in the glory of the clear sky. Back in the world, however, the sky would thicken with clouds and obscure her light behind the bloody legacy of his past, and he wanted to protect her, this young woman so clean and gay, from the lethal wind of his intent.

His vengeance against Pilger was like a storm rampaging on the horizon, threatening to encompass him in a violence capable of obliterating all light from his life. Yet it was a drive he could not deny, an ugly tempest born of blood and demanding blood before it would abate. Maybe then he could think of a new beginning, but even as the thought was born in his hopeful soul, he doubted its truth. The stain of murder was indelible, and though she wore it proudly on the skirts of her yellow dress, her soul was clean and he knew if his love meant anything, he would leave her to find a man worthy of sharing her future.

He figured he could accomplish both his wants by returning to El Paso. Johanna would be home and able to begin putting her life together again, and when eventually Pilger showed up and Seth left on his own, she'd have a foundation to sustain her.

Jade Devery was dead and all his holdings belonged to her now. Not just the brothels and his share of the North Pass Saloon, but the house on Montana Street and whatever bank account he'd had. Seth knew whorehouses to be lucrative enterprises, and he figured with the means at her disposal she could write the lawyer in San Antonio and he'd be only too happy to come to her. But Seth couldn't go back to El Paso so soon, certainly not riding his flashy red sorrel. He decided to return to his friends north of Mesilla. Then he could borrow Ramon's black mare and come into town with Johanna established in her home to give him sanctuary. But when he broached the subject, she was opposed to the plan.

"How can I go back alone?" she asked. "Where will I say I've been?"

She was sitting in front of the hearth and he watched her from where he stood by the window.

Her delicate face was beautiful in the soft glow of firelight, the bloodstains on her dress a reminder of all she'd done for him. "You'll have Joaquín with you," he answered softly. "Tell them you went to San Antone, then when the lawyer shows it'll look like it's true."

"And what will I say about my stepfather's death?"

"That you read about it in the newspaper and came home as soon as you could. That's only partly a lie."

"I was mentioned in the newspaper," she argued.

"Just a girl in a yellow dress is all. No one will think it was you."

"Rosalinda knows. It was her dress."

"She can keep her mouth shut when properly motivated. Fire that fat cow Annie and give Rosalinda the job."

"Do you think I want to own a brothel?" she asked indignantly.

"Then sell it to her cheap," he smiled. "She's not so squeamish."

She studied him across the room. "Will you see her again?"

"I hadn't thought about it," he said.

"But you like her, don't you."

"She's a good whore."

"Is that all I am to you?"

"What do you think?" he teased.

"I don't know, Seth," she answered earnestly. "You make love to me every night but you've never said how you feel about me."

"I owe you my life."

"So it's only gratitude you feel?"

"You think that's insignificant?" he asked, wary of the conversation's direction.

"No, but you feel that towards Joaquín. Am I the same to you, a friend who saved your life, just one that happens to be someone you can sleep with?"

"You want more, do you?" he asked, teasing again in an effort to lighten her mood.

"Yes," she said.

He sorted through his mind for something he could offer that would satisfy her, but nothing presented itself short of marriage. The fire crackled in the silence between them.

"I've been wanting to ask you something," she said with hesitation.

He waited, seeing she was nervous anticipating his answer.

"Will you tell me who Esther is?"

The question was an easy one, given all the things in his past that could have aroused her curiosity, and he smiled. "A woman who thought she loved me."

"You mean she didn't, really?"

"Maybe she did, but it wouldn't have taken her long to hate me if I'd given her what she wanted."

"What was that?" she whispered.

"Marriage," he answered playfully, his smile saying he was aware she wanted it too.

Slowly she said, "And you think Esther and I are the same."

He nodded.

"How can you be sure?"

"You're as young as she was, not quite but close. You've both been hurt by men and I took you both out of a bad situation. I figure what you feel is gratitude and that's not love, as you just pointed out."

"I loved you before you freed me from Jade."

"Not because you were hoping I would?"

"What I feel has nothing to do with him. It has to do with who you are."

"You don't even know me," he scoffed.

"I think I do," she said.

"You think you do, but I'm an outlaw, Johanna. I robbed banks for a living. I've killed men, some of them for no better reason than they took exception to giving me their money. I've raped women, beat hell out of them for my entertainment." He saw the doubt on her face and he laughed. "You don't believe me, do you?"

"You may have been like that once but you're not now," she said.

Again he laughed at her stubbornness. "Okay, I've mellowed some. But I'm the same man who did those things and they're not something that ever entirely goes away. Even if I stay ahead of the law, my reputation beats me everywhere I go and there's plenty of people who hate me sight unseen. My wife would be open to that hatred the same as me."

"I don't care what other people think of us," she answered.

"That's an easy thing to say when you're sixteen."

"How old are you?"

"Thirty-two."

She stood up and crossed the room to stand before him. "I'll love you when I'm three times thirty-two. I'm young and you think I don't know what I'm saying, but I do. Maybe because of your past, because it made you who you are and I love the man I see now. I have since I tried to steal your horse and you gave me a ride anyway. And then when I kept trying to get away from Ramon's, how you'd catch me and laugh. You could have beaten me then, as you say you've done to women in your past. You didn't because even when you thought I was a boy, there was something between us that stopped you. And then when you found out I was a girl, and I told you to go ahead and take whatever you wanted, you didn't because you didn't want to hurt me. You could have left me in the desert or at Ramon's, and when I came to your hotel room you could have told me to get out of your life and closed the door in my face. When I didn't show up after you agreed to take me to San Antonio, you could have gone on without me. Every chance you've had to hurt or get rid of me, you didn't do it. We belong together, Seth. What we feel is true and you know it as well as I do. Why can't you admit that we love each other?"

"I can admit it," he said painfully. "I just can't see it'll do either one of us much good."

She smiled. "Do you think it'll do us any good to ignore it?"

"Maybe not," he conceded.

"Well, then. Why not go for broke? Isn't that what they say in poker when you put all your money on one card?"

"That's what they say."

"I'd rather risk having a chance at happiness with you than a sure bet of anything else."

He looked down at her pretty face lifted so appealingly, her tiny body enclosed in the low-cut yellow dress, and the stains on her skirt left from his blood. If her love was strong enough to come through seeing him at his worst, fleeing the law and hiding out in a hovel south of the border, eating beans and rice everyday and living a month in the same clothes without complaint, if she could hear him confess the crimes of his past and her love could still shine from her eyes as he was seeing it now, he thought maybe they had a chance. But it was a longshot for which she was putting up the stake. He stood to lose only his loneliness, while she was risking her entire future on a chance of happiness so slim it was a thread of silk against the rampage of vengeance. He took her in his arms and held her close to hide himself as he searched for the words to let her down easily. Her arms encircled his waist and held on tight, the scent of her hair enveloping him as if in a dream of feminine succor he had thought he'd forfeited forever. He moaned with the weight of his longing.

She raised her face and whispered, "Nothing could be worse than my loneliness without you.."

He laughed with surprise that she had so aptly expressed what he was feeling. Meeting her eyes and knowing he understood better than she the consequences of his words, he said, "All right, Johanna. I'll marry you tomorrow if you still want me in the morning."

She threw her arms around his neck, happiness shining in her eyes. "I'll never change my mind," she laughed. "I love you."

"I love you too," he said, bending to kiss her mouth, tasting the succulence of submission and knowing, for the first time in his life, that it was his own.

When he had her hot and insistent beneath him in bed, he stopped to ask for the promise he needed from his wife, approaching it slowly so she would understand the severity of what he asked. "Look at me, Johanna," he said. She opened her eyes and they were bright blue beneath him. "Do you think you're tough enough to be my wife?"

"Yes," she answered bravely.

"I need a promise from you," he said. "Don't close your eyes."

"No," she said.

"Don't say that word to me. Ever. Do you understand?"

She nodded, wide-eyed.

"I need a lot of satisfaction," he said. "Are you sure you're up to it?"

"Yes," she said.

"If I pulled you down on the floor in the middle of the day, what would you say to me then?"

"Yes," she smiled.

"And if I woke you in the night and you were tired and mad at me?"

"Yes," she laughed.

But he knew she wouldn't be laughing in a minute. He moved inside her, watching her face as he thrust himself in deep without the solicitude he'd been showing out of gratitude. "Am I hurting you?" he asked.

"A little," she admitted.

"This is nothing, Johanna. This is like playing with a baby. I can be rough, do you understand that?"

"Yes," she said.

"But you'll take it, whatever I give you?"

"Yes."

"And you'll love it even when I hurt you, because you love me?"

Her eyes pleaded to understand him. "What do you want me to say, Seth?"

"I already told you."

"Yes," she whimpered.

"I told you some of the things I've done, but not all of them. Someday someone will tell you stories that'll turn your stomach. Will you love me then?"

"Yes," she said with certitude.

He got to the point. "What if a posse came storming through that door right now? Would you kill to defend me?"

"Yes!"

"If they arrested me and put me in jail, would you bring me a gun?"

"Yes."

He hit her with it. "And if that didn't work would you kill me before you let them hang me? Think about it, Johanna. You'd only have one shot so you couldn't botch it, you'd have to do it with the one. Could you shoot me dead?"

"Don't ask that, Seth," she whispered.

"That's not the answer I want from my wife."

"Yes, I would kill you!" she cried.

"I need your word you'll keep that promise. It's the only dowry I'll ask from you, Johanna."

"I give my word," she answered solemnly.

He smiled and let himself come, flooding her with wetness so he could move inside her with ease. "Is that better?"

She nodded.

"Will you come?"

"I'll try."

"That's not what I want to hear."

"I can't," she moaned.

"Is that what you'll tell your husband?"

"No," she said.

He sat up fast and slapped her, not hard, but enough to make his point. "Tell me again," he said.

"Yes," she sobbed.

"Do you hate me?"

"What do you want?"

"I want you to say yes to whatever I ask. Can you do it?"

"Yes."

"Even when you hate me?"

"I'll never hate you."

He looked at her with warning.

"Yes!" she cried. "I'll love you even when I hate you!"

"Attagirl, Johanna," he smiled. "Move with me now. Will you come for me?"

"Soon."

"Come good for me, Johanna," he urged, pushing in deep and steady, watching her breasts rise and fall with her ragged breath until she moaned with pleasure and trembled beneath him. "Yes?" he smiled, burying his face in the delicate fragrance of her hair.

"Yes," she whispered, clinging to him. "Yes, yes, yes."

14

In the morning he left her asleep and walked out to the stable. With his bowie knife he ripped open a seam in his saddle where he'd hidden ten Gold Eagles. He dropped five of them into his pocket, stacked the other five on a crossbeam in the wall, then curried his horse as he waited for Joaquín to wake up. After a few minutes the kid came from his bed in the loft and stood at the end of the stall watching him.

"Buenos días," he smiled.

"Mornin'," Seth said, turning to face him so he could catch his honest reaction. "Johanna and I are getting married today."

Joaquín's smile spread across his face as happily as sunrise warming a dark dawn. "I'm glad to hear it. She needs a strong man."

"I'm not sure I'm the right one."

"She loves you, that makes you right."

"Maybe," he smiled. "Will you stand up with us?"

"Gladly," Joaquín said.

"Where do we go in this town to get it done?"

"To the padre," he answered as if it were obvious.

He shook his head. "I don't go inside churches."

Joaquín stared at him a moment, then said softly, "Marriage is a sacrament, Seth. It won't be real unless it's sanctified in the Church."

He went back to currying his horse. "Ain't there a judge or alcalde or somebody who can do it?"

"That will make it only legal," Joaquín answered.

"It's enough," he said.

"I do not believe that."

Seth leaned against the strong back of his horse as he met the kid's dark eyes, silently laughing at himself for taking on such a compadre. "Tell you what, Joaquín. Because I owe you my life, we'll do it in a church."

Joaquín's smile was radiant. "It is as it should be," he said.

Seth nodded, taking the Gold Eagles off the wall and walking over and dropping them into Joaquín's shirt pocket. "My share of our keep this last month."

"I asked for no money from you," he said, pulling the pocket out and seeing the gold coins nestled there.

"I know you didn't," Seth said. "That's why I want you to have them."

"I will accept them as a gift, not repayment of a debt," he said.

Seth smiled at the kid's logic. "You think it's too early to go to the padre?"

"No, I think we should go before something stops you."

"You're prob'ly right," he laughed.

Together they walked up the dusty street of Zaragoza. He held Johanna on his left, keeping his gun-hand free for trouble. Both of them were wearing bloodstained clothes and he smiled wryly, recognizing that it was appropriate. He was a killer marrying a near virgin and the blood spoke for their future as well as his past. When they came to the shop of a vulcanadora, he smiled down at her playfully, then stopped in the door.

The blacksmith was already working at his forge and he looked over at the three people blocking the light. "What can I do for you, señores?" he asked pleasantly.

Seth held up a Gold Eagle. "If I shoot a hole through the center of this coin, can you hammer it into a ring for the lady?"

The man came forward, peering at the coin. "Señor, if you can shoot a hole through the center, I will make the ring for free."

"You got yourself a deal," Seth smiled. He walked back into the sunshine, fingered the coin a moment to center himself in his purpose, then threw it straight up, high into the blue sky over his head. When it caught the sun at the apex of its ascent, he drew his gun and fired. The coin lurched when the bullet hit and fell a few yards away.

Joaquín ran and picked it up, holding it between his fingers to show the sunlight shining through.

"Pinche," the vulcanadora whispered.

Seth looked at Johanna and saw her smiling. "Think you could do that?"

"No," she said.

"What did I tell you about that word?" he teased.

"Yes," she laughed. "I'll learn to do it."

He grabbed her around the waist and pulled her close, nuzzling her neck beneath the short-cropped hair. Behind him, he heard Joaquín say to the blacksmith, "They're getting married."

"I will make a beautiful ring that she will cherish always," the man said, coming over to measure her finger with a string.

They stood leaning against the door, Seth holding Johanna in front of him as he watched the broad dusty street of Zaragoza for any flicker of danger while they listened to the hammer working inside. When the blacksmith presented the ring, it had been flattened into a wide band fluted with the markings of the coin. Seth held it in his palm, the gold shimmering in the morning sun. "You did a good job, señor," he smiled at the man.

"Gracias. I wish you much happiness."

"Thanks," Seth said. Then he grinned at Joaquín. "Lead on."

At the mission, Joaquín went in to find the priest as Seth waited with Johanna outside. He looked up the whitewashed building at the cross silhouetted against the sky and felt a sense of doom at entering into the church's darkness. But he'd told Joaquín he'd do it and guessed he was stuck with it now. When the kid came back with a black-clad priest, Seth tried to encourage himself with the thought that it would be over soon.

The priest looked at him and Johanna carefully, noting her youth, the blood on their clothes, and his gun. He spoke softly to Joaquín, who turned uncomfortably to Seth.

"He says you must take your gun off before entering the sanctuary."

"No," Seth said, flat to the priest's eyes.

"It is the House of God," Joaquín argued softly.

"The answer's no," Seth said again.

Joaquín spoke quickly to the priest in a rapid, fluid Spanish Seth couldn't follow. He understood some of the language and he picked up the words pistolero, peligroso, and hermanos de sangre, meaning gunman, danger, and blood brothers, but the rest of the vocabulary wasn't anything he'd ever found it necessary to learn. He watched his compadre putting his heart into convincing the priest, and saw that the priest gave in because of Joaquín's argument but that it bothered him to do it. They followed the man in the black robe into the building.

The church had a hard-packed dirt floor and no benches or furniture other than the altar. The stations of the cross were illuminated by flickering candles in the gloom. Seth watched Joaquín touch the water in a bowl by the door and make the sign of the cross over his chest and he had to stop himself from laughing, not wanting to offend his friend but finding the ritual uncomfortably absurd. Then they all followed the black robe up to the altar. The priest knelt with his back to them for a few minutes and Seth smiled, thinking the man was asking God's forgiveness for what he was about to do. He rose and faced them again, speaking softly to Joaquín.

With worry in his eyes, his friend said, "You should kneel now."

"No," Seth said again, his eyes hard on the priest.

But he could see the padre wasn't intimidated. He spoke to Joaquín and Seth couldn't catch one word of the soft Spanish. His friend argued then looked at him with defeat in his eyes. "He said you must take off your gun and kneel before the altar, otherwise he won't perform the marriage."

Seth looked down at Johanna and saw she was amused. Both of them felt like laughing but he figured the priest would kick them out on the spot, and he also suspected they'd never make it to the alcalde's if they gave up now. He looked at the altar. The wall behind was decorated with a colorful painting of the Virgin of Guadalupe and he decided that kneeling before a woman holding an armful of roses instead of God enduring a gory execution was all the mercy he was going to get. Meeting Joaquín's eyes with a warning that he better appreciate what he was doing for him, Seth unbuckled his gunbelt and handed it over. "Watch the goddamned door," he muttered, letting himself drop to his knees and sliding his arm around Johanna's waist as she knelt beside him.

He felt like a fool, a hypocrite of the worst order, a killer on his knees in a church. The priest droned on, speaking Latin now, and all Seth could catch was domini sanctus thrown in at the end of every phrase. Holy Christ summed up Seth's feelings too, but not in any way remotely close to what the priest meant. Then he looked down at Johanna. She was smiling as she watched him, and her love shone brighter than all the candles on the altar. He smiled back, wishing the priest would hurry up so he could kiss her.

Joaquín whispered it was time for the ring and the priest took it from Seth's hand, studied it doubtfully a moment, then carried it to the altar, holding it high as he blessed it with the Blood of Christ. Seth caught those words because he knew the name of the mountains above Santa Fe, and again he smiled that blood should be such an integral part of this marriage. The priest came back and held his hand over Seth's head, intoning more Latin. Then Joaquín whispered, "Say yes."

"Yes," Seth said.

The priest moved his hand over Johanna's head and droned on some more. When he stopped she didn't need to be prompted, her affirmation was clear and lovely with certitude.

The priest gave the ring back to Seth and he slid it on Johanna's finger, smiling into her eyes.

Finally Joaquín whispered, "You can stand up now." With relief Seth regained his feet, Johanna standing close beside him. The priest held his arms high and intoned more words, then lowered his hands and smiled for the first time. "Es fine," he said.

"Do I get to kiss her now?" Seth asked Joaquín.

He nodded and Seth took her in his arms and gave her a kiss the likes of which he doubted the priest had ever seen. When he'd finished he met her eyes and they both laughed, then he looked at the priest, feeling like a schoolboy flaunting his misbehavior. But the priest smiled and spoke again.

Joaquín translated, "He says your love is deep and it gives him hope."

Seth nodded. "Gracias," he said, giving the priest a Gold Eagle.

"Vaya con díos," the padre said.

Seth laughed, took his gunbelt from Joaquín's hands, and led Johanna back down the aisle and into the sunshine. His first act as a married man was to buckle on his gun again. He looked up and down the wide, dusty street of the village as he did it, then he turned and looked at his wife. "You feel any different?" he asked.

"I'm Mrs. Seth Strummar now," she smiled. "I feel like the queen of all God's creation."

"All God's miscreants is more like it," he laughed.

Joaquín came out holding a piece of paper. "The certificate," he said, extending it toward Seth. "To prove it happened."

"You keep it," he said to Johanna.

She took it happily, studying the Spanish a moment, then holding it close to her breasts with a smile of contentment. As they walked back to the casita, Seth explained their plans to Joaquín. When they stopped in front of the stable, Joaquín looked back and forth between them a moment, then asked, "You're not coming back with us?"

He shook his head. "Not right away. I'll be at the vineyard of Ramon Gutierrez north of Mesilla. You know where that is?"

"Sí," the kid answered, doubt in his voice.

"If anything happens you can find me there. Until then, you stick by Johanna's side. Can you do that?"

"Sí," he said again. "How long before you return?"

"That depends," Seth said, leaving the explanation of Pilger for another time. "Johanna has to sell her holdings in El Paso and wait for an answer from the lawyer in San Antone. Then we'll be leaving Texas for good."

Joaquín nodded thoughtfully. "What will I say about the deaths of Devery and Olwell?"

"You weren't there, you don't know anything about it. What could you say?"

"It will be difficult to lie."

"Not as hard as hanging. If you remember that, you'll do all right."

Joaquín looked doubtful again, but finally he smiled. "Suddenly a lie seems an easy thing."

Seth nodded. "I'll get my horse," he said, turning away.

When he led it out into the sunshine, they were standing as he'd left them, doing nothing but waiting. They seemed so dependent on his lead, he worried how they'd do without him. He stopped before Johanna, lifting her chin to look into her eyes, hearing Joaquín move away from them.

"Do you remember everything I told you this morning?"

"Yes," she said, tears glittering on her lashes.

"You're not going to cry, are you?"

"Yes," she smiled.

"Good girl," he laughed, kissing her quickly. He swung onto his sorrel and spurred it away in a lope, not looking back. He cut south through México, circling below El Paso, then rode north into the badlands of New Mexico toward his friend's sanctuary on the Rio Grande.

15

Rosalinda Sisquieros Montoya was thinking of going back to Ramon's, too. Devery had been dead over a month now and Annie was acting as if she owned the brothel, even demanding a bigger share of the girls' earnings. Rosalinda thought the well had dried up in El Paso and at Ramon's she might hear news of Seth. Mawson hadn't been back to see her but she'd picked up the gossip that he was still in town. She thought if she warned Seth, he might take her with him when he left. If he was still anywhere around.

Annie came into her room without knocking, her face pinched with anger.

"This is still a private room," Rosalinda snapped.

"Huh, that's what you think. Mrs. Strummar's in the parlor askin' to see ya."

Rosalinda felt the blood drain from her face. "Mrs. Strummar?" she whispered. Her first thought was that he was dead and his mother had come to her because somehow she'd learned of their friendship. Ordinarily a good woman would never step foot in a brothel, but when the woman was the mother of an outlaw she might overlook propriety. Rosalinda studied herself in the mirror, wondering what his mother would think of her. "Is he dead?" she whispered.

Annie laughed. "Not unless dead men can get married."

Rosalinda spun on her. "What the hell are you talking about?"

"Go see for yourself," the fat woman laughed, turning and walking out, leaving the door open.

Slowly Rosalinda forced her feet across the floor and down the stairs, stopping halfway as she saw Johanna sitting in a chair, the Mexican kid Joaquín standing beside her wearing a gun. She forced herself forward. "I was told Mrs. Strummar asked to see me," she said, barely able to get the words out.

Johanna stood up. "I am Mrs. Strummar," she said softly.

Rosalinda looked at the pride in the girl's eyes, at the ramrod of her posture in the elegant gray cloak, the gunman beside her where there hadn't been one before, and she knew it was true. Desperately she struggled to make her tongue work. "He married you?" she whispered.

Johanna nodded. "I wish to sell this house and the Rio Bravo. Seth suggested you might be interested in buying them."

Rosalinda turned away, fighting tears and her almost irresistible impulse to slap the girl. Her mind reeled with the knowledge that he, whom she had known and loved for three years, could marry an ignorant girl he'd barely met. She tried to tell herself he was like any other man and wanted a bride who was innocent, but she couldn't believe it. He appreciated savvy in his women and a toughness no child could have. And then it occurred to her that he'd married Johanna for her money. Like an aging whore, he'd reached out for comfort in his old age. That it had been offered by a pretty young girl hadn't been a detraction but he didn't love her, he couldn't. Their offer to sell the brothels meant he still wanted Rosalinda in his life but not attached to his marriage, he wanted her independent and nearby.

Slowly she turned to face the girl, trying to hide her hatred. "I'm afraid I'm not in a position to make such an investment," she said, knowing Seth had a remedy in mind.

"No cash will be required," Johanna replied. "The contract will stipulate that you make monthly payments to a trust fund established to finance a school for poor children."

"That wasn't Seth's idea!" Rosalinda jeered.

"No," the girl said without a smile.

"Does he know you're giving away your dowry to educate poor children?" she asked snidely.

Johanna's eyes were cool. "He suggested I give the brothels to you outright since I don't want the money. But this way, I'll have the chance to take it back if you renege on our agreement."

Rosalinda struggled to understand exactly what she was agreeing to, then she caught on. "Ah. The girl in the yellow dress was at least a witness to murder if not an outright accomplice, wasn't she? A murder by which she profited handsomely. You're right, my silence is worth a great deal. Otherwise your husband may have to visit you in prison and that would be inconvenient for a man with a price on his head, wouldn't it?"

"I'm not afraid of you, Rosalinda," Johanna replied stiffly. "No jury would take your word over mine."

"The word of a whore over a lady, you mean?" she spit out.

"I thought the arrangement would benefit both of us," Johanna said, pulling on her gloves. "If you're not interested, I'll approach someone else."

"Annie knows you were there."

"Even two whores don't make a lady," she smiled. "Besides, Joaquín and I were on our way to San Antonio when we heard the news of my stepfather's death."

"And you just happened to stop off and marry his killer!"

"It seems I'm wasting my time," the girl replied haughtily. "If you're going to speak badly of my husband, I'll bid you good day."

"You little twit! He married you for your money, don't flatter yourself he cares for you."

"Let's go," she said to Joaquín, turning away.

Rosalinda watched her desperately, knowing if Johanna walked through that door, Seth was out of her life for good. "Wait!" she cried, submerging her feelings beneath the facade of indifference she'd learned well in her life as a whore. "I'm sorry," she said softly. "The offer is generous and I accept your conditions."

Johanna didn't smile. "I'll have my lawyer call for you when the contract is ready. It should take only a few days. Barring any problems, the two establishments are yours." She turned and walked out, followed by Joaquín.

Rosalinda stared at the door for a long moment, then she swept a vase of poinsettias from the table and flung it with the full force of her rage to shatter against the wall.

When Johanna walked into the kitchen of her home, Marietta and Armando Chávez, the couple who took care of the house, were standing there with solemn faces.

"There's a man waiting to see you," Armando said.

"Who is it?" she asked eagerly, hoping it was Seth.

"A Ranger named Mawson," Armando answered. "He's in the parlor."

"What did you tell him?" she whispered.

"Only that you were out, señora. He insisted on waiting."

"Nothing of my husband?"

He shook his head. "That is not my place."

"Thank you, Armando," she said, taking off her gloves and cloak. Marietta came to lift them from her hands.

"Would you like coffee brought in?" Armando asked.

"No," she said. "He won't be staying long."

She stopped in the hall to straighten her hair before the mirror, feeling frightened at facing a Ranger alone. She told herself all she had to do was say nothing, remembering Seth's advice to Joaquín. She hadn't been there when Devery died, what could she possibly know? The trick was to not volunteer information and trip herself up. Resolutely she opened the parlor door and walked in.

The Ranger was a fearsome man. He was huge, his chest crossed by a bandolero full of bullets, his face ruddy, his dark eyes unkind. "I'm Johanna Devery," she said, stopping a good distance away.

"Captain Earl Mawson of the Texas Rangers, miss," he said in a gruff tone, assessing her openly.

"What can I do for you, Captain?" she asked, noting that her voice quivered with fear.

He noticed it too and smiled, but it wasn't friendly. "Let me offer my condolences on the death of your stepfather," he said.

"Thank you," she replied. "It was a great shock."

"Yeah, I bet it was. Mind if we sit down?"

"Forgive me," she said, taking a chair that was isolated in the room.

He came closer and towered over her. "I've been investigatin' the killin'. Right after it happened, folks saw two men ridin' hard out of town. One of 'em was on a bay that din't amount to much, but the other rode a flashy sorrel and he had a girl wearin' a yeller dress on behind him. Do ya have any idea who they might be?"

She shook her head, watching him.

"Well, Seth Strummar was in town right about then and he rides a sorrel. I got information the girl in the yeller dress was you."

She smiled. "I was on my way to San Antonio at the time."

"Uh-huh. This person what told me said your stepfather laid a trap for Strummar and got himself caught instead. Do ya have any idea why he'd tangle with a killer like Strummar?"

Again she shook her head.

"Don't know nothin' about it, eh?"

"As I said, I was on my way to San Antonio."

"All by yourself?"

"No, I had a man along for protection."

"Who might that be?"

"Joaquín Ascarate. He works for us."

"Us?"

"My stepfather and me."

"Your stepfather's dead."

She looked down. "A slip of the tongue," she said, sliding her hands inside the pockets of her dress to hide her ring. "It's all rather new to me, being alone."

"I don't think ya are alone, Miss Devery. But I agree it's new to ya. I don't think ya got any idea what you're into."

"I don't understand," she murmured.

"I'm sure ya don't." He walked away as if he would leave, but then turned and faced her again with his bulk silhouetted against the window so she couldn't read his eyes. "Ya know this man, Strummar?"

She shook her head.

"Well, I'll tell ya about him, though there ain't much I can say that's fittin' for a lady's ears." He paused, and when he spoke again the hatred was thick in his voice. "He's the worst killer the Southwest has known. Killed two dozen men, near as we can figure. A woman, too. Hung her. Think of that, Miss Devery. Jus' imagine if it'd been you, feelin' that rope round your neck and then havin' him slap the horse out from under ya and the rope cuttin' off your air as your skirts flapped in the breeze. Ain't a pretty picture, is it?"

"No," she whispered.

"That was kind, what he done to her, compared to what he's done to others. He's violated women, Miss Devery. I'm sure ya know what I'm talkin' about. Had his way with one right in the middle of robbin' a bank. Drug her into the office and took her with the door wide open so's the other people standin' there under his partner's gun had to watch it, hearin' her scream as she fought him. He come out of that room laughin'. What kind of man ya think could laugh after doin' something like that?"

She didn't answer.

"Not a nice man, would ya say?"

"No," she whispered.

"No, indeed. I ain't after him 'cause of all that, though. I'm after him 'cause he killed a Ranger in Austin a few years back. Him and his partner was drinkin' in a crowded saloon when the Rangers tried to arrest 'em. Strummar, he din't have no thought for the innocent people standin' around, he jus' opened fire. Killed my friend, and I'd like to see Strummar hang for it."

She sat in numbed silence.

"Hard to figure a man could shed so much blood, ain't it? But ya know, it's like a disease, killin'. Once it gets hold of a man, he runs rampant, like smallpox through the population. The only way to stop him is with an inoculation of the same lead he's pumpin' into decent folks. I aim to give it to him. Like I said, I'd rather see him hang and I'll arrest him and take him to Austin for trial if I'm certain I can accomplish that. But I don't believe he'll let it happen that way, and I feel sorry for anyone's with him when the law comes down on him again." He paused to let his words sink in. "Ya got anything ya want to tell me, Miss Devery?"

She felt ravaged. Swallowing hard to clear her throat of the tears she wanted to let loose, she said, "I don't know this man."

"Yeah, I believe that. But I suspect ya think ya do. I suspect ya think ya like him, maybe even have feelin's deeper'n that. So bein' as he killed the man who could've protected ya, I thought it my duty to come tell ya jus' what breed of man Seth Strummar is. And if there's anything ya can say or do to help bring him to justice, the whole Southwest'll be in your debt. So ya think about it, Miss Devery, and I'll call again sometime soon and see if ya haven't recollected something that mebbe could help me find him."

She remembered Seth had told her this would happen, warned her she would hear stories that could turn her against him. She thought of that night now, as well as all the days and nights she'd spent in the happiness of his love, and she stood up with resolution. "I'm sorry, Captain Mawson," she said, "I have no information to give you."

He laughed. "If ya see him again, tell him it's jus' a matter of time 'fore we meet. And when that meetin' comes off, only one of us is gonna walk away from it."

He crossed the room, scooping his hat off the table and slamming the door behind him so it echoed in the silence.

Earl Mawson stood on the front porch for a moment, reviewing what he'd just seen. The girl had obviously been shocked by his words, much more so than if she'd been hearing those things about a stranger. And she'd flat out lied about not knowing him, because the desk clerk had said a young girl with short hair had visited Strummar in his hotel room and not many girls wore their hair cropped off like hers. But that she cared for Strummar didn't mean the feeling was mutual. The death of Devery could have resulted from a feud between the two men that drew the daughter in only as a repercussion. Her leaving town with Strummar could have happened only because he wanted to get her away from the scene, maybe to win her loyalty so she wouldn't give evidence against him. That she had lied proved he'd won her loyalty, but he could have convinced her she would be held equally accountable for her stepfather's death and she could be acting simply out of fear.

In any case, Mawson didn't think Strummar would come back to El Paso soon, nor that he'd visit the daughter, no matter what her wishes in the matter were. It was too dangerous. No outlaw stayed alive as long as he had without protecting himself first and foremost right down the line. So Earl Mawson rode over to the stable where he'd quartered his Apache scout and headed back to Isleta. If Strummar showed up in El Paso again, he was sure to hear of it. In the meantime he had to placate his commander that he was still among the garrison of Rangers.

16

In less than a week, Seth was back in El Paso. He rode Ramon's black mare, missing the refinements of his own horse but admitting the mare had enough speed to get him back to his sorrel in a hurry if he needed. It was several hours after dark when he turned behind the big house on Montana Street and rode into the stable where Joaquín was working.

They greeted each other warmly, talking softly as they settled the horse into a stall. Joaquín told him everything was fine, that Johanna missed him but it was the only problem they'd faced since their return.

"Didn't you miss me?" Seth teased as they crossed the yard toward the house.

Joaquín smiled. "Sí, amigo. I lit a candle to the Virgin for your safe return."

Seth laughed. "Ain't there a saint for outlaws?"

"St. Jude is the patron of lost causes," Joaquín answered playfully.

So they were both laughing when they walked into the kitchen. Marietta and Armando were there, sitting over cups of cocoa at the table. They stood up as the two men came in, and Seth looked them over as Joaquín introduced them, seeing a couple in early middle age, rotund with the good food available from Devery's kitchen and shyly circumspect about meeting his eyes.

Joaquín excused himself and returned to the stable. While Marietta went upstairs to tell her mistress of Seth's arrival, Armando took him into the parlor, gave him a drink, and left him alone. He looked around at the ostentatious furniture, feeling his good mood diminishing fast. It wasn't just that the house belonged to a man he'd killed, but that every inch of it reeked with the kind of ornate style he detested. He carried his drink over to the window and looked out, finding some comfort in the darkness there.

In a few minutes, he heard Johanna's running footsteps and he felt better even before she came through the door. She was dressed in a blue velvet wrapper that fell open to reveal a lacy white nightgown. He lifted her high in his arms, spinning around in a circle as they laughed. Then he set her down and kissed her.

"Come up to my room," she whispered, her eyes naughty with her invitation.

"You have any whiskey up there?" he asked, following her toward the door.

She let loose of his hand, crossed to the sideboard and took a full bottle from the stock inside, then slid her other arm around his waist as they climbed the stairs. The hall was wide with numerous doors closed in the darkness. She led him to the far end, into a room that faced the back yard. The bed was huge and canopied with burgundy draperies, the carpet a dusky rose color, the furniture dark and heavy. Again he felt oppressed by the denseness of the furnishings but he tried to shake it off, telling himself it didn't matter.

He took his wife in his arms and kissed her hungrily, then untied her wrapper and let it fall to the floor. Her nightgown was thin, showing the dark circles of her nipples through the white cotton but modestly covering her from neck to toes. He smiled and stepped away, poured himself a drink and carried it over to look out the window, studying the grounds from this new vantage. "So what's been happening?" he asked. "Joaquín said you haven't had any problems."

She hadn't told Joaquín of Mawson's visit and she pushed it from her mind so as not to mar their evening. "Everything's fine," she answered, "now that we're together again."

When he turned around and saw her retying the wrapper around her waist, he started to object then smiled at himself, realizing a wife wasn't someone he could order to walk around a cold room nearly naked just because he enjoyed seeing her body.

She caught his smile and asked, "Did you tell Ramon and Esperanza about us?"

He nodded.

"What did they say?"

"Ramon spouted the usual curses about my stupidity, then brought out his best champagne."

"And Esperanza?"

He sipped his whiskey, remembering. "She crossed herself and said a prayer."

"That was sweet," she smiled.

It hadn't been sweet but he didn't tell her that. Esperanza had been frightened by the news, and she'd repeated her earlier prediction that Johanna was death riding behind him. Whether Joe or Johanna, smart aleck boy or pleasing young wife, Esperanza felt an ominous dread that nothing good would come from the union. Seth credited it to the superstitions of an old whore whom marriage had passed by. "What's happening with the brothel?" he asked.

"Rosalinda accepted the offer and my lawyer's drawing up a contract." She remembered the woman's harsh assessment of Seth's motives but refused to give them credence by repeating them now, as if she needed him to deny the accusation, so once again she avoided the truth. "She was surprised at our marriage," was all she said.

"Don't reckon she thought I'd ever do it," he said, suspecting Rosalinda's reaction had been as caustic as Esperanza's had been melancholy.

"Are you sorry?" she whispered.

He shook his head. "Are you?"

"No." She smiled mischievously. "Am I allowed to say that word now?"

"As long as you mean you love me."

"I love you," she said.

"Let's go to bed," he smiled.

Her body was even smaller than he remembered, tenderly obliging and striving to please but delicate and easily wounded. Far different from the whores he was used to who could take anything he cared to dish out. Several times he stopped himself when he felt her resistance or saw her wince, tempering his hunger in an effort to find a common ground for their pleasure. Johanna was trying hard and he held his passion in abeyance to what he believed he owed his wife. When he felt unsatisfied after their gentle lovemaking, he told himself it was an accommodation that was his to make.

She felt his discontent. "Is something wrong, Seth?" she whispered.

"What makes you ask that?"

"You feel tense. Didn't I satisfy you?"

He kissed her with a smile, then got up and pulled on his pants. "Reckon I'm just edgy being back in El Paso. What was said about Devery's death?"

"It's practically forgotten," she lied, again refusing to allow the ugliness of Mawson to intrude on the first night of their reunion. "Men die of gunfights nearly every week here, so it wasn't unusual. And being the man he was, he had a lot of enemies. I don't think the marshal is spending any time worrying about it."

He poured himself another drink, carried it over to the window and stood looking down at the dark yard and stable.

"You're not sleepy, are you?" she asked from the bed.

"No," he said, feeling so pent up he knew he was hours from sleep.

"What would you like to do?"

"Truthfully?" he asked, turning to look at her.

"I always want the truth from you," she said, feeling guilty for withholding it from him.

"Okay," he said. "I'd like to go to a saloon and have a drink among men." He could see she wasn't happy with his answer. "But I won't," he added.

"Not tonight anyway," she said softly.

"Not in El Paso," he agreed, watching out the window again. "Have you heard where Pilger is?"

She shuddered that his thoughts had turned to Travis Pilger so soon. "My lawyer has written him in San Antonio," she sighed, throwing the covers off and climbing out of bed. "Let's not talk about all that tonight, Seth," she pleaded.

He caught the unhappiness in her voice and turned around to watch her slender body disappear beneath her nightgown and wrapper again. "It's hard to make plans if I don't know what's been happening," he said, feeling a loss of control though he couldn't name what was wrong.

She crossed to her dressing table and sat down to run a brush through her short hair. Then she sighed again and turned on the stool to face him. "Simon, he's my lawyer, Simon Weisenhall, he says Travis owns a half interest in the saloon and that I'm partners with him now, as Jade's heir. I've told Simon I want to sell everything but he says I have to offer Travis first right of refusal before I can sell my share of the saloon. He says Travis doesn't own anything else and he expects him to return soon."

She wanted to take his mind off Pilger so she stood up and crossed to her chiffonnier, opened it and took out a stack of shirts. "I got these from Jade's room. His suits will be too small for you, but these shirts might fit. Would you like to try one on?"

"No," he said sharply, refilling his glass with whiskey.

"It's silly to let them go to waste, Seth. They're quality work and the colors are wonderful. Look at this chalky purple one, it's like the blossoms on those thistles that grow in the mountains." She looked at him across the room. "I don't think he ever wore it," she added hopefully.

He was having trouble understanding why she thought he'd want them, but he tried to make a joke to cover his annoyance. "You hinting I should get dressed?" he laughed, standing there barechested.

"I like seeing you like that," she smiled. "I just thought it was something we could do until you're sleepy."

He crossed the room and looked down at the stack of shirts, the dull purple on top, the others pale yellow and blue and tan and green. They were all linen and soft to the touch, the clothes of a gentleman, not the rough saddletramp he'd always been. "How about that lawyer in San Antone?" he asked, moving away to sit on her dressing stool and lean his elbows on his knees, holding his drink and staring at the floor, trying to get a handle on what was going on. "You hear from him?"

"Not yet," she answered, nervous about his mood.

"You take any steps toward selling this house?"

"Simon's working on finding a buyer. He says the market is speculative right now so we shouldn't have any problems. As soon as I hear from San Antonio, I'll be ready to leave." When he didn't answer, she asked, "Have you thought where we'll go?"

"I hear California's pretty," he said without conviction.

"I've heard that, too," she smiled, though he wasn't looking at her. She knelt on the floor in front of him. "What is it, Seth?"

He met her eyes, both of them recognizing that something had erected a barrier between them. "Lot of changes, is all," he said. "Reckon I'll get used to it."

"It's hard to give up old ways, you mean?"

He nodded, studying the innocence of her young face. "I've been an outlaw half my life, Johanna. Not sure how I'll do as a husband."

"You'll do fine," she smiled. "I love you as you are."

"You don't even know me," he scoffed.

"That's not true," she argued. "I met you as a boy, knew you as a girl in trouble, as a woman in your bed, and now as your wife. Maybe I know you better than anyone."

"For a part of me that's true," he conceded, looking into the whiskey in his glass, "but it's not the part that's governed who I am."

She watched him carefully. "This part you say has governed you, is it something you want more than the tenderness you've shown me?"

"It's not a question of what I want," he answered impatiently.

"Why not?"

"You don't understand," he said, setting his drink aside and leaning back with his elbows on her dressing table.

She rested against one of his knees and ran a finger around the edges of his belt buckle. "When you say that, you close me out."

He assessed her harshly. "You know what I'd do right now, ordinarily?"

She shook her head, watching him.

He laid it on thick because he felt trapped by their sudden lack of affinity. "I'd have you suck my cock, whether you wanted to or not. Then I might hit you for it afterwards just to let you know you hadn't pleased me, even if you had. Then I'd fuck the bejesus out of you and when we woke up in the morning you'd have a few bruises for souvenirs. Then I'd get on my horse and ride away and never think about you again."

She didn't believe him. She was aware he'd been holding himself back in their lovemaking but she felt she could learn to handle his passion and that it wouldn't be as awful as he was trying to make it sound. "You can do all that, Seth," she smiled, "if you promise not to leave in the morning."

"I don't want to," he answered roughly, standing up and walking away from her.

She stared at him, afraid she'd lose before he'd given her a chance. "Will you go to Rosalinda and do it to her? Is that how you'll stop yourself from hurting me?"

"Maybe not her, but I can't figure any other way out of it," he said.

"I can!" she cried. "Give it to me, whatever it is. I'm your wife, it's mine."

"Then I don't want a wife," he said. The pain on her face made him realize he'd hurt her much more than if he'd hit her. He laughed at himself. "I'm caught, Johanna," he said gently. "A man ought to honor his wife, not demean her."

"Your love could never demean me, Seth," she argued. When he was silent, she pleaded, "Teach me to please you. I'm not Catholic, there's no separation in my heart between the madonna and the harlot. I can be both."

He was surprised at her words but admitted ruefully, "I'm not sure I can let you."

"You let me act like a boy after you knew I wasn't. Isn't it the same?"

"It didn't matter to me that you were passing yourself off as a boy. It didn't have much to do with me. My wife is something else."

"To the world, your wife will be a lady with all the refinements I can master. Only in our bedroom will I be your whore."

"Do you think you can be a whore in my bed and walk out in the morning without remembering the things we'd done?"

"I'll remember them," she smiled. "I'll remember I'm Mrs. Seth Strummar and let the world be pleased to think what it will."

"You say that like I'm the king of England or something," he laughed.

"Something," she smiled. "Will you come back to bed now, and try to forget I'm your wife and treat me like a woman who wants only to please you?"

He knew that was the problem, he couldn't forget she was his wife and he didn't want to drag her down into his pain. He could do it with whores because it was a reality they shared, the roughness that came from living on the edge of decent society. A wife, though, was akin to a mother, women who deserved to be protected from brutality. But he did as she asked, making love to her gently again, insisting he wanted it that way then lying awake long after she'd gone to sleep, doubting that he could accommodate himself to marriage. Already he could feel his grief building inside him, and he knew if he didn't find a whore to share his pain it would accumulate until he might kill Johanna with the force of it breaking loose.

In the morning, he left her asleep, walked downstairs to the kitchen where Marietta was working and asked her for breakfast. She was a short, plump woman with her hair tied in a thick silver-streaked bun at the back of her neck. He could see she was afraid of him, but he didn't know if it had to do with him or her memories of Devery. It was evident she was uncomfortable sharing the kitchen as he ate, but he knew he'd feel uneasy in the windowless dining room and he figured he had some rights in the house. When he'd finished his ham and eggs, he asked for more coffee and smiled at her as she brought the pot to refill his cup.

"Have you worked here long?" he asked, watching her carry the coffee back to the stove.

She turned to face him from across the room. "A few years."

"Did you like working for Devery?"

She shook her head. "My husband was looking for another job when Señor Devery died. Working for the girl, I mean, Señora Strummar, will be easy."

"It's a big house to keep up."

"Sí, but it was never the work that bothered us."

"What was it?"

"I'm sure Señora Strummar has told how he treated her," she answered cautiously.

"I've heard some of it."

"He kept her locked in her room much of the time. It was hard, seeing her cooped up as if in prison. And then, many times, I heard her crying when they were alone. Pobrecita. I'm glad she found someone who cares for her. Armando and I will try to please you in all ways, Señor Strummar."

"You should please her, not me. The house is hers."

"You are her husband and master here," she answered, dropping her gaze.

He stood up. "Thanks for breakfast," he said.

"De nada," she murmured.

He felt ill at ease walking down the baronial hall to climb the sweeping staircase back to his sleeping bride. Just as he was crossing the foyer, the front doorbell rang. He stepped back half-obscured in the shadows and watched Armando come from where he had been stacking firewood in the parlor.

Armando saw him. "Buenos días, Señor Strummar," he said.

"Mornin'," he said.

"Do you wish to open the door?"

He shook his head, continuing up the stairs. He had made it to the first landing when the sunlight flooded the hall below him and he felt so edgy he had to work at not drawing his gun.

"Buenos días, Señor Weisenhall," the servant said. "Pasa usted."

Seth looked down at the lawyer, who looked up and met his eyes. "Mr. Strummar?" he asked.

Reluctantly Seth retraced his steps to the foyer and extended his hand to the small, wiry man. "Pleased to meet'cha," he said, though he wasn't.

"The pleasure is mine. I've been hoping to have a talk with you."

"Why?"

"Perhaps we can go into the parlor?"

"All right," he said, looking at Armando.

"Would you like coffee brought in?" the servant asked.

He looked at Weisenhall. "Please," the lawyer said. Armando bowed and retreated toward the kitchen. Seth followed Weisenhall into the parlor then walked over to look out the window at the broad street and the desert beyond. When he turned around again, he saw the lawyer still standing holding his satchel and realized he was waiting for an invitation to sit down. He felt like an idiot. "Have a seat," he said.

"Thank you," the lawyer replied, choosing a place on the horsehair settee, opening his briefcase and pulling sheaves of papers out, spreading them on the low table before him, then looking up at Seth. "There are a few documents which require your signature."

"Why mine?"

"You're Johanna's husband."

"So?"

"Under Texas law, Mr. Strummar, the responsibility of her affairs resides with you."

"I don't want it," he said.

The lawyer was surprised. "Nevertheless, her actions aren't binding without your approval. She has a large estate and there are matters that need to be resolved."

"Such as?"

"The sale of the house on Utah Street and the Rio Bravo Dance Hall. The contracts have been drawn up, but without your signature they're not binding."

"I don't have any interest in Johanna's property," he argued. "It belongs to her."

"Morally and ethically you're correct. Legally, even, to a moot degree. The property remains in her name, but she can't sell any part of her estate without your approval."

"Just because I married her?"

"Yes," he answered slowly. "It's rather a large holding."

"How large?"

"The house on Utah Street is worth two thousand, plus another eight hundred for the furnishings. The dance hall, though a larger building, is worth less due to its location. The lot and structure are valued at approximately twelve hundred. The furnishings consist of the bar stock, one brass bed, and a collection of whips."

"Whips?"

"Yes. Fifty-three, to be exact. No two alike. They're worth, approximately, three hundred dollars. These are round figures, you understand. I can give you the exact amounts if you wish."

He shook his head.

"This residence and furnishings are worth thirty-five hundred, though if you hold onto it until the railroad comes it will be worth considerably more. But that's true of all the El Paso property. The North Pass Saloon, as a building, is worth about seven hundred including the furnishings, though the business, of course, is worth more. It's held in partnership with a Mr. Travis Pilger. Have you met him?"

"Not yet."

"He's a pleasant gentleman. I don't anticipate any problems dividing the business but where money is concerned it's hard to predict how people will act." He shuffled through some papers. "Then there's the bank account in St. Louis. The present balance, as of the first of last month, is fifty thousand, eight hundred seventy-five dollars and three cents. There's a portfolio of stocks and the still somewhat mysterious trust established by Mrs. Strummar's grandfather. We've written the attorney in San Antonio handling that but have yet to receive his reply."

"Fifty thousand?"

The lawyer nodded, watching him. "Didn't you know you had married a wealthy woman, Mr. Strummar?"

He shook his head.

"How fortunate for the young lady. I must confess, when she told me of the marriage I suspected unkind motives on your part. I'm greatly relieved to learn you acted out of affection rather than avarice."

"I don't want her money," he said.

The lawyer smiled patiently, letting his gaze slide down the form of the man standing before him, then meeting his eyes again. "Nevertheless, Mr. Strummar, for all intents and purposes, it's at your disposal."

"Do you know who I am?"

"Yes," he answered, drawling the word.

"And you'd still hand her money over to me?"

"The decision is not mine to make. If she wished to limit your use of it there are means by which that could be done. But she's told me you're to have access as easily as she herself."

"She's practically a child. Do you think she's competent to make that decision?"

Again the patient smile. "Under the laws of Texas, a married woman is no longer a minor. The law considers her competent."

"You mean I could take the money and leave her?"

The lawyer looked unhappy. "If you did and she chose to do so, we could fight you in the courts to regain control. Provided we could find you."

Seth turned away and stared out the window, thinking Johanna was a fool to trust anyone that much. But then he didn't guess she'd known all this when they were married in Zaragoza. He looked at the lawyer watching him. "Isn't there some kind of paper you could write up that would prevent me from touching the money?"

"You could settle it all in a trust for her but I wouldn't advise it."

"Why not?"

"It would freeze the capital so neither one of you could touch it. That would handicap your investment possibilities, leaving you only a stipend to meet living expenses."

Armando knocked on the door and came in carrying a silver coffee service on a tray. He set it on the sideboard then said, "Señora Strummar will be down in a few minutes," and turned to go.

"Nice meeting you," Seth said, starting to follow him out.

"Mr. Strummar, may I have your signature on these documents?" the lawyer asked quickly. When

Seth balked, he added, "The sale of the Utah Street house and the dancehall can't be completed without your signature."

"Then leave them incomplete," he said, walking out, down the hall and through the kitchen, feeling the servants' eyes on him as he left the house. Only when he reached the stable did he remember his sorrel wasn't there. He stood at the gate to the stall and stared in at the black mare he'd borrowed from Ramon, wanting to saddle it and ride back to his friend, retrieve his horse and disappear into the wilderness where he felt he belonged. Then he looked up and saw Johanna closing the door, and he knew he didn't want to leave her.

She came toward him and he pulled her deeper into the stable, into an empty stall and down on the floor covered with fresh straw over the odors of horse piss and shit, where he tore her drawers off and fucked her fast without one kiss or word of endearment. As they lay together breathing hard, he raised himself above her and met her eyes. "Now I feel like myself again. How did you like it?"

"I loved it," she smiled.

"You sonofabitch," he laughed, rolling off her. "Why didn't you tell me you're so rich?"

"Are you going to hold it against me?" she asked, laughing too.

The barn door opened and Armando called, "Señor y Señora Strummar?"

"Go away," Seth shouted angrily.

"What shall I tell Señor Weisenhall?"

"The same thing," he yelled, falling back on the straw and staring up at the loft.

She watched him in confused silence a moment, then asked, "What difference does it make, Seth?

It only means we can buy ourselves a ranch in California."

"I have enough money to buy us a ranch. Did you think I was going to let you keep me?"

"No," she said carefully. "I never thought that. But . . ."

"But what?"

"The way you live, I didn't think . . . I mean, you always seem to have money in your pocket but you don't work. I guess I thought you made enough to get by gambling or something."

"I robbed banks, Johanna. I told you that."

She remembered Mawson's story about what Seth had done during a particular bank robbery and she looked away.

"Are you going to tell me you don't want my ill-gotten gains?"

She pushed Mawson out of her mind and smiled at her husband. "Isn't that what you're telling me?"

"We're talking about your inheritance," he argued.

"But it's mine because we killed him," she said. "You killed him. Don't you think you earned it as much as the money you consider yours?"

"It belongs to you."

"So you made it possible for me to have it. Why does that bother you?"

"'Cause your lawyer says it's under my control."

"So am I," she smiled. "If I trust you with my life, what do a few dollars matter?"

"It's more'n a few."

She shrugged. "I trust you, Seth."

He looked at her, realizing the enormity of what he'd done. He had married her out of loneliness and a hunger for the felicity of her love, but all those years he'd been a renegade hadn't prepared him for what he'd taken on with a wife. He'd still been thinking as a desperado when he married her, worried only that he was opening both of them to attack by admitting to the world there was someone he loved, someone his enemies could threaten, knowing he'd come to her rescue. He'd told himself he could handle that, but this daily responsibility, this nurturing and caring for her welfare was something he hadn't considered. He said, "I hope I don't let you down, Johanna."

"You won't," she smiled.

"I don't know," he said. "I've never been a husband."

"No man is until he gets married," she answered.

He looked into her blue eyes shining with absolute confidence that he could take care of her if he'd just stop fighting his past and admit everything was different now. And he had to admit it, whether he wanted to or not. His only alternative was to leave her and he couldn't see that he'd feel any better if he did that. "I used to think I was pretty brave," he said, looking into her eyes as deep as the sky, "but this scares the shit out of me."

She opened her arms and pulled him close. "Don't worry about it, Seth," she murmured, kissing his cheek, his ear, his hair where it fell against the collar of his shirt. "Just love me, that's all I need."

"I can do that," he said, sliding his hand up under her skirt again.

"Yes," she smiled. "I know you can."

17

Joaquín lay motionless in the hayloft, afraid if he moved he would send dust filtering down on Seth and Johanna making love in the stall beneath him. The loft was his usual refuge when he felt out of sorts, because the repetitious murmurs of the palomas high in the rafters helped him regain the calmness of mind which allowed him to think clearly again.

He had looked forward to Seth's return with keen anticipation of the pleasure of his company, yet now Joaquín burned with embarrassment when he compared himself to his friend. Even in the joking of their reunion the night before, his contribution had been an awkward admission that he'd lit a candle to the Blessed Mother. Seth had laughed with affection and Joaquín had laughed too, but out of gratitude that his friend hadn't ridiculed him. Now as he struggled to reconcile his lifelong beliefs with the obvious superiority of Seth's wisdom, he saw the impotency of his response to the world.

Long before he'd come to this country, Joaquín had hated Jade Devery. Yet he had put himself in the man's employ and then been trapped there by his desire to help Johanna. Instead of helping her, though, he had soothed his rage with the promise of divine justice. Even when she'd been raped, he had controlled his anger by telling himself that vengeance was not a human endeavor.

Remembering Seth's clean grace as he killed Beau Olwell, his silent efficiency as he stepped from the shadows, clamped his left hand over the villain's mouth then took his life with one swift stroke of the knife, Joaquín was suffused with envy. He remembered, too, Seth's smile as he stood up from cleaning his weapon on the dead man's clothes, and the satisfaction of that smile was an emotion Joaquín coveted.

He lay motionless in the loft as he listened to the sounds of love reaching him from below, paralyzed not only with his wish not to disturb his friends but also with the enormity of what he saw as his mistakes in interpreting the world. Joaquín had witnessed the sex act many times growing up in the brothel where his mother worked, yet never had he known the tenderness he was overhearing now, the shared compassion and nurturing expressed in the same act he had found so ugly as a child. He realized his rejection of sex had been born of a rightful abhorrence of the abuse of women, yet that rejection also crippled his understanding of what it meant to be a man.

Joaquín wanted to emulate Seth in all ways. To own the confidence to act on his judgment without hesitation or regret, to kill cleanly and swiftly and walk away feeling only satisfaction, to humble himself on a stable floor as Seth was doing now, then walk out beneath the sky with as much ease as he had walked the road that day in Zaragoza, possessed of a wry humor at all his shortcomings countered by the firm conviction that he could match any man God threw in his path.

In the weeks of Seth's recovery, when Joaquín and Johanna had spent their evenings talking softly by the fire, she'd told him of Seth's friendship with Devery's favorite whore. On one occasion Joaquín had seen her naked in Devery's bed and he'd admired her beauty even from within his monkish stance of chastity. Now he formed his resolve as he waited in silence until his friends had left their rustic bed in the stable, then Joaquín Ascarate climbed down from the loft and walked out under the sky.

He called at the brothel once owned by the man he had helped to kill, intending to take lessons in love from the woman whose expertise Seth had sought on his first night in town. She wasn't there and Joaquín sat down in the parlor to await her return.

The woman in question had passed him on the street, though neither had seen the other. She rode in a carriage with the windows covered by heavy draperies and alighted in front of the offices of the law firm of Weisenhall and Thorp, then entered the anteroom in a great commotion of silk skirts and overpowering perfume. Simon Weisenhall stood behind his desk as she was ushered into his office, taking in the expensiveness of her white gown, the fine wool of her forest green shawl, the matching broad-brimmed bonnet decorated with white silk flowers, the nearly combustible fragrance of her French perfume, and his smile covered his trepidation. But Rosalinda sensed he was unhappy to see her in his office. She accepted the chair he held for her, declined his offer of coffee, and got right to business. Before he could even sit down behind his desk, she asked, "What's holding up the contracts?"

"Only the necessary signatures," the lawyer answered carefully, leaning back and lacing his fingers across the front of his vest.

"Has the little twit changed her mind?"

Weisenhall winced. "I assume you're referring to Mrs. Strummar?"

"Call her what you want. Why hasn't she signed?"

"She has," he answered slowly.

"Then what's the problem?"

"I met with Mr. Strummar today and, unfortunately, he refused to put his signature on the documents."

Her heart beat faster at the knowledge Seth was back in town. "Did he say why?" she asked breathlessly.

"No, he didn't. I can only assume he will eventually agree to the arrangement. However, there's no guarantee of that, of course."

"Then what makes you assume he will agree?"

"He expressed an opinion that Mrs. Strummar's property was not his concern."

"Hah! All he wants is the money, you mean, and what she does with the buildings he doesn't give jackshit about."

Again, Weisenhall winced at her language. "I believe you've misjudged the man. He seemed immensely surprised at her holdings and his responsibility as her husband. I believe he married her solely from affection."

"Then you're mistaken!" she cried. Rising to her feet, she struggled to control herself. "How long must I wait to have title?"

Slowly the lawyer stood up. "Since you've given no money to effect the transaction, I can't see, Miss Montoya, that you have any grounds for complaint."

"We had an agreement, she and I!"

"Yes, but it requires his signature to be legal. I'm sorry, that's the law."

"The law! As if he ever cared one whit for the legality of anything! Maybe his dumb little wife doesn't know how to properly motivate a man like Seth Strummar. You tell him my brothel is at his service and I await his pleasure. If he doesn't come see me, I'll go to the marshal and raise holy hell. They'll know what I'm talking about."

She spun her silk skirts and departed, leaving a cloud of perfume behind. Simon Weisenhall slowly sank back into his chair, wondering if he could in all good conscience deliver such a message, but as the attorney standing between them he knew he was duty bound to do so.

When Rosalinda walked back into what she had come to regard as her house and saw Joaquín sitting in the parlor, she assumed he had come from the woman she habitually called the little twit. "What do you want?" she asked rudely.

Joaquín stood up and tried to think of how Seth would answer such a question. "I thought this was a brothel," he laughed, picking up his hat. "If not, I can take my money down the street."

Her smile was conniving. "You've come for a whore, have you?"

"I've come for you," he smiled. "But like I said, one is as good as another."

Her smile deepened, adding a sparkle to her eyes which wasn't kind, though it flashed with a wicked delight. "I'm expensive, Joaquín. I wouldn't think a stableboy could afford me."

"I am no longer a stableboy but the protector of my compadre's wife."

"And you make a good salary, do you?"

"Enough to afford you," he replied.

She looked him over and her entire demeanor softened. "Will you come upstairs, please?" she purred.

He followed her, wondering if he could pull this off without her guessing how frightened he felt. The only thought which gave him courage was the suspicion that Seth had probably done it when he'd been even less experienced. But once he was in the room and she had closed the door, he didn't know what to do. He watched her take her bonnet off and place it in the hatbox, then slide the box on top of her chiffonnier, watched her remove her dress and corset and petticoats until she stood before him in only her shimmy, and then he faltered, not remembering how to begin.

Her smile was solicitous and he felt certain she'd guessed his secret. Suddenly she was kind, coming forward to drop on her knees before him, open his pants and take him out. He watched his manhood disappear in her mouth and in a few quick strokes of unimaginable pleasure he had come and felt ashamed. She smiled with encouragement. "Now we can do it properly," she said, taking his hand and leading him to her bed.

Rosalinda was mistaken in the source of his trepidation, thinking his fear-rose from ignorance rather than a premature exposure to carnal knowledge. She had discerned his motive in choosing her, however, and she served him as she would the man he was trying to emulate. It wasn't easy. When they were naked on the bed, Joaquín was shy and clumsy, making no move to fondle her or assert his dominion over her body in any way. She uttered a few silent curses in her mind then smiled and lifted his hand to her breast.

"Don't you like it?" she teased.

"Sí," he said. "It's soft and warm."

"Yes," she cooed. "Why don't you kiss it?"

His dark eyes flashed up at hers a moment, then he lowered his head and as gently as butterfly wings his lips brushed across her nipple. She wanted to scream with impatience but kept her voice perfectly in control as she murmured, "I won't break, Joaquín."

"I have no wish to hurt you," he said.

"No?" she laughed. "Well, let's try something else then." She grabbed hold of his hair and slapped him hard, laughing at the shock on his face. "Come on, Joaquín. There's a man in there somewhere. Let him out." She slapped him again, then punched her fist into his belly.

He was angry now, she could see it in his eyes, but instead of giving it back to her he was getting up to leave. "Oh no," she said, catching hold of his hand and stopping him. "Come on, give it to me, whatever you're feeling. That's what whores are for."

"I don't want a whore, then," he said, standing by the side of the bed.

"Yes you do or you wouldn't be here." She reached a foot out and rubbed it lightly against his thigh, then slid her hand between her legs and caressed herself. "Come on, Joaquín," she moaned. "Don't leave me all alone after you've made me so hot." He just stood there, staring down at her. She squirmed around so her spread legs were directly in front of him, knowing she had him because he hadn't moved any farther away. "Come on, Joaquín," she begged. "I need to feel your cock inside me, hot and throbbing." She reached up and touched him, coaxing his response. "There's the man coming now. See, he wants me, why don't you?"

"I don't like you," he said.

She laughed. "Then fuck me, Joaquín. That's what you do to people you don't like. You fuck them." She tugged him down on top of her, maneuvering herself beneath him. "Haven't you ever been fucked, Joaquín?" she whispered in his ear. "I'm talking about all the shit other people lay on you. Give it back. Give it to me."

He moaned and she brought her knee up hard into his ribs. When he recoiled away from her she slapped him again.

"Pinche puta," he said, slapping her back.

"Yeah, do it again," she laughed. "Let me feel the force of your anger. Come on, you've got a lot in there, I can feel it bustin' to get out."

He thrust himself inside her and rode her hard. She circled his hips with her legs and clung to him, sliding her hand around behind and sticking a finger up his ass. He jerked rigid and recoiled away from her again, his eyes so pathetically confused she almost felt compassion. "It's all right, Joaquín. Everything's all right with a whore," she cooed, giving him a wet kiss on his mouth, moving her tongue down his chest, dawdling her way until she licked her own juice off the tip of his cock. He let her suck him then grabbed her and threw her down beneath him, thrusting himself in deep and hard, watching her face as she faked an orgasm, thrashing in the agony of her pretense, then he filled her with his hot, wet semen.

"Oh God," she moaned. "Jesus. Holy Mary." She laughed. "Jumpin' Jehovah, I haven't been fucked like that in a long time, Joaquín."

He was watching her with his dark eyes full of bewilderment and she laughed again. "Didn't you like it?" she cooed, snuggling close. "Please say yes. I couldn't bear to know that giving me such pleasure wasn't the same for you."

"I liked it," he said, but his voice was hurt.

She reached down and touched his cock, wet and limp in her hand. "Want to do it again?" she murmured, feeling it grow beneath her caresses.

He didn't answer and she sucked him hard again, guided him inside her again, let him dawdle with his pleasure, anticipating his rhythm, matching it, dragging their ascent out until he came again and lay breathing hard on top of her. "Jesus," she laughed. "You're some lover, Joaquín." She wriggled out from beneath him and crossed the room to the whiskey on the sideboard.

"Would you like a drink?" she asked from her distance.

He shook his head, watching her.

"Don't mind if I have one, do you?"

"No," he said.

She brought the glass back with her and sat down beside him as she sipped at it, then she dunked her finger in the whiskey and let it drip onto his cock, watching it stir with her fresh attentions. "Shall we do it again?" she smiled.

"I don't think so," he said.

"You gonna keep me hungry, Joaquín?" she pouted.

"I have to get back," he said.

"Aw, will your compadre miss you? He won't mind, he understands how a man needs a woman."

But he stood up and looked down at her, his face puzzled. "I have to go," he said again.

"Will you come back?" she asked sweetly.

"Perhaps," he said.

"Say yes, Joaquín. I'll keep my evening free just for you. After this afternoon I couldn't bear to let another man touch me. Won't you promise that you'll come back after dinner?"

"Maybe," he said, pulling on his clothes.

"Perhaps, maybe," she sighed. "You know how to tease a woman, don't you? Won't you promise, please?"

"If I can," he said, buckling on his gunbelt. "How much do I owe you?"

"It was on the house," she smiled. "I can't remember when I've spent such a satisfying afternoon."

Joaquín regained his composure as he walked down the stairs. By the time he felt the warmth of the sun on his face, he'd forgotten his confusion at the holy words she'd uttered in the heat of passion. By the time he'd turned onto Montana Street in his ambling walk toward home, he was congratulating himself for having pulled it off. He laughed, thinking Seth certainly knew how to get across in the world. That the madam of the best brothel in El Paso would enjoy him so much she wouldn't even charge him, but instead beg him to come back and do it to her again, affirmed not only that his decision to imitate Seth had been the right one but that he was able to do it with aplomb.

When he walked into the stable, Seth was saddling the black mare. "I'm glad you're back," he said, pulling the cinch tight.

"Thanks," the kid answered with an odd smile as he sauntered past towards his room.

Seth took in the heavy fragrance following him and looked up. "Did you have a good time?" he teased.

"What do you mean?" he asked, turning at the door.

"You smell like a whorehouse," he laughed. "I hope you plan on taking a bath before seeing my wife."

Joaquín lifted his sleeve to his nose, then grinned. "Pretty obvious, huh?"

"You'd have to be dead to miss it," he said, dropping the stirrup over the tied cinch then leaning on the saddle as he smiled at him. "I thought you didn't like women that way."

"I changed my mind," he shrugged.

He nodded thoughtfully. "Well, now it's my turn. But I don't expect to enjoy my visit. Stay with Johanna, will you?"

"You sure you don't want me along?"

"Haven't you had enough for one day?" he laughed.

"I could stand guard," he winked. "Keep your back covered while you're busy."

Seth studied him, noting the new cockiness in the boy's demeanor. "I don't intend to turn my back," he answered. "And when I can't handle a vindictive whore, I may as well be put out to pasture with the rest of the steers."

"That'll be the day," Joaquín laughed.

Seth smiled at the change in him. "Try not to trip over anything," he advised. "It still fits in your pants, you know."

The kid blushed as Seth swung onto the horse and looked down at him with affection. "I'll be back for supper. We'd be pleased if you'd eat with us."

"I'll be there," he answered.

"Good. Hurry up with your bath. I don't like leaving Johanna alone."

"Do you think she's in danger?"

"Anyone connected to me shares the same risks I do," he said. "Right now, that includes you."

"I'll be careful," he said.

Seth nodded, then turned the horse out of the barn and west toward the tenderloin.

18

When Earl Mawson walked into the office of the commander of the Rangers at Isleta, George Baylor frowned as he looked up from his desk. "What can I do for you, Earl?" he asked, leaning back in his chair and tossing the letter he'd been reading aside. It landed among the other papers scattered so thickly that the desk top was obliterated beneath orders from the high command in Austin, questions from Washington as to why the Apaches hadn't been defeated, and pleas from citizens for protection.

Earl sat down and put his feet on the corner of George's desk, pushing a letter from a rancher in the bootheel of New Mexico aside. "I jus' got the news I've been waitin' for," he said.

Baylor frowned again because the rancher had written complaining that the army was ineffective in protecting him against Geronimo and he wanted the

Rangers to intercede, jurisdiction be damned. "And what news is that?"

"Seth Strummar was seen ridin' into El Paso last night."

Baylor stood up and walked over to crouch in front of the hearth, pulled the coffeepot out and filled his cup with the strong, bitter brew. "Want some?" he asked over his shoulder.

"No, thanks," Mawson said, watching his commander's back for any clue as to what he was about to tell him.

Baylor stood up, sipping the coffee as he stared into the fire. "You know, Earl," he finally said, still not looking at him, "Strummar's just one man. We've still got two hundred marauding Apaches we've been ordered to stop."

"He's more dang'rous than any Apache," Mawson said.

Baylor turned around and studied the captain, then carried his coffee over and sat down again, trying to formulate his words in a way that the man wouldn't take offense. He leaned back and put his feet up too, square in the middle of the letter from Austin implying he'd been sitting on his duff since the death of Victorio. "You're one of the best fighters I've got, Earl. I'd hate to lose you."

"Who's sayin' anything about that?"

"I am. It seems to me you've become obsessed with Strummar, and it's not good in a fighting man to hold a personal hatred for his enemy. You know that."

"He's a hard man not to hate," Mawson growled.

Baylor sipped his coffee, looking away from the heat in the man's eyes. "Why is it you've got such a burr up your ass over him?"

"He killed Johnny in Austin."

"That was ten years ago."

"Johnny's still dead."

"The Apaches have killed more'n a few of our men. Why don't you help me go after them?"

"I been helpin' ya. Now I wanta do this."

"I'm having trouble understanding why, though."

Mawson jerked his feet to the floor and walked over to stare out the window at the dusty courtyard of the compound, the cottonwood trees bare and stark against the gray winter sky. "Did ya know Jeremiah Strummar was lynched by a mob in Austin?"

"Of course."

"Was eighteen years old, innocent as a babe. Mob was after the outlaw for killin' Johnny, hated him so much they lynched his brother instead. That was wrong, I know that. But what kind of man would let it happen?" He turned around and faced Baylor. "What breed of man would let his baby brother take the rope for him? It sticks in my craw every time I think about it. He was right there, in the city, and he let the mob kill his brother while he jus' sashayed his way outta there, prob'ly laughin' with his cutthroat buddy, Ben Allister."

"I doubt if he's ever laughed about it," Baylor said.

"Ya give him credit for bein' human but he ain't. He's killed more men than you and I personally put together and we're soldiers. He's got a taste for blood and I bet he ain't wasted no grief on any of 'em, includin' his brother."

Baylor turned away from the hatred in his eyes and stared into the fire again. "So what are you asking, Earl?"

"Give me leave to catch him."

"Probably have to kill him."

"I'm prepared to do that."

"All by yourself?"

"I'm askin' for Cha, too."

Baylor looked at him. "He's our best scout, Earl."

"So? What're ya doin' now? Nothin'!"

"The men are worn out. Soon as we're rested, we'll be going after Geronimo again."

"Let me have Cha in the meantime."

"What do you need a tracker for if Strummar's in El Paso?"

"He won't stay. I ain't figured yet why he come back, but I got a hunch it's got something to do with one of two women he's got there."

"You know who they are?"

Mawson nodded.

"I'll give you three days," Baylor sighed, knowing Mawson would go without permission and then he'd have to dismiss him for insubordination. "Three days, Earl. Then I want you back here ready to fight Apaches."

"How about Cha?"

"If he's willing, you can have him. Remember what I said, though. Three days. That's it."

Mawson smiled. "If I ain't back, consider it a resignation."

Baylor stared at him. "You've been a Ranger half your life, Earl. Are you saying you'd quit to get one goddamned outlaw?"

"Goddamned is the right word, George. I'm gonna see he gets the retribution the Good Lord's been a little late deliverin'."

Softly, the quiet of his voice adding weight to his words, Baylor said, "When a man starts seeing himself as God's avenger, that man's as dangerous as the killer he's fighting."

"That's what it takes," Mawson said, walking out.

He found Cha in the village of wickiups behind the compound. The wiry Apache followed the huge Ranger into the bosque along the river and they stood staring across into México as they talked.

"I'm goin' after Strummar agin," Mawson said. "Baylor told me I could have ya, if you're willin' to go."

Tcha-nol-haye looked into the small eyes of the man asking for help, curious about this outlaw who could inspire such hatred from so heartless a man as Mawson. Softly he asked, "Before I say, I would like to know why you chase him so hard."

"That's fair," the Ranger said. "I'll answer ya with a question. What do your people do to a bad Apache that goes around killin' his own kind?"

Tcha-nol-haye thought a long time, then said, "I have never heard of such an Apache."

"Ya tellin' me murder don't exist among heathens?" Mawson scoffed.

"Sometimes a brujo who sees his own death will witch another to take it instead," he answered. "And sometimes a drunken man fights another because he has lost his wits to poison. But no Apache warrior kills his brother."

"Well, white men do," Mawson answered impatiently. "And this one I'm after is the worst of the lot. He's killed more of his brothers than Geronimo's got horses. He's gotta be stopped and I aim to do it."

Tcha-nol-haye looked away from the Ranger's hatred, across the river toward the Sierra Madre where the last of the war chiefs were probably sitting around a campfire, perhaps thinking of the scouts who rode with their enemies. His heart was with the renegades, but his soul was with his wife and children who lived in safety because of what he did. As he had before, he decided he would rather track a bad white eyes than his brothers. "I will go with you," he said.

"Good!" the Ranger grinned, clapping him on the back. "Get your pony and meet me at the gate soon as ya can."

Tcha-nol-haye watched him walk away, then he scooped dust from the ground and swept the remnants of the Ranger's touch off his shoulder.

While the Apache scout was saddling his mustang, Seth was riding Ramon's black mare down Utah Street to Rosalinda's bordello. He tied the horse in back then walked up the steps and into the kitchen. Several young women sat around the table, drinking their morning coffee though it was afternoon. They greeted him with tentative smiles.

"Don't get up," he smiled back. "I know my way."

He could feel their eyes on his back as he left them behind, and also that they were still half-asleep and wouldn't follow him. He climbed the stairs and pushed through the door without knocking.

Rosalinda sat before her dressing table brushing her long auburn hair, wearing a wrapper of ivory-colored silk. The wooden shutters were closed against the sunlight beyond the windows and a lone candle illuminated her reflection in the mirror. Their eyes met in the looking glass but she didn't break her rhythm with her hairbrush. He closed the door and stood leaning against it, recognizing that the perfume filling the air was the same he'd picked up off Joaquín.

Finally she laid the brush down and turned on the stool to face him. "It's good to see you, Seth," she said sweetly.

He snorted. "I heard you caused a ruckus at the lawyer's office."

"You know how impatient I am," she smiled.

"You should learn to curb it."

"Should I?" she asked, rising and crossing to stand in front of him. "I was patient waiting for you to feel inclined to get married and it didn't do me any good."

"I never gave you reason to think it would."

"Didn't you?" she murmured, running her fingers down the buttons of his shirt. When she reached his belt, she slid her fingertips beneath it.

"Get your hand out of my pants, Linda," he said.

She laughed, moving away. "That's right. You're a married man now. And the honeymoon's barely over, not time yet for you to seek the solace of a woman who understands you."

"You think you do?"

She smiled. "Would you like a drink?"

He shook his head.

"If you don't want to drink with an old friend and you don't want my hand in your pants, why did you come?"

"Maybe to tell you to stay away from Joaquín."

"He's just a customer," she replied with a smile. "Are you going to tell me how to run my business? Or is it yours now?"

"Why didn't you give him a girl closer to his own age?"

"Ooh, an insult. You're angry with me, aren't you, Seth?"

"I don't like you messing with what's mine."

"And that includes him?"

"Right now it does."

"And her, too, of course. The little Mrs. Strummar."

"That's right."

She crossed to the chiffonnier, took off her wrapper and hung it on a hanger. She wore only a white teddy and black silk stockings held up by white ribbons. When she turned to face him, her breasts were full and voluptuous over the tight garment. She saw his eyes on them and smiled as she moved back to her dressing table, knowing he could see them in her reflection in the mirror. She raised her arms and began brushing her hair again, smoothing it behind the brush, her breasts threatening to escape with each stroke. "You didn't come here to talk about Joaquín," she said.

"Why do you think I came?"

"I told Johanna she wouldn't be enough for you." When he didn't answer, she said, "She's so small, and young. Not experienced enough for a man of your hungers."

"We're doing all right," he said.

She continued to run the bristles through the length of her thick hair glistening with fire in the candlelight, a regular, hypnotic rhythm. "You mean you're managing to hold yourself back," she smiled, laying the brush aside. She stood up and crossed to the bed, turned the covers down then sat on the edge in a seductive pose. "I can take everything you have to give, Seth."

"I can take a lot from a woman too, except threats to go to the law."

"I didn't mean it," she whispered quickly. "I just wanted to see you."

"A dangerous way to go about it."

"Would you prefer me to call at your home?"

He shook his head.

She smiled, standing up and moving to the sideboard, taking a bottle of whiskey and two glasses back to the bed and arranging them carefully on the table. She slid the drawer open and took out a short black quirt ending in a small braided tassel, laid it across the white sheets, then sat down and pulled the bow loose on one ribbon, peeled the stocking off her leg and tossed the silken bundle to him still standing by the door.

He didn't move and the stocking bounced off his chest and onto the floor. She laughed, thinking most men would have caught it as a reflex but Seth Strummar kept his hands free for his gun. She unrolled her other stocking and tossed it on her dressing table then picked up the whip, leaning back on her elbows and slapping the leather against her thigh. "I'll bet your wife has an aversion to whips," she smiled.

"She's not a whore," he answered.

"No. She's a good girl, isn't she."

"Yes."

"It must be touching, watching you try to be gentle with her. I wonder if she has any idea how hard it is for you."

"Some," he said.

"Then she should understand, and be glad even, if you bring your need to me."

"Maybe I don't need it any more."

Her laughter was a deep, throaty sound. "You don't believe that any more than I do." She continued to slap the whip against her thigh, watching him as she wet her lips with her tongue.

He laughed. "You're good, Linda, I'll give you that."

"You helped train me, Seth. I was a child like she is when we met."

"Not quite."

"No, I wasn't rich."

He frowned and she dug deep. "That's okay, Seth. All whores look around for a sugar daddy when they slip past their prime. I imagine it's the same with gunfighters."

"I didn't marry her for her money, but I can see that you'd like to think so."

"I do think so, whether you admit it or not. You are past your prime, you know. Over thirty now, starting to lose the edge that's kept you alive." She slid the whip down the inside of her thigh, rubbing it against her crotch.

"You gonna fuck that whip, Linda?" he laughed.

"Do I have another offer?"

He shook his head.

"No?" she asked, slipping the quirt inside the teddy, rolling it lazily between her legs.

He walked across the room and poured himself a drink then stood looking down at her as he drained the glass and set it aside. "Is that what old whores do when they can't get a man?"

She pulled the whip out of her teddy glistening wet, raised it to her mouth and licked it off.

He laughed. "I didn't teach you that."

"I've had the advantages of a well-rounded education," she smiled, sitting up and touching the buckle on his gunbelt.

He backed a step away.

She laughed softly. "Come on, Seth. I'll never tell."

"I got a wife to take my wants to now."

Her anger flashed in her eyes, quickly submerged beneath a wicked smile. Again she reached to touch his buckle. His hand snaked out and slapped her so hard she sprawled on the floor. She picked herself up on her knees and smiled again. "Not something you can do to the little wife, is it, Seth? Go ahead, hit me again. I like it."

"Why?"

She sat back in confusion.

"Maybe if you thought about it," he said gently, regretting having hit her, "you'd see we were only hurting each other."

"But we're good at it," she argued earnestly. "Who else can match your pain as well as I do?"

"Not many," he admitted.

"It used to please you."

"I changed."

She studied him a moment, then laughed. "You just think you have," she said, getting up and sitting on the bed again, smiling her invitation. "I'll do anything you want."

"All right. I want your promise not to go near anyone connected to me."

"Aw, but I enjoyed Joaquín so much. Such an innocent. I had to work hard to make him mad enough to hit me."

"But you managed, I reckon."

"I even got him to say he liked it," she smiled.

"Jesus, Linda. He's a good kid."

"He doesn't want to be good. He wants to be like you. How can he do that if he doesn't learn to enjoy hurting women?"

"I'm not like that anymore," he told her again.

"Since when?" she scoffed. "I know you, Seth. You need me to pick a fight so you can justify giving me your grief."

"I'll give it to you," he warned. "If you go near the law, you'll see a side of me even you won't like."

She laughed. "Is that supposed to be a threat?"

He pulled her to her feet in front of him. "I'll kill you if you cross me."

She loved the iciness in his gray eyes, the rough grasp of his hands. "Say it again, Seth," she begged, her lips moving against his throat as she pushed her body against his. "Tell me you'll kill me."

He held her close with compassion and murmured into her hair. "I mean it, Linda. I'm not playing now."

"I mean it, too." She leaned back and met his eyes. "I need you to hurt me."

He looked down at her breasts, at her hips hot against his, and he wanted her with a hunger that twisted inside him like a knife. With a growl of rejection, he pushed her away. "You're poison," he said.

"Fuck you!" she retorted from where she lay on the bed.

"If you cross me or anyone connected to me, I'll hurt you in spades. And I guarantee you won't like it."

"You sonofabitch!" she hissed.

He nodded. "That's right, I am." Then he pulled the contract from the inside pocket of his jacket. "Remember that," he said, dropping it on her belly and walking out.

The whores were still in the kitchen and they smiled at him as he came in again, their faces as sweet and fresh as Johanna's. But it was only because they were young. After a few years they'd be as hard as Rosalinda, if they were lucky. If not they'd be working the cribs on the border and no vestige of youth would remain. He couldn't muster a smile to give them back.

They watched him walk out. In a few minutes Rosalinda came in, looking worse than they'd ever seen her. Her beauty was ravaged with a hatred that made them want to cringe away from her. She looked at each of them, then settled on one. "I need you to run an errand for me, Sally," she said, biting off her words. "Go to the marshal and tell him I want to see that Captain Mawson of the Rangers." The girl just sat and stared at her until Rosalinda snarled, "Do it now!"

When Seth got home and found Johanna sitting at her dressing table, he couldn't help comparing her to the woman he'd just left. The love shining from his wife's face made him feel incredibly lucky. "What are you doing?" he asked, coming close to rest his hands on her shoulders and meet her eyes in the mirror.

"Looking at my hair," she said. "I wish it'd hurry and grow out."

"I kind of like it like that," he smiled, bending to kiss her neck beneath the short cut.

"Rosalinda has beautiful hair, doesn't she?" she whispered.

He stood up and met her eyes again, amazed at her naiveté in complimenting the whore he was having a hard time resisting. "It ain't real," he said, moving away. "It was black when I knew her before." He crossed to the tray of whiskey on the bureau, the only mark of his possession in the room.

"I can smell her perfume on you," she said.

"I'll take a bath," he said as he poured himself a drink.

She smiled. "We've been waiting supper for you."

"Let me finish this," he said, then turned to stare out the window, thinking of Rosalinda. When they'd first met, she had made a big point of how lucky they'd been to come together when they were both in their prime. They were past that now, but while she had grown more vicious, he had mellowed. About the only thing that hadn't changed for him was his pursuit of Pilger.

Johanna came up behind him and slid her arms around his waist, reminding him of another change: the fact that he had a wife now with high expectations for their future. "I was so afraid," she murmured, her breath warm on his back.

"Of what?"

"That you'd want her more than me."

"I could have had her, if that's what I wanted."

"I was afraid you'd change your mind."

He pulled her around beside him, smiling down at her fear. "You shouldn't worry, Johanna."

"How can I help it? She's so much more experienced than I am."

"You think that's in her favor?"

"Something about her attracts you."

"She's part of my past, is all," he said.

19

It was near midnight when Joaquín left Rosalinda's bordello. As he walked down the stairs and started up Montana Street toward home, the muscles of his legs felt loose, his entire body warm and limber from the hours of lovemaking. Each time he remembered how her eyes had flashed with such fire, he was aroused anew. If he'd followed his own inclination he'd still be in her bed, drinking her whiskey and watching the candlelight flicker on her pale flesh. She had thrown him out, however. Gracefully and with veiled hints that tomorrow would be an important day in her life and she needed her sleep.

Joaquín thought she had a wealthy gentleman coming to town, and for a moment jealousy flared inside him. Then he'd reminded himself he owned only the time he bought, and as she had said before, she was expensive. The evening he'd just enjoyed in the rhapsodies of her pleasures had cost him half a week's salary, but the only anxiety he felt at spending such a large amount was that he'd nearly left home without enough. At the last moment he had taken most of his savings from the hiding place in his room, hoping she might allow him to buy her dinner.

They hadn't eaten any dinner, unless he counted the juices he'd licked from her body. He smiled at her wickedness, feeling strong in his belated discovery of carnal pleasure. She had praised his prowess with such delicate obscenities he blushed even now, remembering the things they had said and done. He even laughed aloud as he walked along the street, causing others to turn and look at him curiously.

The street was still bustling with activity. Torches outside doors closed against the cold lit the faces of the crowd with eerie shadows, making the men appear comical or hideous, depending on how the light fell across their features. Sometimes a smiling man would appear demonical, and sometimes an angry man seemed beatific in his scowl. The world was topsy-turvy all of a sudden. Joaquín laughed at himself again and saw the nearest faces turn toward him, some with understanding that he was drunk, others with fear that he was out of control. He met all their eyes with a challenge.

He was a man now. His harlot was the best in town, his compadre the boldest in the world, and he himself a crack shot who stood aside for no one. It was definitely not a night to be alone, and his room in the stable was a place only for sleeping, not for feeling alive. So he turned south and in a small cantina bought himself another bottle of whiskey then walked on down to the river and sat in the bosque to have a drink with himself.

The moon was full, huge and pale in the winter sky, already nestled on the peaks of the western mountains. He uncorked the bottle and took his first drink, then watched the jagged ridges notch the belly of the moon and eat away its wholeness.

The noises of the town were a mere drone behind him, the river silver with reflection, México dark and empty on the other side. As he stared into the desert of his homeland, Joaquín suddenly remembered his mother, and his memories took the joy from his heart. She had been a woman like Rosalinda. Nothing like Rosalinda, really, but she had lain beneath the weight of many men, and she had laughed and praised them as Rosalinda did, until the disease of their lust killed her. Suddenly Joaquín felt swamped with shame. He had vowed never to abuse women as his mother had been abused, and he felt weak for having broken that vow.

He argued that Rosalinda had taken pleasure from him. Certainly there had been no hint she was suffering from his attentions, and he struggled to see the harm he had done in enjoying his sexuality which, after all, came from God. It was not God who said a man should not be a man, it was the priests who collected money from the pobres and then made them suffer the anguish of eternal hell if they disobeyed the rules of the Church. All his life he had followed their rules, striven to be pure despite the squalor of his youth, and all that discipline had done nothing except make him impotent.

Joaquín felt angry at the priests' deception. He scoffed at the mercy they taught, their constant forgiveness and turning the other cheek. So that a man like Beau Olwell could rape Johanna, and then marry her and rape her for the rest of her life. So that a man like Jade Devery could become rich selling the bodies of women, so that priests could be fat and safe while the pobres starved. Seth had said he never went inside a church and Joaquín had been stunned, but now he felt embarrassed that he had argued for the necessity of the sacrament.

He remembered Seth's eyes when he'd handed over his gunbelt then dropped to his knees in front of the altar. The mockery in them, the scorn, his muttered instruction for Joaquín to "watch the goddamned door." Watch reality, he had been saying, while I play this game for the sake of my innocent compadre. To be Seth's compadre was the greatest honor of Joaquín's life, and it had nothing to do with God or the sacraments, it had to do with real power in the real world.

Joaquín lay back in the prickly tules along the Rio Bravo and looked at the stars, so cold and distant, brightening with the setting of the moon. He could hear the river whispering against its banks and he thought about how Americans called the river "great" and Mexicans called it "brave" and what the difference was. A man or a deed or a thought could be brave and still not great, but no creature could be great without courage.

Suddenly he became aware that he wasn't alone and he sat up abruptly, reaching for his gun. A short distance away a man had been walking along the river and he wheeled around at the noise of Joaquín's movement. Their eyes met and held in the metallic starlight.

He was an Apache, wearing moccasins and white trousers with a breechclout hanging between his knees and a blue soldier's jacket buttoned against the cold. His hair was long and lustrous black, his forehead circled by a wide band of red cloth, and he held a rifle propped against his hip ready to fire. They stared at each other a long moment, two men alone on the riverbank with their hands holding guns.

Finally Joaquín spoke. "Buenas noches, amigo," he smiled.

The Apache merely nodded.

"It's a fine night for watching the water," Joaquín said.

Still the Indian was silent.

"I mean no intrusion," Joaquín said. "Do you mind if I stand beside you so we can watch the river together?"

The Apache lowered his rifle and Joaquín took that for assent. He stumbled slightly as he pulled himself to his feet, laughed and bent down to retrieve his bottle then carried it over to where the other man watched him. He offered him a drink. The Apache shook his head.

"Sí," Joaquín said, "it is poison, I know. But it makes me feel good. Most of the time." He looked at the liquor barely catching light from the stars then tossed the bottle back into the darkness of the bosque and smiled at his companion. "I've had enough anyway."

They stood in silence facing the river, not looking at each other but ready to be enemies at the least provocation. Joaquín pointed with his chin across the flowing water. "I come from over there."

The Apache nodded. "I, also," he said.

"You are Chiricahua, no?" Joaquín asked.

"Yes. How do you know that?"

Joaquín smiled. "I knew a Chiricahua slavegirl when I was a boy. She had a face like yours."

The Apache turned away again.

"I did not make her a slave," Joaquín said.

"Did you not use her as one?" he asked in a quiet voice.

Joaquín shook his head. "We were children, that's all. I thought she was pretty."

The Apache looked at him and said nothing.

"Another time," Joaquín said, "you and I would have killed each other tonight. The first moment our eyes met would have been death for one of us. I'm glad it's no longer so. I was lonely and it feels good to stand here and watch the river with another man."

"I could still kill you," the Indian said.

"And I could still kill you," Joaquín laughed. "But why should we?"

"We are enemies," came the reply.

"Once our people were," Joaquín argued softly. "But you wear the coat of an American soldier so you are American now. I was born in México but now I speak English and live here so I am American too. We are brothers, no?"

"No," the Apache said.

"Well, maybe not very much brothers," Joaquín conceded. "But we are both men who came alone on a cold night to watch the river, so we have something in common."

The Apache smiled. "You smell of cheap women and whiskey and stumble when you walk. I do none of those."

"She was not cheap," Joaquín said.

The Indian laughed. "Was she worth the price?"

"I haven't yet learned the truth of that," he answered earnestly. "But when I do, I think the learning will be worth the price." After a moment he said, "My legs are tired. Would you like to sit down?"

He shrugged.

"I would like to," Joaquín said. "Will you sit with me?"

"If you wish," he shrugged again.

They watched each other, neither wanting to lower himself into a less defensible position before the other.

"Let's do it, then," Joaquín smiled, bending his knees to begin his descent. In unison they lowered themselves to the ground, both sitting crosslegged on the cold sand. The Apache held his Winchester across his lap. "That's a fine gun," Joaquín said.

"The man I follow gave it to me," he answered.

Joaquín nodded. "I also follow a man."

"What has he given you?"

He thought about that a long moment. "Pride," he finally said.

"No man can give you that," the Apache scoffed.

"Perhaps not," he admitted. "It is more right to say that he taught me to find my own."

"Did your father not teach you this?"

"I never knew my father."

The Apache nodded. "Mine was killed by Mexicans, so my uncles taught me to be a man."

"I had no uncles either," he sighed. "Only my mother who died when I was young."

"What of your people?"

Joaquín groped in his mind to understand what the Indian meant. "You mean my tribe?"

"Your kin," he said. "The people who share life with you."

Joaquín shook his head. "There was no one, until I met this man I follow now. He is all."

The Apache's dark eyes softened with compassion. Finally he said, "It is good that you found him."

"Ah sí," Joaquín said. "He is bold and strong and moves on the earth with a power that comes from inside. I want very much to be like him, but for many years I was lost in false teachings."

"Who taught them to you?"

"The priests."

"And now you think them false?"

"Many of them. Mercy, for one."

"Mercy is not always false."

"Perhaps not. But if there is doubt, it is better to decide against it."

The Apache smiled. "I would have killed you if I believed that."

"I'm glad you didn't try," Joaquín smiled back. "It is much more pleasant to sit here and talk."

"I have never done it before."

"What?"

"Talked with a Mexican like this."

"I have never talked with an Apache, either."

They smiled at each other.

"If one of us had killed the other," Joaquín said, "the one who survived would be afraid now, worried that trouble would come from the death."

"The need for vengeance comes from death," the Apache said, "that is all."

Joaquín looked across the river twinkling with the reflection of stars. "It is odd, don't you think, that men kill to achieve peace yet, as you said, achieve only the need to kill again?"

"There is no honor without vengeance."

"Maybe there is no honor with it," Joaquín suggested.

"There is always honor in war."

"But never peace. And isn't that what men seek most of all?"

"Without honor, peace is submission."

"With vengeance, peace is impossible."

"That is why we need mercy," the Apache smiled. "It avoids the wrong that demands vengeance."

Joaquín laughed. "I think you are right."

The Apache nodded, then looked at the stars. "It is time I go. The bear is halfway to the horizon. Tomorrow we ride against our enemy and I must be fresh."

Slowly they stood up, holding each other's eyes.

"I am glad," Joaquín said, "that you sat and talked with me."

"I also enjoyed it," he answered. Then he turned silently in his moccasins on the sand, jogged back toward town and disappeared.

Joaquín stood a long time alone on the riverbank. He found his bottle of whiskey and took another long drink, feeling proud that he had made friends with a Chiricahua Apache, the most feared enemy of his people. They had talked of mercy and vengeance, and Joaquín felt he'd gained an understanding of himself from the conversation. Maybe it wasn't that all his former beliefs were wrong, but that he had to test their lessons and temper their wisdom with the potency he admired in Seth. Maybe then he could truly be his friend's equal, able to share the power of both action and mercy.

The next morning Seth walked out to the stable to have a talk with Joaquín alone. He hadn't wanted to say anything in front of Johanna, and immediately after dinner Joaquín had disappeared again. His room was a small one attached to the tack room, which was full of the pleasant smells of leather and horses. Joaquín answered Seth's knock half-dressed, smelling strongly of liquor.

"Mind if I come in?" Seth asked.

Groggily, Joaquín took a step back, gesturing him forward. Seth walked in and stood leaning against the door, watching him splash water on his face in an attempt to revive himself.

"It's not my habit to give advice," Seth began, watching the kid's clumsiness with the buttons on his shirt.

He looked up with bloodshot eyes. "Anything, Seth," he said.

"You really tied one on last night."

"Sí," he grinned. "I'm not used to liquor, I guess."

"I guess," Seth agreed. "She's pretty potent, too."

"Who?"

"Rosalinda Montoya."

The bleary eyes met his quickly, then Joaquín laughed. "I decided to start at the top," he said.

"You know she and I go back a ways?"

"That is why I chose her," he admitted.

Seth winced. "It took me a while to get to women like that. You think it's smart to start off with her?"

"I thought I should make up for lost time."

"What's your hurry?"

"Death is always near," the kid smiled.

"She is death," Seth said.

He walked over to the small window and looked across the desert to the mountains towering above the city. "I'm not sure I can put it together for you in any clear way, but I'm gonna try." He paused, gathering his thoughts as he moved around the room. He saw the tintype of a pretty, young woman on the bureau. The photographer's address in México City was printed on the corner of the frame and he guessed her to be Joaquín's mother. He smiled at the kid watching him from his dark, solemn eyes. "I don't know much about madonnas," he said, "but

I've had plenty of time to study whores, and they ain't just one thing but there're lots of different kinds. Some are sweet and some just try hard to please. A woman like Rosalinda, though, she likes to fight."

He moved back to the window and watched the sun cresting the peaks, then looked at the kid again, thinking he was in need of protection. "Even when I knew her before, and I ain't no angel, Joaquín, you know that, but even then I saw she was mean enough to be dangerous. There wasn't much she could do to me 'cause I had her beat when we met, and I guess that's part of why I was attracted to her, 'cause I knew I couldn't hurt her and she couldn't hurt me. We could trade all the cruelty we could muster back and forth and the only difference when we were done was our weapons were honed a little sharper." Seth paused, wondering if that were still true. He looked at the crucifix over Joaquín's bed, then met his eyes again.

"What I'm trying to say is, a kid like you ain't got nothing to gain from a woman like her. She doesn't know the meaning of love and that's what you deserve from a woman. You don't have to marry one to get it. Like I said, some whores are sweet and some of them know a lot more about love than most wives. All Rosalinda has to offer is meanness. If you spend much time in her company, she'll make you mean too. It's her talent, bringing that out in a man. Was a time when that's what I wanted from a woman, but it ain't anything you want or need. Can you understand what I'm saying?"

"I think so," Joaquín answered slowly. "She does make me feel mean, but there's a part of me that likes it."

He grunted, looking at the kid's gunbelt hanging on the wall. "Reckon it's in all of us to some degree." He met his eyes again. "But I'd hate to see that part win out in you, Joaquín. You got a lot of decency and the right woman, whore or not, could make you a better man. Rosalinda's a killer's whore, and unless you want to be a killer, I suggest you stay away from her."

Joaquín nodded. "I think maybe you are right."

"Enough said," Seth smiled. "Come on up to the house for breakfast, if your stomach can hold it."

He walked out and crossed the yard, thinking the kid was moving in fast company, too fast to do him any good. Seth wasn't sure how he'd fallen into having a kid brother all of a sudden, but since that was the case, he figured he owed him more than teaching him how to kill a man or hurt a woman, and he decided it was time they all got out of El Paso.

He went back upstairs and woke Johanna. She tugged him down toward the covers again, smelling warm with sleep. "It's broad daylight, Johanna," he laughed.

"Are you shy?" she teased.

"In a hurry," he answered, pulling himself away from her. "I want to go see your lawyer."

"What about?"

Studying the view from the window he said, "I want you to give him power of attorney so he can handle things without us."

"Why?" she asked, moving to sit at her dressing table and brush her hair.

He could hear the short stroke of the bristles, and it reminded him of the long, tangled silk of Rosalinda's hair on the sheet beneath him. "So we can get the hell out of here," he said.

She looked at him as she crossed to the washbowl, wondering if he'd forgotten about Pilger. If he had, she wouldn't remind him. "Are you going to invite Joaquín to come with us?" she asked, pouring water into the bowl.

"Figured I would," he answered, watching her now. "Does that bother you?"

"No," she said, looking up from the basin with a smile. "He was my friend first."

They ate breakfast in the dining room for a change. As soon as the servants had left them alone and closed the door, Seth asked Joaquín if he was interested in going with them to California. The kid looked at Johanna, then back at Seth.

"You really want me along?"

"Wouldn't ask if I didn't."

"I'm honored," Joaquín said. "I'll try to live up to your expectations and never disappoint you or make you sorry you took me."

Seth smiled. "If you make it out of El Paso, you'll do fine."

The kid blushed. "I won't see her again," he said.

"Good. You want to come to the lawyer's with us? Since you're in, you might as well know all the arrangements."

"I'll come," he said.

"Don't mention California, though. We're hoping that as far as El Paso's concerned, we just disappeared."

"I understand," he said.

20

The three of them arrived at Weisenhall's unannounced, but the lawyer came out of his office to greet them with enthusiasm. "Come on in," he said. "Mr. Pilger's here."

Johanna looked at Seth quickly and saw the light change behind his eyes. She wished she had pulled him back into bed and delayed their arrival, or that Pilger could have stayed gone the few more days they would be in town, but Seth was already moving and she followed him, her heart pounding.

Travis Pilger was a dapper gentleman in his early forties, with sandy-colored hair and blue eyes. He and Seth had never met, so he came forward to greet Johanna having no idea that the man at her side was his enemy. "Johanna," he murmured, taking her hand and kissing it. "I'm so sorry about the unfortunate death of your father. It must have been a great shock."

"Thank you," was all she could think to reply.

He straightened up and held out his hand to Seth. "This must be your husband. I'm mighty pleased to meet you. Simon was just saying that I have a new partner but he hadn't gotten around to telling me your name. Travis Pilger, sir, at your service."

"Seth Strummar," he said, not taking the hand nor returning the smile.

Pilger took a step back, his hand falling helplessly at his side. "I'm unarmed," he whispered.

Weisenhall laughed. "You're letting yourself become intimidated by Mr. Strummar's reputation, Travis. I assure you, he's capable of being civilized."

"Is he?" Pilger croaked.

"Please sit down, everyone," the lawyer smiled. "We have many things to discuss."

"Another time," Seth said, not taking his eyes from his brother's killer. "Sell my wife's interest in the saloon at any terms he wants. We'll be leaving El Paso."

"But, Mr. Strummar," Weisenhall objected, "surely you'll want to negotiate."

"Some things ain't negotiable."

Again Pilger took a step away from him. "Leaving, did you say?"

"That's right. Just a few more things to wind up before I put Texas behind me."

The man was struggling to regain his composure. "Perhaps you'll allow me to explain. What happened was unfortunate, an act of passion, the heat of the moment. Surely a man such as you can understand what I'm talking about."

Seth smiled. "You'll have plenty of time to tell me all about it."

Hope glimmered in Pilger's eyes. He looked at Johanna and seemed to find her presence reassuring. "Perhaps I could call at your home later?"

"You step foot inside my wife's house and I'll shoot you on the spot. I'd rather not use a gun but if you push me I will."

The silence in the room was painful. Finally Pilger whispered, "It's reprehensible that you're still free."

"I can understand that you'd think so," Seth smiled. He turned to the lawyer. "When you've finished with this scum, come see us."

"Certainly," Weisenhall murmured.

Seth took Johanna's arm and led her from the room, hearing that Joaquín stayed behind to watch Pilger until they were out the door. Just as Joaquín was coming out behind them, Seth heard Weisenhall call, "Boy, bring me some whiskey!" and he smiled.

Johanna clung to his arm, trembling as she looked up at him on the street. "Let's go now," she pleaded.

"Go ahead," he answered, letting loose of her. "Joaquín, take her home, will you?"

"Where are you going?" she cried.

"Haven't had a drink among men since I got back," he answered. "Feel like I want one now."

"Don't, Seth," she moaned.

"Nothing's gonna happen yet, Johanna. I'll be back directly."

"Please," she whispered. "This town is full of his friends. I don't want you to be alone."

"Maybe she's right, Seth," Joaquín said quietly. He looked back and forth between them. "Go on, leave me be."

"No," she said. "I won't. If you go into a saloon, I'm coming with you."

"Me, too," Joaquín said.

He studied their faces of fierce determination. "Makes me wonder how I lived so long without you," he laughed, taking her arm again. "Reckon I can have a drink at home."

When they got back, Seth sent Johanna away. Her eyes were baffled at his rejection and he told her impatiently there were times he wanted a man's company and she had to understand that. She looked at him forlornly a moment, then turned in silence and walked up the stairs alone.

Seth looked at Joaquín. "Have a drink with me, compadre?"

"Sí," Joaquín said, following him into the parlor. "But perhaps it is not a good idea to get drunk."

"It's never a good idea and I don't intend to do it now, but I need something to take the edge off."

Joaquín watched him pour two glasses full of whiskey, then accepted the one Seth handed him.

"Salud," Seth said, drinking a third of his down.

"Salud," Joaquín murmured, sipping at his then setting the glass aside. He watched Seth walk over to the window and stand looking out as he worked at the whiskey. "Will you tell me," Joaquín asked, "who this Pilger is to you?"

Slowly he turned around, his eyes cool with an anger Joaquín hadn't seen since they'd killed Devery. "Reckon you got a right to know," he said, walking across and sitting on the settee, putting one foot on the low table in front of him, his knee crooked and his gunhand draped across it. He stared at his hand a minute, closed it into a fist then slowly spread the fingers wide again.

"Ten years ago," he said in a soft voice, "me and my partner were in Austin having a good time. Some Ranger took exception to our fun and tried to arrest us. He was a fool coming up to both of us, thinking he was such hotshit he could do it alone. I killed him there in the saloon and Allister and I made it out to our horses, but the Rangers came back for more. There was a running battle through the streets and a shopkeeper was killed, too. He was another fool, pointing a shotgun at men fighting for their lives. He paid with his own life for that act of stupidity."

He stopped and sipped at his whiskey, watching Joaquín.

"Go on," he said, sitting on the hassock a few feet away.

"Allister and I made it out of town and we felt we'd done pretty good for ourselves. But we knew, too, that the Rangers wouldn't let it rest, so we hightailed it down to México and laid low for a while. When we came back we fell in with a bunch of desperados that were rougher than most and our life went on degenerating into the gutter until Allister started dealing in whores. I decided I didn't want to crawl that low so I left on my own. I wandered around for a while, even took a job for wages but that didn't work 'cause my reputation was a magnet for the breed of man I was trying to avoid, so I decided to head north and maybe out-distance myself. That ain't the way it worked, though."

Again he stopped and sipped at his whiskey, then set the glass down and returned to the window, staring out as he spoke. "In Colorado I ran into a sheriff who knew my father. They'd been in the war together and this sheriff figured he owed me a debt 'cause of their friendship and we spent some time together. One of those times he told me what happened in Austin after Allister and I hightailed it for the border."

He was silent so long, Joaquín prompted him. "What happened?" he asked softly.

Seth shuddered, looking over his shoulder abruptly as if he'd forgotten Joaquín was there. "The good citizens," he said, his voice flat, his eyes like ice, "took offense at my killing a Ranger in their fair city and decided they needed some vengeance. As it happened, my family was living in Austin then. I didn't know it, I thought they were still on the farm a hundred miles northwest of there. If I had known, I might've visited them and not been in the saloon when that Ranger spotted us. But I was, and he died, and the good, law-abiding citizens formed themselves into a mob and went to my father's house looking for me. They took a rope along and when they didn't find me, they couldn't let that rope go to waste, so they hung my brother instead."

"Madre de díos," Joaquín whispered.

"He was eighteen," Seth said. "And just like you, he'd committed no offense against man or God."

Joaquín could imagine how the boy must have felt, taking the wrath aimed at his brother as if it were his own. After a moment, he said, "So this Pilger was with the mob?"

"He led the mob," Seth answered with venom, turning to stare out the window again. "Ever since I found out what happened, I've been asking everywhere I went for news of that night. And gradually I've put it all together. My mother, as brave a woman as I've ever known and twice the man my father is, she followed that mob and begged them not to hang Jeremiah. But they wouldn't listen, and when they were done she begged them to cut him down. Pilger hurled my crimes in her face until she fainted right there on the street."

Joaquín leaned closer to the table, lifted Seth's glass and drained the whiskey from the bottom. Then he wiped his mouth with the back of his hand and stood up, trembling with the weight of what he knew was his to give. "So now you think you should kill Pilger."

Seth whirled on him, his eyes incredulous. "What would you do?"

"I would leave him to God," Joaquín said with conviction.

He snorted. "Like you did Devery?"

"Sí. God did not fail me."

"I killed Devery. God didn't have anything to do with it."

"I know you killed him. I was there and saw you. And you killed Olwell and I admired your grace in doing it with such silence. But tell me, Seth, what you gained by those killings."

"I freed Johanna."

"Sí, and now she is your wife. What will she gain if you kill Pilger?"

"This doesn't have anything to do with her."

"You are one person now, everything you do touches her heart. Do you wish to give your wife the bitterness of vengeance?"

Seth laughed with amazement. "You think I should let him get away with it?"

"He will pay the price of what he has done."

"He's not paying any price! He's fat and dapper living off his whores. You saw him."

"I saw a man eaten up inside with terror, with guilt and regret. To live with such remorse is a punishment worse than death."

"So it's been a long time coming. That just makes it all the sweeter."

"Sweet? You can call murder sweet?"

"In this case I call it justice and it'll taste god-damned sweet."

"I think you are wrong. I think it will poison everything in your life that is sweet."

"That's a risk I'm willing to take."

"You are taking it not only for yourself but also Johanna."

Seth turned away from him, but not before Joaquín saw the doubt flicker in his eyes. "If your brother were here now," he asked softly, "what do you think he would tell you?"

He laughed with self-mockery. "The same thing you're saying, Joaquín."

"I am a Christian," he said. "I believe Jesus died on the cross for our sins. It seems to me that perhaps your brother died for your sins, and you should not destroy his sacrifice by seeking vengeance."

Seth turned around and stared at him, his eyes hot with pain. "Jeremiah didn't choose to be executed in my place."

"Neither did Jesus," Joaquín said. "God chose it. I think you should leave Pilger to God."

"You think I should just ride out of Texas and let him be."

"Sí. I think you should take care of your wife and leave your past behind."

Seth looked at his empty glass on the table and walked across to where Joaquín had left his nearly full one, lifted it and took a deep drink. He set it down and stared into the amber glow of the whiskey a moment, then he shook his head and looked at Joaquín, the old coolness in his eyes again. "How'd I ever get hooked up with a priest for a compadre?" he laughed gently.

"You are a good man," Joaquín smiled. "I always said so."

"I never believed it."

"Johanna does."

"Maybe you're both fools."

"Isn't it the fool who laughs last?"

He remembered telling himself that, way back when Johanna had first come to him for help. "Okay," he sighed. "You got me inside a church to marry her. I guess I can go along with you again. But it cuts against the grain with me, Joaquín."

Joaquín wanted to embrace him, but he merely smiled from his distance. "I think when you are clean of your past, you will discover the grain goes a different way."

"We'll see," he said, walking across the room and opening the door, looking up the stairs that led to his wife. He smiled back at Joaquín. "Thanks," he said.

"De nada," Joaquín smiled.

21

Seth walked up the stairs thinking he'd pull Johanna into bed and reward her for leaving him alone with Joaquín. She'd looked so hurt at being excluded that he wished now he could have phrased his request a little more gently. But he'd been angry then, and he was thinking Joaquín was right and he had to learn to leave all that behind if he was going to become any kind of decent husband. He'd made it to the first landing when the back door was flung open and footsteps came running down the hall. He retraced his steps and saw Marietta, her face red with exertion, her rebozo askew and the bundle she held crumpled in her grip.

"Señor Strummar!" she cried between gasps for breath. "The Rangers are at the marketplace asking for men to help them. They are coming here to arrest you! I heard them say so."

Joaquín was in the door now. "I will get your horse," he said, already moving down the hall.

"Thanks," Seth told both of them, then took the stairs two at a time and strode quickly down the hall and into Johanna's room.

She stood before her chiffonnier, Devery's shirts in her hands. Tossing them aside, she turned to face him. "What is it?" she asked, worry in her voice.

"I have to leave again," he said, moving across the room and picking up his rifle.

"Why?" she cried.

"The Rangers are in town. They're coming here."

"Take me with you," she pleaded.

He shook his head. "Meet me at Ramon's. Don't leave sooner than tomorrow or they may track you. They may anyway, but when they don't find me and if they don't see you hightail it out of here as soon as they're gone, my guess is they'll leave you alone. Don't bring anything you can live without."

Quickly she crossed to block the door. "I feel afraid, Seth," she whispered. "Take me with you."

"No. There's apt to be shooting and I won't drag you into it."

"I can shoot," she argued.

"At cactus," he smiled. "Lawmen are different."

"Will you be at Ramon's, then?"

"I said I would."

"You won't let anything stop you?"

He set his rifle down and took her in his arms. "It'll take the Devil himself to keep me from you."

"Do you truly love me, Seth?"

"Didn't I just say that?"

"I need to hear it," she begged.

"I love you, Johanna." He smiled. "You're my wife. But if you don't let me out that door, you're gonna be a widow."

She clung to him. "Don't speak of your death," she whispered. "It's bad luck."

"Watch out for yourself," he said, setting her aside. "Do everything Joaquín tells you. Promise me?"

"Yes."

He kissed her, a long and lingering kiss though he felt impelled to hurry. Then he picked up his rifle and walked out.

Joaquín had the black mare ready in the stable. Seth slid his rifle into the scabbard and swung on. "The Rangers have no cause to arrest you, Joaquín. Remember that and don't fight them. Tomorrow take your best horses and enough food to last three days. Tell anyone who asks that you're going to San Antonio and ride east. At Hueco Tanks circle northwest toward Mesilla and meet me at Ramon's. Johanna knows where it is. Make sure you're not followed. Keep your eyes open and don't trust anyone. You got all that?"

"Sí," he said solemnly.

"Stay alive," Seth said, leaning down to shake his hand. "You won't be any good to her dead."

He spurred the horse through the door and rode out the back of the yard, skirting the mountains toward the river and the quickest route to New Mexico. He pushed the mare hard and she didn't disappoint him, covering ground in long, nimble strides that carried him into the bosque as the sun was just beginning its descent toward the horizon. He edged her into the current and they swam the river. When they came out on the other side, he was safely beyond the Rangers' reach, if they chose to abide by the law.

Joaquín stood at the window looking out from the parlor. All was still and empty though it was just past noon and people should have been on the street. He told himself to remember this moment of deathly silence, this heaviness of time passing, to learn to recognize and nurture it in his heart as a fighter's last chance to pray for courage.

Seth had left him in charge, it was Joaquín the others looked to for leadership, and he longed for the black robes of priesthood or the red blood of victory, any talisman to prove he had earned through discipline or success the right to stand in Seth's stead. He who pleaded for mercy, argued for the integrity of the sacrament and against the spoilage of vengeance, yet had never been tested.

Far down the street he heard the approach of the enemy, many horses moving fast. Johanna gave a cry of fright and rose to her feet. He crossed the room to stand beside her, not touching her though she was a friend and both of them needed comfort then, but knowing he had to help from the pinnacle of authority not the dust of defeat. They could hear the hooves of the enemy's horses surrounding the house, a noose of death trapping everyone inside. He waited, not moving, hearing the front door thrown open and a moment later the kitchen door, imagining Armando and Marietta greeting the enemies with downcast eyes, protected in their submissiveness, as he must be for the sake of survival.

The door was opened with rude arrogance and a man stood framed in its emptiness. A huge, ugly man with a bandolero across his chest and a .45 in his hand, wearing a scowl so cruel Joaquín almost took a step away. He held his ground beside his friend's wife, feeling the fear within her. The enemy's men ran up the stairs, violating the sanctity of her home with weapons ready in their hands.

In a trembling voice, Johanna said, "Captain Mawson . . ." then her words stopped, her intended objection to his intrusion silenced by his approach.

"Told ya I'd be back," he growled, turning his eyes on the man at her side. "Who are ya?"

"Joaquín Ascarate," he answered, meeting the dark eyes without flinching.

The Ranger grinned, his free hand outstretched palm up. "I'll take your shooter," he said. "Pull it out with your left real slow."

Joaquín congratulated himself for having known Seth's enemy would be a formidable foe. But he was his ally, chosen to keep his wife safe, and Seth's courage bred his own. He extended the gun toward the lawman. "What is it you want with us?" he asked coldly.

"With you? Nothin'," the man retorted. "We're lookin' for a killer."

"There were no killers here before you arrived," Joaquín replied.

Mawson snorted then jerked his head at the door. "Outside," he ordered.

Joaquín took Johanna's arm and led her down the hall, through the kitchen where he managed to give Armando and Marietta a smile of encouragement, into the yard crowded with horsemen all holding rifles propped on their thighs, their faces hard with readiness to kill. He led her past the line of entrapment to the sanctuary of shadow before the stable, then he let go of her to hold himself from within.

Shouts of anger came from the house, doors flung open, men fierce with failure storming back into the yard. Several ran past where he and Johanna stood and he heard the horses in their stalls whinny and stomp at the noisy invasion. Mawson came to stand in the kitchen door, glowering at Johanna, and from above him Joaquín heard a man shout from the loft that the stable was empty.

Across the yard, sitting a scruffy mustang beside a riderless, towering bay, an Apache watched Joaquín. Their gaze met amid the turmoil of the search, two pairs of dark eyes claiming calm in the frenzy.

"Cha!" Mawson barked.

The Apache threw his leg over the neck of his pony and slid down. He walked toward Joaquín, holding his eyes until nearly the last moment when he looked at the ground, and Joaquín realized he was searching for tracks. The boots of the Ranger thudded in the dust as he came near. Before Joaquín suspected what was happening, the lawman's huge hand swung across the space and slapped Johanna.

She recoiled away from him, kept her feet, stared her hatred. Joaquín held himself inside.

"Where is he?" Mawson shouted.

"Who?" she asked, and Joaquín had to suppress a smile at her audacity.

"You know goddamned well who!" Mawson bellowed. "Where'd he go?"

Johanna's cheek was red with the imprint of the lawman's hand, her own hands clenched into fists nearly camouflaged in the folds of her skirt. "You have no right," she said, "to strike a lady in her home."

"You're an outlaw's whore!" he jeered.

"I'm his wife!" she retorted.

Mawson laughed. "I know that. Did ya think ya could bed a man like him and stay a lady?"

Joaquín saw her hand rise from the folds of her skirts, felt her desire to strike the ugly man echo in his own heart. He stepped closer and touched her waist lightly. "There is no one here but us," he told the Ranger.

The florid face nodded, the dark beady eyes squirming with hatred. "I'll get him," he uttered. "It's jus' a matter of time."

Behind him, Joaquín heard the Apache moving nearly silently in his moccasins.

"What'd ya find, Cha?" Mawson barked.

"West," the scout said.

"How long?"

"The wind has not dusted his tracks."

"Let's go," Mawson said, stomping toward his horse.

Joaquín turned around to face the Apache. For a long moment their eyes held, then the scout looked at Johanna. She raised her head higher beneath his scrutiny and Joaquín saw the barest flicker of a smile on his mouth. He nodded at Joaquín, then sprinted across the yard to his horse and rode out with the Rangers, leaving Joaquín and Johanna alone in the silence of the settling dust.

Seth followed the road north toward Mesilla a short way, then pulled off in a grove of palo verde trees thick enough to obscure him. He stopped and tugged his boots off to empty the water, then checked over his guns to make sure they weren't clogged with mud. As he was sliding his rifle back into the scabbard, he heard a horse on the road, someone traveling along at a brisk trot. He pinched the mare's nose to keep her quiet and waited for the rider to pass. Then, through a gap in his sanctuary, he saw it was Pilger.

A deathly desire swamped Seth's mind, obliterating everything but his hunger for justice. He waited until he couldn't hear Pilger's horse, then swung into the saddle, shook his lariat loose and spurred the mare in pursuit, riding in the soft sand to muffle his approach.

It had been a long time since he'd roped anything, but a target the size of a man's body wasn't much of a challenge. If he missed he could always shoot him but he'd rather take his vengeance slow. He urged his horse faster, whirling the loop over his head, and saw Pilger sit up straighter as he heard him coming, saw him swiveling around to see who it was, then Seth let go of the rope and watched it sail across the space between them and settle pretty as pie around Pilger's chest. He yanked the mare up sharp and Pilger fell into the dirt.

The mare wasn't trained as a cowpony and Seth had to keep backing her up to hold the rope taut. He smiled watching Pilger struggle to his feet, noting he wasn't wearing a gun but had traveled unarmed except for the carbine in his scabbard, useless to him now. "Afternoon," Seth said.

Pilger's eyes searched frantically up and down the road for help, but they both knew from the silence they were alone. "What're you doing here?" Pilger cried.

"Did you expect me to be on Montana Street fighting Rangers right about now?" he smiled.

"I didn't send for them. I just heard they was coming, is all."

"So you thought you'd make yourself scarce 'til it was over."

"Can't blame me for that. I didn't send for the Rangers, Strummar, I swear it."

"Who else would care?"

"Rosalinda Montoya did it for the bounty. Mawson told me himself."

"Who's Mawson?"

"A captain of the Rangers. He's the one after you, the one went to your hotel room and roughed up Rosie. Went to Montana Street, too, and questioned your wife, but he didn't know you were married or he wouldn't have needed Rosie to betray you. I had nothing to do with it, Strummar. I knew if I acted against you I was as good as dead. You gotta believe me!"

"No, I don't," Seth said, trying hard to understand why Johanna hadn't mentioned a Ranger questioning her. Unless Pilger was lying. He jerked the horse around and kicked it into a trot, making Pilger run to keep up, following the river even after the road curved away from it. When he felt a sudden lurch, he looked back and saw Pilger had fallen and was being dragged. He reined up, waited for the man to regain his feet, then rode on.

It didn't make any sense that Johanna wouldn't tell him something like that, but he couldn't see any reason for Pilger to invent it. Mawson, Captain Mawson. The name meant nothing to him. If Pilger was telling the truth, the Ranger had come to the hotel right after he'd left to get breakfast before meeting Johanna. So Rosalinda had known all along that this Mawson was just steps behind him. He had no reason to expect her loyalty, but Johanna was entirely different.

There were only five people in El Paso who knew. Armando and Marietta were loyal. The lawyer would hurt himself by getting his richest client in trouble. Pilger had the most cause but his protests were beginning to make sense. Apparently Rosalinda hadn't told Mawson anything when he'd roughed her up in the hotel or she wouldn't have made that threat at the lawyer's. At that point she still wanted Seth back in her life, not dead or arrested. When he'd visited her the last time, she was trying hard to gain his affection but he'd turned her down, said he loved his wife and had no need of a whore, even called her poison. It was after that she'd gone to the Rangers. He understood it all now, except Johanna not telling him the law had been to her home and questioned her.

He couldn't fathom why she'd kept that from him, and then he caught on. Mawson had told her things she didn't want to confront, neither in her husband nor in herself. He'd raised doubts in her mind and she wasn't strong enough to throw them on the table so they could sort them out. She'd backed off instead, and helped Mawson pull the noose a little tighter.

Ahead, Seth saw a cottonwood tree that would serve his purpose. He spurred the horse faster, hearing Pilger fall and not stopping this time, wanting the man already down. When he swung off, Pilger lay on his side, his mouth open as he tried to suck enough air 'into his lungs. Seth took a few quick strides toward him and kicked him hard in the gut. The man was definitely no problem then. Pilger curled into a ball, puking and coughing, writhing in the dirt as he clutched at his belly. Seth yanked the lariat off him and threw it over a limb of the tree.

He left the noose the way it was, just a simple slip knot that would slowly close against weight, then he wound the end of the rope around the saddle horn so he could play with the slack. He walked over to Pilger, picked him up by the shoulders and threw him toward the tree. Before the man could shake the sense back into his head, Seth cut the conch strings off his saddle and bound Pilger's wrists behind him, then slid the noose around his neck, retreated to his horse, and took up the slack.

After a few minutes Pilger came around, standing up and looking at him with confused, bleary eyes. Seth took the slack out of the rope.

"For God's sake, Strummar," he pleaded. "Can't we talk about this?"

"You got something to say?" he mocked.

Pilger struggled to find the words that would grant him mercy. "I've regretted what happened to your brother," he said, his voice thick with tears. "It was wrong, I know that now. But I was drunk and all het up. You know how that is."

"I've never hung an innocent man," he answered, "so I can't say I do."

"Your brother died brave," Pilger said, hope resonating in his voice. "He had a lot of sand." He tried to laugh, a mangled sound. "Runs in the family, I guess."

Seth didn't say anything, the accumulated weight of years of intention impelling his vengeance.

"He died without a curse," Pilger offered in desperation. "Someone in the crowd asked just before the end if he didn't curse you now. You know what he said? He said, 'I love my brother and nothing you say or do can change that.' Wasn't it sporting of him?"

Seth turned away, remembering Red McDowell saying Jeremiah had cursed him. He believed Pilger, but knowing Jeremiah had died professing his love and loyalty only strengthened his resolve.

"Your brother wouldn't want you to do this," Pilger pleaded, then begged, "For God's sake."

Joaquín's words were resurrected by Pilger's voice, but Seth shook himself as if someone had thrown cold water down his back, then turned and faced his brother's killer. "God ain't here," he said.

"Do it then," the man pleaded. "Stop stalling."

"If you'd taken a little more time lynching my brother, you might've seen it would lead to this."

Pilger lost hope, hearing that. He lifted his knees, trying to end it, but the noose only shut off his air. After thrashing a minute, he regained his feet, gasping for breath.

"Do it again," Seth smiled.

"Kill me!" he screamed.

"Jeremiah never said those words to you, did he?"

Pilger lost control, crying openly. "I'm sorry," he sobbed. "I've been sorry for near ten years now. Doesn't that mean anything to you?"

"No."

The afternoon dragged toward dusk until the sunset stained the cottonwood the color of blood. Pilger cried and begged, struggled to keep his feet but lost them again and again. Always at the last moment he regained the strength to stand. Darkness fell and the already risen moon slowly moved across the cold winter sky.

"Please," Pilger moaned, his voice faint in the pale light.

From the foothills a coyote yipped and was answered by another. Seth smiled, listening to them call back and forth. "How you feeling, Pilger?"

"God have mercy," the man begged again.

"Is that what my mother said when you put the rope around my brother's neck? Or even after it was done and she just wanted you to cut him down? Can you remember her voice? Please, she must've said. God have mercy. But God wasn't there either, was He?"

The moon was setting now, leaving the world in darkness. From the mountains the coyotes howled forlornly at the impending loss of light. "They're gonna eat you when I'm gone," Seth said. "What do you think of that?"

The man sobbed, barely able to keep his feet.

"If I let you go, you gonna spend your life doing good deeds?"

"Yes," the man gasped. "I swear it."

"Too bad you didn't give Jeremiah that chance. 'Course he would've done it anyway. That's the way it is with good deeds. They come from the heart. Bad ones just the same. A man can make all the pretty promises he thinks sound good but it won't change who he is. 'Cause once he takes that first ride with death there's no turning back. He can kid himself that he can change, and maybe even get other people to believe in him. But the truth is, once a man kills it's in his blood and nothing good comes after."

He watched the light fade from the river as the moon sank beyond the distant mountains, telling himself it wasn't too late. He could let Pilger loose and it would be dawn before the man regained enough strength to find the road. By then he would be halfway to Ramon's. Johanna and Joaquín would be there by another nightfall. They could go to California and everything would be okay. But he didn't believe it. She'd been too afraid to repeat the things Mawson had told her, too afraid to speak the truth. And if she couldn't speak it, she couldn't live with it.

Without looking at Pilger again, Seth led the horse away, listening to the man choke and strangle behind him. Slowly he turned around, forcing himself to watch Pilger dangle kicking from the noose. He watched him struggle for a long time, then finally the man was dead.

Seth tied the rope to the trunk of the tree, leaning against the weight so the corpse wouldn't fall. Looking into the face of his vengeance, he didn't feel better because he knew he had another killing before he could ride to Ramon's. He swung onto his horse and headed south toward El Paso.

He tied his horse at Rosalinda's back porch and walked quietly up the steps, jimmied the lock on the kitchen door and crept along the hall and up the stairs. Her door was unlocked and he stepped into the semi-darkness sultry with her perfume.

She was deeply asleep and he sat down wearily in a chair by the door, wanting to gather his strength before he moved against her, though he knew he shouldn't tarry because Mawson could come back to tell her their trap had failed. But then he smiled, thinking that might be the best way it could happen. The Ranger wouldn't expect to find him here and there was no sense leaving town with a bloodhound on his trail. If that's the way it fell, he'd take his chances which man walked out alive. Right now he wanted to rest, and Rosalinda, sleeping so peacefully, brought back memories of the time he'd been content with whores. He told himself he should have left it that way, and not kidded himself that just because he'd been married in a church he could make a decent woman a good husband. He watched the light grow behind the wooden shutters closed against the sun.

After a long time, Rosalinda opened her eyes. She sat up abruptly and stared at him. "Seth," she laughed, too late and too tense to be convincing, "what a pleasant surprise."

"It shouldn't be," he answered, gaining his feet.

"What do you mean?" she asked, her voice falsely sweet.

"Were you gonna come to my hanging, Linda? Or do you love me too much to watch me die?"

"I don't know what you're talking about," she said, reaching for her wrapper at the foot of the bed. The white silk shimmered in the shuttered light as she moved toward her dressing table.

He figured she had a gun in the drawer and caught and held her, staring down into her lovely face hardened by fear. "I know you betrayed me to Mawson. Pilger told me with almost his dying words." She twisted trying to escape him, and he asked incredulously, "Did you expect to get away with it?"

"I expected you to be dead," she hissed.

"I'm not," he smiled.

"You will be. You made a mistake, Seth. The oldest one in the world: you fell in love."

"But with the wrong woman, isn't that what you mean?"

"I'm more a match for you than she'll ever be."

"In cruelty is all."

"That's your strong suit, Seth," she smiled.

"Maybe you're right," he said, letting his gaze slide down her body. He let loose of her arms and tore her wrapper open, then ripped her nightgown down the front so he could see the rise of her ribs over her flat belly.

Her laughter mocked him. "You always did get horny when you're mad."

"Am I gonna have to rape you?"

"No," she smiled, leading him backward toward the bed. "I love your fucking when you're angry. The true Seth Strummar comes out."

"You like the true Seth Strummar, do you?" he asked, pushing her onto the bed.

"I love him," she smiled, lifting her arms to invite him closer.

He pulled his knife from the sheath on his belt and slid it in at an angle beneath her ribs, thrusting the tip upward into her heart. Her eyes opened wide and her lips moved, but there was no breath to give her curse strength.

22

Johanna had cried in her empty bed for hours after the Rangers left, feeling as devastated as if they'd raped her. But finally she'd pulled herself together and gone downstairs to see Joaquín. The sweetness in his eyes had helped her hold on. Seth would be waiting for them at Ramon's, he'd said. Once they were out of Texas, his past would evaporate like a mirage on the desert. She had clung to his words, and this morning she'd risen and packed her satchel and dressed for the journey with hope in her heart.

But they had to wait until the express office opened. If she hadn't been so lost in devastation the day before, she could have done it then. She'd wasted those precious hours crying, and it had been late afternoon when Simon had come and only then had she remembered all she had to do. Sitting with her lawyer in the parlor she had him draw up the power of attorney and then made the arrangements to keep

Marietta and Armando on salary until the house was sold and pay them a final bonus for their loyalty.

As she sat across from the lawyer discussing money, she felt despair because she had no cash in the house. Embarrassed, she had told Simon her predicament. He had smiled as if she were a child as he explained she could arrange an advance transfer through the Butterfield Express, that he would certify her holdings and with the power of attorney, he could later settle the account. It was no problem, he'd said, but by the time they'd finished their business and reached that point, the express office had been closed and they had to wait until morning.

Now she stood holding a small satchel as she watched Joaquín saddle their horses. She had followed Seth's advice and packed only things she couldn't live without, mostly the documents proving who she was, thinking they could buy whatever else she needed along the way. She wore a split riding skirt she'd ordered from Boston, apparel definitely risqué for the Southwest, but she couldn't see why she should care what people thought of an outlaw's wife.

Finally Joaquín led over the little gray mare Seth had bought for her and she swung into the saddle. He had chosen a tall Chestnut gelding and together they rode into town and he waited outside the express office while she went in and collected a five hundred dollar advance from her account in St. Louis. Simon had made all the arrangements and the clerk was expecting her. He gave her the money in a small cloth bag with the transaction slip inside, and she smiled at him, then held the bag clutched in her hand even after she'd remounted her horse, feeling in control again now that she had money enough to take care of herself if somehow it happened that Seth wasn't at Ramon's.

Joaquín led her through an alley, taking the most inconspicuous route to the San Antonio road, hiding even the lie about their destination. She had told everyone the lie, Simon and Armando and Marietta, even the express clerk when he'd asked if she was taking a journey. "Yes," she smiled. "I'm going to San Antonio to see a lawyer about my grandfather's estate."

The alley led behind Rosalinda's brothel. With a lurch of her heart, Johanna recognized the horse tied at the back door. It was the black mare she'd tried to steal from Ramon so long ago, the horse Seth had borrowed to ride back to El Paso. She turned her mare in and stopped beside it, looking up at the windows she knew to be Rosalinda's. She heard Joaquín come back but she didn't look at him until she'd swung down and was handing him her reins.

"You shouldn't go inside," he warned.

She guessed he was probably right. There was nothing inside she would be better off for having seen, but her husband was there and she wanted to know why. Without answering Joaquín, she walked quietly up the steps and pushed through the door into the kitchen, still holding the small bag containing the money for her journey.

The house was silent. Just as silently she crept down the hall, past the parlor and up the stairs. She knew the room, she had been there before. Her hand moved as if by its own volition to grasp the knob and push open the door.

Seth whirled, his knife thudding onto the carpet, his gun in his hand before the knife had completely fallen. They stared at each other across the silence. She looked at Rosalinda, at all the blood drenching the bed beneath her, then at the knife on the floor, blood still on the blade, then at her husband watching her with a gun in his hand, and she opened her mouth to scream.

He holstered his gun and crossed the room quickly, pulling her inside, closing the door and covering her mouth with his hand before a sound could escape. "What are you doing here?" he whispered roughly.

She searched his face for a hint of love but couldn't find any in his cold gray eyes. She looked at the woman on the bed, blood still seeping from her body, and she felt tears hot on her cheeks. Without even being aware of it, her hand opened and she dropped the bag of money on the floor.

Seth didn't notice it either. He was watching the horror on her face, knowing he deserved the loneliness he felt at that moment. He let go of her and retrieved his knife, wiped it clean on the bedsheets and resheathed it, then met Johanna's eyes. "What are you doing here?" he repeated.

She swallowed hard, afraid of him now. "I saw your horse."

"On your way to Ramon's?"

She nodded.

"You still want to come?"

She looked at Rosalinda. "Why did you kill her?"

"She betrayed me."

"Have you no mercy?" she cried.

"Be quiet!" Then, incredibly, he laughed. "Now I need you to be quiet, Johanna. But that's not what I needed yesterday. Why didn't you tell me about Mawson?"

She didn't answer and he moved to the window, opened a slat of the shutters to look down on Joaquín and the horses below. He walked quickly back across the room, listened through the door a moment, opened it and looked up and down the hall, then turned his eyes on her. "You coming?"

She looked at Rosalinda, knowing only that she couldn't stay in the same room with all that blood. She nodded and he took her arm and led her back down the stairs, through the dark, silent hall and kitchen, out into the bright sunshine.

Seth took the reins of her horse from Joaquín, meeting the kid's eyes for a moment, wanting to tell him about Pilger. Joaquín gave him a sweet smile of encouragement and Seth saw his brother in the love of his friend, both lost in the bloodlust of vengeance. He turned away and watched Johanna pull herself into the saddle, then tried to meet her eyes as he handed her the reins, but she wouldn't look at him now. He swung onto the black mare and turned west down the alley toward New Mexico.

At the east end of the narrow passage, the hoof-beats from a huge bay and a small scrubby pony echoed off the walls. Seth heard them and jerked around to see his enemy for the first time. "Move!" he told Joaquín, pulling his rifle from the scabbard. "Run for the river and don't look back."

But he was too late. The cold wind of a bullet whined past his ear and Johanna's mare grunted and fell over. She screamed as she jumped clear and Seth opened fire on the men in pursuit, making them abandon their horses and scramble for cover. Joaquín spun around and returned for Johanna as Seth kept the Ranger and his scout pinned in the other end of the alley. She grabbed her satchel off her fallen horse and took Joaquín's hand, leaping nimbly up behind. Joaquín dug in his spurs and rode hard.

Seth followed them a short distance then whirled around, listening to their horse galloping away as he cocked his rifle and fired again and again at the two men obscured behind packing crates. Their horses had bolted and he kept them trapped until his gun was empty. Mawson shot back but he'd lost his rifle with his horse and Seth had gone just far enough to put himself out of the sixshooter's range. He yanked his horse around and galloped after his wife and compadre.

He overtook them crossing the river. They waited on the far bank until he gained dry land then he led them on a twisting, circuitous path through the desert, looking for rocks that wouldn't betray the passing of their horses' hooves, camouflaging the trail every way he knew how, riding west into the badlands for an hour, then turning south before finally honing in on his destination.

Johanna rode with her arms around Joaquín, watching Seth ahead of them. She shuddered every time she remembered Rosalinda's dead face, all the blood swamping the bed beneath her, the blood on Seth's knife as it fell from his hand.

He had warned her. That night before they were married, he had said someday she would learn the things he'd done, and he'd asked if she would love him then. Yes, yes, yes, she had said. Anything to have his love. Now she felt the truth stabbing her to the quick, and she hid her face in Joaquín's back so she wouldn't have to look at her husband.

She was trembling violently and Joaquín looked over his shoulder and asked, "Are you hurt, Johanna?"

"No," she managed to say. "Only frightened."

He thought now that they were away from danger she had let her fear surface. She had a lot of sand for a girl, but she was still female and didn't have the courage of a man. He wished he could hold her in his

arms and speak soft words of comfort, but all he
could do was cover her hand with his own. She made
no response, and he knew it was nothing in the face
of her fear. The comfort she needed would have to
come from Seth but he was riding ahead and didn't
look back, as if he'd forgotten they were there.

He hadn't forgotten, he needed only to hear the
horse coming behind to know they were still with
him. Johanna's eyes had been so full of horror in
Rosalinda's room that he suspected what her thoughts
were now, and he berated himself for thinking she
could love him for long. He'd fallen into a trap, as
Rosalinda had said, fallen in love with a young girl
who thought him wonderful because, in her ignorant
innocence, she refused to see who he was. He should
have done what he had done before, sent her away
with one cruel stroke to break her heart cleanly so
it would heal. He'd even had Joaquín, as he'd had
Angel with Esther, but he'd thought he had a better
chance with Johanna, that she was stronger, that she
could take it. He would know soon if he'd been
wrong.

When they rode into Ramon's yard, Seth swung
down and stood holding his reins, watching his wife
slide off from behind Joaquín and come close to him.
But she wouldn't meet his eyes. He slid his arm
around her waist and felt her resistance though she
was trying hard to hide it. Trying out of fear. Seth
was familiar with fear and knew he wasn't mistaking
what she felt now as he had earlier, thinking her
infatuation was love because he wanted it to be. He
greeted Ramon and introduced Joaquín, then said he
was tired and wanted to sleep. He took Johanna's
hand and led her into the room he had once shared
with Rosalinda.

She lay down on the bed and hid her face. He stood watching her a moment, then set his rifle aside, took off his coat and hat, rolled up his shirtsleeves and poured water into the washbasin. He remembered that he'd shared this room with Johanna before too, when he'd thought she was a boy. He wished he could go back to that day and let her steal Ramon's horse and ride out of his life. He didn't wish he'd let her steal his sorrel because then he would have gone after her. With the black he could have paid Ramon and called it even, laughing at the scruffy boy who'd pulled something over on him. He didn't expect to be laughing any time soon.

He crossed the room and crouched beside the bed, his gunbelt still buckled around his middle. He thought he should take it off but he couldn't be totally friendless in what lay before him. "Johanna?" he said softly.

"I'm tired," she whimpered, her face in the pillow.

"Look at me," he said.

It took her a long moment but finally she rolled over and met his eyes. Hers were the soft color of the bluebonnets that grew in the fields on his father's farm, as painfully haunting as all the goodness he'd left behind. He raised his hand to her hair, saw her flinch at his touch and try to control it out of fear. "I'm sorry you saw Rosalinda," he said.

"It doesn't matter whether I saw her or not!" she cried, her words coming scattered through her ragged breath. "It only matters that you did it."

"I won't hurt you."

"Unless I give you reason?"

He winced, knowing she was right. "I never lied to you."

"No," she said. "I lied to myself."

He stood up and retrieved his coat, buttoning it as he watched her silent crying, her face buried in the pillow again. Picking up his rifle he said, "I'll ask Ramon to take you home in the morning." He had opened the door and was halfway into the darkness when she called him back.

"Seth?" she cried, her voice broken.

He turned to look at her.

"Where are you going?" she whimpered.

"I'll sleep in the stable," he said, closing the door.

She stared at the wooden barrier, feeling alone. His eyes had been so hurt when he'd looked at her, as hurt as she felt. So it was something they shared, this pain that seemed unbearable to her. She thought since they shared the hurt, perhaps only together could they learn to bear it. He was a hard man with a capacity for cruelty she couldn't condone, but he was her husband, whom she loved. She hurried after him, catching him halfway across the yard.

He turned at the sound of her running footsteps and she stopped in front of him, looking up with her face wet with tears. "Don't go," she pleaded. "I'm sorry. It was awful and I hated you for doing it."

"Maybe you're right to hate me."

She shook her head. "In Zaragoza you asked if I would love you even when I hated you. I said yes and it's true, I do. Please come back and make all the ugliness go away."

"I can't do that. I'm not a magician, Johanna."

"Then I'll learn to live with it," she argued. "Forgive me, Seth. I was weak. I won't let it happen again."

"Maybe I'm the one who shouldn't let it happen," he said.

"You can't expect me to see something like that and not be horrified! If I did I'd be as hard as you and that's not what you want, is it?"

"No."

"Then come back inside. Give me another chance."

He hesitated and she stood on tiptoe and kissed his mouth. "Don't you want me, Seth?" she pleaded.

"Yes," he said.

"Then come back inside," she smiled, tugging him toward the door.

He followed her, thinking she was struggling valiantly to accept him despite the horror she felt. Maybe if he could convince her of his logic, he could redeem the love in her eyes. If in hers, maybe in Joaquín's when he learned of Pilger. Maybe everything wasn't lost because his past had reached out and found him on the road to a new life, caught him with the old, familiar hand of death and trapped him in his need for vengeance. If he could rekindle Johanna's love, maybe he could still free himself and not disappoint these two innocents who had thought him worth saving.

Turning to close the door, he saw Esperanza in the shadows by the kitchen, her dark eyes glimmering in the ripe glow of the already setting moon. He remembered her prediction that Johanna was death riding behind him, and he looked toward the wall separating his sanctuary from the Ranger on his trail, then back at the woman watching. He gave her a small smile, acknowledging that the odds were on the side of her prophecy, then closed the door.

Johanna was kneeling before the hearth, building a fire to take the chill from the air. He leaned his rifle in a corner and took off his coat, sat down in the only chair and watched her. She stared into the flames long after their blaze lit the room, and he knew she was afraid to look at him, but he let her take as much time as she needed. Finally she stood up and faced him with a smile that tore at his heart. "Everything feels different," she said.

He nodded. "Why didn't you tell me about Mawson?"

"I wanted to, but we were always so happy, and the things he said were so ugly."

"What did he say?"

She shrugged, as if it didn't matter, then crossed to sit on the bed and stare into the fire. "Stories from your past," she said softly. "About the woman you hung, another one you raped, the men you've killed."

"Did you believe him?"

Her eyes were bright with hope. "Wasn't it true?"

Patiently he asked again, "Did you believe him, Johanna?"

"Yes," she whispered.

"I told you most of those things. Didn't you believe me?"

She gave him a small, sweet smile. "Everything sounds all right when you say it."

He nodded, then took a deep breath. "I killed Pilger," he said, watching her eyes flare with hurt again. "After I left you yesterday I ran into him on the road. I caught him with my rope and dragged him to a tree and hung him long and slow. Took all night. Before he died he told me about Mawson and that Rosalinda had betrayed me. So in the morning I rode back to El Paso and killed her, too. Does that sound all right because I say it?"

"It might," she whispered, "if I hadn't seen her."

"You think I was wrong to kill Pilger?"

"No," she answered slowly. "It was wrong what he did to your brother. That was justice."

"And Rosalinda? Wasn't that justice because she betrayed me?"

"But you laughed, Seth!"

"I laughed at us. Because you were quiet when you should have told me about Mawson, and when I needed you to be quiet you were ready to scream your head off. Not a woman I need shadowing my life."

She wound her arms around herself as if she were cold. "Are you saying it could happen again?"

"What could?"

"Seeing you, my seeing you kill someone."

"It's likely, if you share my life."

"But I thought all that was behind you. I thought we were going to California and you would be different."

"Yeah," he said, looking into the fire. "Reckon I thought that, too."

"It's not true, then?"

He looked at her again. "I can't just walk away from my past, Johanna. There'll always be someone like Mawson showing up."

"He's a Ranger," she argued. "He can't touch you outside of Texas."

"I wouldn't count on that. Anyway, he's just one man. I could kill him and someone else would come along to take his place."

She stared at him with horror. "So you'll kill and kill and kill," she whispered, "and it'll never stop?"

"Reckon not, 'til someone kills me."

"God, Seth," she moaned, hanging her head, her tears catching firelight as they fell. He let her cry alone, knowing he had no solace to offer. Finally she looked up and hope shone from her eyes again. "We could go to México."

He smiled with melancholy. "You think that would be far enough?"

"South America, then. Europe. We have money, the world's a big place."

He studied her a moment. "What were you thinking on the ride here?"

She looked away, betraying her thoughts in that gesture of avoidance.

"You were afraid of me, weren't you?"

"Yes," she admitted, still not looking at him.

"You think you could live with that? You think I want to?"

She met his eyes across the distance. "I love you, Seth."

He nodded. "I love you, too. But it ain't enough, is it."

"Come to bed," she pleaded. "We can make it be enough if we try real hard."

"You think so?"

"Yes."

He sighed and stood up, then walked across to her, unbuckled his gunbelt and hung it on the bedpost. She was staring at the fire. He reached down and tilted her face to look into her eyes, and he saw the fear there. "I used to like bedding women who were afraid of me, but I've lost that."

"I'm not afraid of you," she answered bravely.

"You're lying," he smiled.

"Help me, Seth," she moaned. "I keep remembering Rosalinda and all that blood."

"You think fucking me is gonna help you forget?"

"Yes!"

He didn't believe it, but he said gently, "Take your clothes off. Let's find out."

She didn't move and he pulled her to her feet, unbuttoned her skirt and let it fall to the floor, unbuttoned her blouse and slipped it down her arms, dropping it too. She stood before him in her camisole and pantaloons and boots. "You gonna do it with your boots on?" he smiled.

She shook her head, but she couldn't look at him. He moved to the other side of the bed and undressed, watching her strip herself naked and slide under the covers. He lifted the blankets and slid in beside her, feeling her tremble against him. When he kissed her, her response was buried beneath her barely contained compulsion to escape. "I'm the same man I was before," he said, meeting her eyes. "This is your husband up here, remember me?"

She sobbed and clung to him, though her body was rigid. He tried everything he knew about loosening up a woman, but she was dry when he touched her, and he rolled away to crook an elbow over his eyes, leaving a chasm of emptiness on the bed between them. After a long time she curled close to him. He turned eagerly, craving her love, thinking maybe she was right and if he came inside her he could claim her again. He wet her with spit to ease his entry, rode her gently, and let himself come. She was flooded now with the heat of his love and he caressed her tenderly, trying to kindle some response, but she was beyond him. He stopped and lay still, then rolled his weight off her, holding her close beneath the covers.

"I'm sorry, Seth," she whispered. "I need time."

He kissed the top of her head as if he understood, and he did, he just couldn't share his life with a woman who held death against him.

23

In the morning, Esperanza was working at the stove when he came into the kitchen alone. He crossed the room and kissed her cheek. "How've you been?" he asked.

"Better'n you," she answered.

He moved away from her, to the cupboard where Ramon kept a bottle of whiskey, poured himself a drink and downed it fast, then put the bottle away.

"A little early, isn't it?" she asked with compassion as he met her eyes.

"I had a rough night," he said.

"Umm. And more to come. Did you accomplish what you went to El Paso to do?"

He nodded, turning away to stare out the window.

"I like your company more than any man's," she said softly, watching him, "but you better make yourself scarce in these parts."

"You're right," he said, not moving.

"I told you she'd be your death. Didn't I say that?"

"Yeah, you did."

"Then why aren't you saddling that sorrel you love so much? He serves you better than the girl."

"I should," he said.

"Why aren't you?"

"I don't know. I'm tired, I guess."

"Huh! a young wife will wear any man out. You don't have time for such foolishness. The law can track you here, then what will you do?"

"I don't know," he said again.

"I'd hate to see you hang."

"So would I," he laughed.

"Is no joke, Seth. Leave her here. We'll take care of her."

"You said you didn't want me to," he answered, facing her now.

"That was before she was your wife. I'd keep the Devil himself if you asked. Didn't we keep Rosalinda for you?"

He turned away again.

"Did you see her in El Paso?"

"Yeah."

"She's a crazy bitch. I'm surprised she didn't kill Johanna when she found out you were married."

"She tried to collect the bounty on me."

"And?"

"I killed her."

She concentrated on laying bacon to sizzle in the skillet. "How many does that make, Seth? Devery and his gun, that's two. Pilger, three. Rosalinda four. Do you think they won't work hard to track you?"

"There was another one," he said. "Rosalinda's lover."

"Ay, Seth. Sometimes I think you want the hand of God to strike you down, only you're so bad even He can't reach that far."

"Maybe He thinks this is more fun."

She crossed herself. "Your luck won't hold forever, Seth."

"I was a fool to get married, wasn't I?"

"Yes. And so was she. But you still have a chance, if you leave now and never come back. It pains me to say that. I'll miss you but I'd rather think of you alive someplace else than hung here."

"It's strange about Pilger," he said, watching Joaquín come from the stable and cross the yard to the outhouse. "I thought when he was dead, I wouldn't care what happened after."

"Now you find it's not true, eh? I'll tell you something else. Johanna's probably already pregnant. Think of your child. You want him to grow up without a father? The girl's only sixteen, how do you think she'll do on her own? Some other man will come along and claim her and her money. And he will hate the child of Seth Strummar. Think of that."

"You're full of cheer, ain't you, Esperanza?" he laughed bitterly.

She shook her head. "I'm full of dread. You should go now. I'll give you food and Ramon has a whole carton of .44's he bought just for you. Take them and go, Seth, so you have a chance to stay alive."

He watched Joaquín come out, stare across at the kitchen a moment, then return toward the stable. "You're right," he said. "Pack them up, will you?"

"They're already packed," she said, but he was out the door.

He caught Joaquín at the stable and laid his arm across his shoulders as they walked into the comforting smells of leather and horses. When they reached his sorrel he went into the stall alone and backed the horse out. "I need to ask a favor," he said, smoothing the blanket then tossing his saddle on.

"Anything," Joaquín said.

Seth looked at him over the back of the horse, wanting to tell him about Pilger but unable to bear the hurt in his eyes that he'd seen in Johanna's. He looked down to pull the cinch tight and tie it, then dropped the stirrup and met the kid's eyes again. "I need you to take Johanna to my father's in Austin. Can you do that?"

"Sí," the kid answered hesitantly. "Are you not coming with us?"

He threw a lock of his sorrel's red mane across its neck to lie smooth with the rest. "Sharing my company ain't healthy right now, Joaquín. I need to know she's taken care of."

"In such cases," he answered, his face brightening, "it is always best to turn to family."

"Why?" Seth asked bitterly.

Joaquín studied him carefully. "A person is stronger with kin. Do you not think this is true?"

"Not always," he said, "but I hope so for her."

Again, Joaquín watched him for a long moment. "Are you certain you wish to leave her behind?"

"Ain't a question of what I want," Seth replied tersely. "That lawman's right on our tail. He'll follow me and leave you alone."

"You also will be alone," Joaquín said.

Seth slid the bit into his sorrel's mouth then secured the bridle over its ears. "I can handle it. Can you?"

"Sí," he said again. "But I would rather help you."

"You are helping me. It's what I need you to do." He tied his saddlebags and bedroll on, then faced him. "There're plenty of vermin between here and Austin who could profit with my wife in their hands. You understand what I'm saying?"

"Sí," he said cautiously. "I won't let you down."

"There's only one way you could, and that's to quit and leave her alone. I want your word you'll see her safely to Austin."

"You have it," he said.

He smiled and held out his hand, knowing he was doing the kid a favor by parting ways with him. "Been a pleasure, Joaquín."

They clasped hands a long time, and even then Seth hated letting go of him. "Take care of yourself," he said gruffly, leading his sorrel out the door and across the yard, tying it in front of the room where Johanna was.

He went inside and saw she was half-dressed, washing her face in the bowl on the bureau. Their eyes met in the mirror and for a moment hers flashed with fear, then she hid it behind a smile.

"I'm leaving," he said from the door. "I've asked Joaquín to take you to Austin. Did you bring that paper the priest gave us in Zaragoza?"

"Yes," she said, drying her hands and crossing the room to pick up her blouse.

"Show it to my father and he'll take you in. I want you to stay there until you hear from me. Will you do it?"

She nodded, buttoning the blouse then stepping into her skirt and fastening it as she watched him.

"I'll get word to you soon as it's safe. It'll be a while, but don't think I've forgotten you."

"Take me with you," she pleaded from her distance.

He shook his head. "You'll slow me down."

"That isn't why you won't," she said.

"If I don't put a lot of distance between me and that Ranger, it'll mean a fight and I won't drag you into it." He looked out the door and saw Joaquín with Esperanza and Ramon by the kitchen, then looked again at the child he had made his wife. "Don't go back to El Paso. Get out of here today and take the northern route."

She crossed the room to stand before him. "Take me with you, Seth. Give me another chance."

"I don't want to do this, either," he lied. "But it's for the best."

"Do you promise to send for me?"

"As soon as I can see my way clear."

"I've forgotten your father's name."

"Abraham," he smiled. "He'll be happy to have you in his home." He bent his head and kissed her quickly. "Do everything Joaquín tells you. Promise me."

"I promise," she said, biting her lip.

"You're not going to cry, are you?"

"Yes," she said.

He smiled, but he couldn't bring himself to kiss her again. He turned his back, led his sorrel across the yard and shook hands with Ramon, thanking him for being a good friend. Esperanza held out the bag of supplies and he took them, then leaned down to kiss her cheek.

She held him close a long moment. "Vaya con díos, Seth."

He laughed, met Joaquín's eyes for one brief, final moment of regret, then swung onto his sorrel and rode away from the rising sun into the desert of New Mexico, toward Tombstone and the wide open territory of Arizona.

It didn't take Mawson and Cha long to catch their horses and go after the outlaw and his companions, but as soon as the tracks led across the river and into the Territory of New Mexico, Mawson stopped. The day was crisp and clear and nothing would disturb the trail the running horses were leaving behind, so he reined around and went back to Rosalinda's bordello.

"I want ya to come in with me, Cha," he said, dismounting and tying his horse to the porch. "Nothin' like an Apache to strike fear in a woman's heart, even a woman who beds a killer."

The kitchen was full of whores, hastily dressed and wide awake after the gunfight in the alley. They stared silently at the Ranger coming in, but when Cha followed, gasps were audible.

"Relax, ladies," Mawson smiled. "He ain't gonna hurt ya. Where's Rosalinda Montoya?"

After an awkward pause, one of the women said, "She ain't come down yet."

"None of ya thought to check on her?" he barked.

"She don't like bein' disturbed," another woman said.

"Well, don't let me disturb *you*," he retorted, stomping out of the kitchen, down the hall and up the stairs. He pushed her door open then stopped on the threshold. "Godalmighty," he breathed, taking a few steps closer then stopping again.

Cha followed him, quickly asking his Power for protection from the ghost. As Mawson moved to the windows and flung open the shutters, Cha watched the sudden flood of sunlight illuminate the corpse on the bed. He stepped closer and bent over the wound, noting there was just one slit beneath her ribs where a knife had slid upward to puncture her heart then been pulled out along the same path through her flesh. He looked up and met Mawson's eyes.

"Yeah, it's his work, ain't it," Mawson growled.

Cha nodded. "A man experienced with a knife," he said.

"Where d'ya think he learnt it? He's a bandit and a shooter."

Cha shrugged, looking down at where the blade had been cleaned on the bedsheets. Then he saw the blood on the carpet. "He dropped his knife," he said.

"What?" Mawson came around to the side of the bed. "Where is it?"

"He took the knife but there is blood from when it fell."

Mawson squatted down and saw what Cha had seen standing above it. "That means he was interrupted, don't it."

"Probably," Cha said.

Mawson looked up at the door from where he was, then he saw the express bag on the floor against the wall. He crossed and picked it up, opened it, stared in at the money, then pulled the transaction slip out. "Johanna Devery," he said to himself, putting it together that she had been the one to interrupt Strummar. If he'd had the money he wouldn't have left it behind, so the girl had it and in her shock at seeing her husband standing over a woman he'd murdered, she'd dropped and forgotten it. That told him two things: she was traveling broke and she'd seen the truth about the man she'd married. Mawson smiled. "What d'ya think, Cha? Think a li'l girl like we saw yesterday can love a killer like Strummar for long?"

The Apache met the beady eyes of the inferior man he followed. "A man with Power can achieve anything," he said.

Mawson frowned, then jerked his head toward the door. "Run down to the marshal's office and fetch that lazy no-account back here."

When he was alone, Mawson closed the door and stared at Rosalinda on the bed. "Ya should've vamoosed with Pilger like I told ya," he said to the dead face. "But ya wanted to stay and see him in chains. Well, ya saw him agin, din't ya? Only he wasn't wearin' no chains."

He walked over to the window and stared down at the two horses tied to the back porch, wondering how Strummar had found out that Rosalinda betrayed him. No one had heard the conversation, no one could have known outside of himself and the whore. Then he remembered he'd told Pilger when he advised him to hide out until it was over. "Goddamn," he muttered. "That means he got Pilger, too."

For one brief moment Mawson doubted himself. The outlaw seemed to have the luck of the innocent, always managing to stay one step ahead of the law, enlisting the help of nearly everyone he met, finding his enemies when there was no way he should have, killing them at the moment they should have been safest, riding out of town leaving a trail a fool could follow, then having it obliterated by a herd of goats or some other freak occurrence that no justice in God's creation should have provided. He turned around and looked at Rosalinda again, thinking he was the one using whores and heathens to bring the man down.

"There ain't nothin' supernat'ral 'bout it," he told Rosalinda as he stood in the bright sunlight, staring into the coagulated river of blood from her corpse. "He's right cozy with death, is all. But I ain't no stranger to it neither, and he and I are gonna share our blankets 'til one of us wakes up with a bullet in his brain."

When Marshal Campbell came into the room alone, Mawson looked out the window again at Cha standing with the horses, then threw the bag of money at the marshal. "Found it on the floor," he said. "The name inside is Devery but Mrs. Strummar dropped it. So when ya get the judge to write up the warrant, be sure he puts her name on it too." He moved toward the door.

"Wait a minute," the marshal protested. "What proof you got Strummar did this?"

He turned on the threshold. "She was helpin' me and he took his vengeance. If ya check along the Mesilla road, I think you'll find some more dirt he left behind for the law to clean up. Jus' look for buzzards and they'll lead ya to whatever's left of Pilger."

"Where you going?" the marshal asked.

"To kill a killer," Mawson said.

As he'd expected, the trail was easy at first. Then it led into the badlands and Cha had to walk along leading his horse to follow it. The sun went down when they were still way out in the desert and there was nothing they could do but camp and wait for light again. In a blustery wind under the gray sky of morning, the Apache led the Ranger up to the yard of a vineyard north of Mesilla. Cha assured him the outlaw was gone but had been there. Mawson didn't question how he knew that. He didn't care about the Apache's methods but had learned to trust his conclusions as if they were writ in blood. He yelled for whoever was inside to open the gate in the name of the law.

A short, fat Mexican well past his prime opened the wooden gate and stood in the narrow crevice with the wind blowing his serape across his belly, eyeing the two riders with suspicion.

"We're lookin' for a man travelin' with a young woman and a Mexican kid. Ya seen 'em?" Mawson barked.

The man shook his head. "We have seen no one since before Christmas, señor."

"Who's we?" Mawson asked.

"Me and my woman."

"Can ya give us breakfast, think?"

He could see the man wanted to refuse, but he opened the gate wider and let them pass. The compound was small and snug, the adobe wall nearly blocking the cold wind that swept across the valley with a bone-rattling chill. Cha took their horses into the stable as Mawson followed the man into a warm kitchen where a rotund woman stood cooking at the stove. Her eyes were black and hostile.

"Captain Earl Mawson of the Texas Rangers," he said, taking off his hat. "I'd be obliged for some warm vittles for me and my scout."

"This is New Mexico, señor," she said for an answer, her voice as unfriendly as her eyes.

"Yes, ma'am, I know that. I'm ridin' as a private citizen."

"But not for sport on such a cold day."

"No, I'm trackin' a man. Can ya see your way clear to feed us?"

"Sí, I can feed you," she said, turning her back as she worked at the stove.

Mawson dropped his hat on an empty chair and sat down at the table, taking in the rustic kitchen, the two doors leading to other rooms in the house, the man watching him from where he leaned against the wall. After a moment, Cha came in and hunkered down by the door, his sharp eyes watching the Mexicans for any treachery.

"This here's my Chiricahua scout, Cha. I din't catch your names."

"Ramon Gutierrez," the man said. "My woman is Esperanza."

"I heard of ya," Mawson said in a friendly tone. "Seems to me ya used to ride with the man I'm after, seven, eight years ago, down on the Rio Bravo near Laredo."

"I been there," Ramon answered.

"I'm lookin' for Seth Strummar. Ya know who I mean."

Ramon shook his head with an expression of stupidity. "I rode with many men," he shrugged.

"I'm sure ya've seen him since. We tracked him here."

"Like I said," he replied with an ingratiating smile. "We have seen no one since the end of December."

"That's peculiar, bein' as Cha tracked 'em right to your gate. And Cha's never wrong."

"Maybe he came," Ramon shrugged again. "But I didn't see him. Did you, mujer?"

She shook her head from where she stood frying fatback at the stove.

"I don't take kindly to bein' lied to," Mawson said.

"I have no reason to lie," Ramon answered.

"Mebbe ya been gone. Mebbe that's how he come and ya never saw him."

"No, señor, I never go no place," Ramon answered thoughtfully. "But a night or two ago I had too much tequila and forgot to lock the gate. In the morning I noticed some feed gone from the stable, but I heard or saw nothing. I slept like a baby all night, didn't I, Esperanza?"

"Huh. No baby ever snored like you, Ramon."

Ramon grinned at the Ranger, who didn't crack a smile. The woman began slapping tortillas flat and laying them on top of the stove to singe with heat. She flattened and browned several, tossing them aside as they were done, then cracked eggs into the sizzling pork fat. The pleasant aromas filled the warm kitchen as she poured two cups full of rich, dark coffee, then carried them to her guests. The one she set on the table well away from the Ranger, the other she carried to the Indian where he hunkered against the door. She held the cup down to him and smiled with her back to the man at the table. The only change in the Indian was a slight lessening of the coolness in his eyes.

"This man I'm trackin'," Mawson said, slurping the scalding coffee, "is a dang'rous desperado. He's killed at least two dozen men, near as we can figure."

The woman crossed herself, then turned the eggs in the skillet. The man shrugged. "Never heard of him," he said.

"Travelin' with his young wife and a Mexican kid, on jus' two horses, a black and a big chestnut."

Ramon shook his head.

"There's several rewards on his head. Comes to two thousand dollars all told, guaranteed by banks and the State of Texas. I'll give it to anyone gives me information I find out to be true."

"For such money, I wish I could help you," Ramon said.

Esperanza carried the plates of food to the men, sliding the Ranger's down the table and handing the other to the Indian hunkered on the floor. She waddled back to the stove and poured herself a cup of coffee, then stood sipping it with her feet planted firmly, not leaning against anything.

Mawson dug into the food, watching both of them, knowing they were lying. "All I'm int'rested in," he said around a forkful of eggs and fatback, "is where they might be goin'. Cha here can find out which direction they took, but if I knew their destination it might be I could cut 'em off."

There was no answer.

"This man, Strummar," Mawson said, "is gonna get his sooner or later. Jus' a matter of time. The thing of it is, if it's sooner, a few more people will be livin' out the time God give 'em." He watched them as he chewed.

The kitchen was silent except for him and Cha eating and the fluttering of the flames in the stove. Quietly Cha set his empty plate down, met the woman's eyes and nodded his thanks, then slipped out the door. Mawson pushed his plate away. "Can I have some more coffee, think?"

Esperanza carried the pot to the table and refilled his cup, avoiding his eyes.

"I know ya folks know this man," Mawson said, blowing on his coffee to cool it. "I admire loyalty, but it ain't like he's kin of your'n, and a friend like him is trouble." He pulled his sixgun and laid it on the table. "I could show ya what I mean."

"We know nothing, señor," Ramon said, putting a tremble of fear in his voice.

Mawson slurped his coffee, watching them. He picked up his gun and opened the chamber as if he wasn't sure it was loaded, then snapped it closed again, but didn't lay it down. "Ya love your woman, Ramon?"

"Sí," he answered miserably.

"If I was to shoot her foot, she wouldn't be able to do much work for a long spell. Even helpin' her back and forth to the outhouse would be a mighty inconvenience, wouldn't it?"

"Please don't hurt her, señor. We are pobres, if we knew anything we would tell you for the money."

"Well, ya know, I kinda doubt that," he said, pulling the hammer back with his thumb. The woman stared hatred with her black eyes.

"If this hombre is such a desperado as you say," Ramon argued in a wheedling tone, "do you think he would be so stupid as to tell us where he's going?"

"If he trusted ya he might," Mawson said, taking aim down the long silver barrel of his .45.

"No one can stand up to torture, señor. Desperados understand that."

"Ya know a lot about how desperados think, don'cha, Ramon?" he smiled.

"They are men, like all of us," he answered.

"Like you, mebbe."

"And you, señor, if you would shoot an innocent woman to gain what you want."

The door opened bringing in a gust of cold with Cha's return. He looked at the gun in Mawson's hand, then at the woman watching without fear. He thought she would have made a good Apache.

"What'd ya find?" Mawson asked.

"The girl and Mexican rode north on one horse. The man west alone."

"West, eh?" He stood up, still holding his gun aimed at the woman. "He ever mention a fondness for any town that way? Some li'l whore mebbe who tickled his fancy?"

The woman stared her hatred in silence until Mawson pulled the trigger. Then she fell with a cry and lay curled in a ball, holding her foot as blood seeped through her fingers.

"Pinche cabron," Ramon muttered.

"She's still got one good foot, Ramon," Mawson smiled. "If ya tell me now, mebbe ya can rig up a crutch to help her walk."

Except for Esperanza's moans, the kitchen was silent.

"I could turn Cha loose, ya know. Apaches don't use bullets."

Through his teeth, Ramon said, "We know nothing."

Mawson lowered the hammer on his gun and smiled at the Indian. "I believe we'd have to kill these two to get 'em to talk, and I don't guess even then they'd have much to say. Let's ride." He holstered his gun and picked up his hat. At the door, he turned back and smiled. "Thanks for the vittles," he said.

24

The desert of southwestern New Mexico stretched red beneath the sunset, the distant mountains in all directions shrouded with clouds. Seth was headed for Carrizalillo Spring where he knew he could replenish his water, but he wouldn't make it until long after dark. He reined his sorrel up on a promontory and scanned the terrain behind him with his spyglass. The two riders were still coming, so closely following his course he figured they must be tracking him.

A blocky man on a big bay with a smaller man on a buckskin. An Indian pony probably carrying an Apache by the accuracy of the tracking. Seth turned his horse and cantered down the slope and on toward the spring. His sorrel was in top condition and could push on through the night, which is what he intended to do. But he didn't delude himself that he was likely to lose the men behind him. He had two choices: keep pushing and hope to outdistance them through a calamity not of his making, or stand and fight.

The latter was always his inclination. He didn't like riding with trackers breathing down his neck, and he was curious as to who would care enough. If it was a bounty hunter, Seth figured he was doing the world a favor by eliminating him from the breeding stock. If a lawman, he'd already outdistanced his jurisdiction and was no better than a bounty hunter if he rode seeking another man's death. If it was Mawson, and he figured it was, he knew the Ranger wouldn't give up and he may as well choose his spot for the fight to come down. He was outnumbered two to one, but he'd faced worse odds than that often enough.

So Seth rode with his eyes open for a good place for an ambush. He wasn't in any hurry, figuring the farther they were from Texas, the less sympathy the Ranger would merit if word got out what happened. And it probably would, one way or another. Either Seth would be dead and Mawson crowing about it, or Mawson would be missing and Seth didn't think he had come without telling someone his intentions. He must have borrowed the scout from the garrison at Isleta, so Baylor probably knew what he was up to. As for the scout, it was anybody's guess who he thought he was tracking.

He stopped to rest his horse periodically, shivering in the cold while the sorrel munched on whatever dry fodder it could find. In the early light of dawn he reached the spring and filled his canteen, let the horse drink its fill, then moved on. Twice he filled the feedbag and waited until the horse had emptied it. That left him no more grain, and he knew he'd have to find a town to buy some. The next closest settlement was Fort Bowie but he wasn't eager to mingle with soldiers. Beyond that was Tombstone.

In between were the Chiricahua Mountains, country any Apache over twelve years old knew well. He wasn't likely to pull off a successful ambush among their narrow canyons and eerie hoodoos, so he circled south, flirting with the Méxican border. Easy enough to cross over and be safe from all but the boldest bounty hunter. But it behooved him to count the man behind him among their company. Whoever he was, he had already tracked him out of Texas, across New Mexico and into Arizona. The finer points of international law wouldn't likely stop him.

At dusk, he reined up in the foothills of the Pedregosa Mountains to survey his backtrail. They were still coming, slowly and inexorably, men who yielded to no temptation of warmth or whiskey to stop their pursuit. Seth was out of food and nearly out of water. His sorrel had been eating the scrub forage for two days now. He was pushing his limits and he knew it. Knew, too, that the men behind were in no better shape. He turned his horse and kicked it into a lope across the low valley toward Tombstone.

The desert spring he had sought was dry. He was surprised in the dead of winter, hoping to find at least some ice to melt. He'd risk a fire for water, not anything else. He stood in the sandy creekbed and rubbed his sorrel's nose. The horse nickered at his touch. "I know," he said. "I'm thirsty, too. But that sonofabitch won't let up. You think I should meet him in town?"

The horse gave no answer and Seth laughed. "Keeping quiet, eh? I don't blame you. You've never been tracked this hard, but I have. Back with Allister, it seemed like Rangers were always on our tail. They never followed us out of Texas, though. I wonder why it is this Captain Mawson hates me so much."

He stepped around to the side of the horse and ran his hands down the warmth of its long, lean legs. They were sound and he knew he was doing it as much for comfort as anything else. He stood up and looked back through the darkness, then swung on and headed toward the lights of Tombstone illuminating the sky. After a while, he said, "I sure would enjoy some rough whiskey right now."

The sorrel snorted as if in disapproval.

"Yeah, you're right. Stupid thing to be thinking about when I got death trailing me, ain't it? Guess I'm getting punchy without food so long. I'd try shooting something but the noise would only help that bastard behind us. Besides, I couldn't build a fire and I ain't hungry enough to eat raw meat. I've heard Apaches eat cactus. He's prob'ly cutting some right now. Wish I knew which ones would help and which kill me. Apaches can run through the desert all day holding a mouthful of water. Ain't that something? Not that I'd want to run through the desert, but I can appreciate the discipline it'd take. They're tough, that's for damn sure. Don't have much respect for us, though. They think we're stupid."

The sorrel snorted again and he laughed. "You don't have to agree with them, Rojo. You're lucky you're a horse and don't have to think about nothing but your next feed. You've even been cut so don't have to worry about your cock driving you crazy half the time. I had me an Apache whore once. Well, she was only half-Apache. I learned some of their ways but nothing that seems helpful right now. She taught me most of what I know about using a knife, though. She was a fine little lady. Had that long black hair.

Apaches are vain about their hair, you know that? They consider it a source of power. Lot of other things, too. Carvings of animals they've decided are kin, signs and such, prophecy and magic.

"Did you hear what Johanna said? 'Make all the ugliness go away,' she said. Makes you wonder what she saw when she looked at me, doesn't it? Married herself a killer then cried 'cause she saw a little blood. Well, it was more'n a little but goddamn what'd she expect? I shouldn't blame her, though. I'm twice as old and the one to blame. Shouldn't have told Joaquín I wouldn't take my vengeance, either. You know, for a while I thought he was Jeremiah come back to me. Not the same man, I know that, but kin just the same. He made me think about what I was doing the way Jeremiah used to, how when I'd be mean back when we were kids and he'd look at me with his blue eyes all full of hurt. It was worse than if he'd cursed me. Joaquín's eyes are dark as midnight but they're the same as my brother's in that respect. Damn! I wish I could explain about all those years I searched every hellhole in the Southwest for Pilger, all those times I listened to that ugly story told again in some gloomy saloon. A man doesn't just let go of something that strong 'cause of pretty words spoken in a parlor. Any more than he becomes a good husband 'cause he was married in a church."

Tombstone was so close he could hear the mariachis singing in the cantinas on the outskirts. He remembered a woman he'd known who sang in one of the saloons there, sad ballads of love and death. "Johanna has the deepest blue eyes," he said with sudden longing. "When she'd look at me with all that love, I felt like the goddamned sun in the blue sky of her eyes."

He reined up and stared back through the darkness for a long time. "Apaches worship the sun, you know that, Rojo?"

The sorrel flicked its ears toward the sound of renewal in his voice. Seth looked beyond the lights of Tombstone to the Dragoon Mountains, where the mighty Cochise had once had his stronghold. "There won't be anyone else up there," he said. "Just the three of us and a lot of ghosts." He smiled and turned his horse toward the foothills.

All night they climbed a narrow canyon. Under the starlight he spotted a bank of snow and swung down and ate some, watching back in the direction he'd come. The sorrel pawed the snow away and munched on the frozen grass beneath. Seth let him eat a while, then continued their ascent into the homeland of the Chiricahuas.

They were on the west side of the mountains when dawn came with a gray light and little warmth. Finally the sun crested the ridge and began to thaw the frozen air. He stopped and let his horse rest, watching down the way he'd come for any sign, any flight of bird or flash of metal to tell him his pursuers were close behind. They were coming, he had no doubt of that, but tracking by starlight was slow work even for Apaches.

A jumble of boulders caught the sun and he moved toward them, thinking to rest in the comfort of their warmth. Then he stopped dead still. On a flat rock a rattler was coiled, stealing the warmth he'd intended to take for himself. It was early yet and he knew the snake couldn't move fast, and also that he could stomach snakemeat raw, he'd done it before. So he drew his knife and approached from behind. He stuck his blade in behind the snake's head and with the patience of a predator held it pinned to the stone until the long body stopped writhing in the agony of its death throes. Then he skinned it carefully with just one long slit down its belly, and hunkered in the sun working to chew the tough flesh.

If he hadn't been so hungry, it wouldn't have tasted at all good, but it was pure protein and he could feel himself start to revive as soon as it hit his stomach. Still, he didn't eat much. He threw the rest into the forest and ate more snow as he stared down at the skin with the rattlers and head still attached, the jaw open as if in warning. In the forest he found a fallen branch taller than he was, and he carried it back and planted it deep in the sandy bed of the arroyo.

He picked up the snake and cut a notch under its jaw, being careful not to sever the head by connecting the fatal cut with the one he was making now, and he hung the skin on the stick facing downhill. With the tip of his knife he pried the jaws open wider and wedged a Gold Eagle between the fangs, the uplifted wings of the bird of prey still shadowed in the morning light. He smiled into the dead eyes of the snake. "Thanks, compadre," he said, then he caught his horse and rode higher into the mountains.

When the sun was at its apex, he spotted bear scat on the ground and reined up sharp. "Careful, Rojo," he warned. "Don't step in it." He edged the horse sideways until its hooves had cleared any danger of marring the pile, then he swung down and led the horse over to a slope of wild wheat bobbing in the wind. The sorrel nickered as it lowered its head to graze. Seth tied his reins to ride the horse's neck and went back and stared down at the scat on the ground. He dug into his pocket again and pulled out another gold coin. Carefully he placed the eagle face up in the center, then he looked down the mountain and smiled again.

A little farther on he finally found water, a spring gushing from high on a red cliff. Ice had crusted all around it, but through its center bled a flow still warm with the heat of the earth's heart. He swung down and lay on his belly and drank deeply from the pool, his horse's face close to his, both of them taking in the refreshing liquid of life. In the bright sun of afternoon, the wet sand around the pool was soft. Seth stood up and looked down at all the prints in the mud: deer, coyote, fox, rabbit, even a few smudged pawprints from bear and some from birds large enough to be eagles. He drew his knife and in the center of the clearest print left from his own hand, he etched a half-moon with the tip of his blade.

He left that message for the scout who was such an excellent tracker, in the hope he'd see it both as a compliment and an invitation. Then he rode higher into the mountains until finally he reached the top. He unsaddled his horse and hobbled it to graze so it could replenish its strength for the descent, then carried his rifle onto the highest promontory in all the range and sat down in the falling sun to wait.

In the gray light of dawn, Cha stood up from where he'd been studying the ground and said, "He has gone into the mountains."

"That don't make no sense," Mawson argued. "All night we been seein' the lights of Tombstone. Why would he turn away from whiskey and women to go back into the wilderness?"

Cha shrugged, watching the Ranger stare toward the town.

"Goddamn," Mawson said. "He must be as thirsty and horny as I am."

The Apache waited to see if the Ranger's lust would be stronger than his hatred for the man they were tracking.

"Ya sure?" Mawson asked.

"He went into the mountains," Cha said.

Mawson stared up at the peaks still hidden in darkness. "Sonofabitch," he said. "Okay, lead on."

As soon as Cha was sure the man they were tracking was following the arroyo, he climbed back on his mustang and rode again, watching only the sides of the canyon for any hint that a horse had clambered over its walls. He saw none, and often enough to keep him honed in the right direction, he found the evidence that he was still on the trail.

All morning they climbed through the narrow passage, and when the sun was almost overhead he caught a flickering of gold catching its light. He studied the metallic gleam as he edged his pony forward, then reined up abruptly at sight of the snake. He dismounted and walked slowly up to the skin hanging from the stick. Within its jaws he saw the golden eagle shining in the sunlight, its beak open and its wings lifted for flight.

Mawson edged his horse forward and sat staring at it, too. "What's it mean?" he growled.

"That he knows we are following him."

"Course he knows. He ain't stupid. But why'd he leave this here?"

The Apache looked up at the scowling face of the Ranger. "What does it mean to you?"

Mawson shrugged. "A threat, mebbe, or a hint of a bribe."

Cha mounted his horse, edged it forward to come abreast with the Ranger and meet his eyes. "A deadly snake, so a threat, yes. But not money: an eagle between its fangs."

"So?"

"He's telling us we are tracking death."

"His death," Mawson barked.

"Perhaps," Cha said, nudging his horse higher up the canyon.

They rode for hours, their ascent laborious through the cold day. In mid-afternoon, Cha reined up and stared down beneath his mustang's belly. Mawson stopped beside him and looked at the shit with another gold coin stuck in the center.

"What's that mean?" he asked with ill-humor.

"It is the sign of a bear."

"So?"

Cha looked up the canyon in the direction of the man he was tracking. Bears walked on two feet and were kin to men. No Apache would willingly kill one for fear of harming a relative, someone who had been so bad he wasn't allowed entrance to the eternal world but was condemned to walk the earth again. Cha didn't know how the white eyes knew that, but he knew the man was telling only the Apache who followed that they shared knowledge. And again, unlike the Ranger he was serving, Cha saw not money placed in the sign, but the Power of an eagle.

"What's it mean?" Mawson bellowed belligerently.

Cha met his eyes. "Maybe that money is shit," he joked.

"I ain't after money but blood," Mawson said. "Let's go."

In the dying light of day they came to the spring. Mawson dropped to his belly and drank eagerly with the horses, but Cha stood staring down at the palm print with the half-moon etched in its center. The line was so fine it could only have been drawn with the tip of a knife, and again Cha looked up the canyon, appreciating the compliment and marveling that a white eyes would know that a man seeking to share the ways of wisdom drew a half-moon in the shaman's palm. Cha smiled, wondering who was the possessor and who the seeker of Power.

Mawson raised himself on his knees and saw the smile. "What'd ya find?" he asked.

Cha nodded down at the sign. Mawson stood up, walked over to look down at the handprint of his enemy in the mud, and shrugged. "So he was thirsty, too," he said.

Cha stared at him a moment, realizing the white eyes hadn't even seen the sign drawn in the palm, then he moved aside to drink from the spring. He had to work at not laughing because the Ranger was so stupid. He risked his life fighting Apaches yet had never bothered to learn the secrets of their hearts. The man they were tracking had not only learned, he understood. And Cha felt an affinity for his prey.

He mounted his mustang and rode on toward the crest until finally they came to the highest plateau. Shimmering in the red light of dusk they saw the man's horse grazing on the brown grass. Cha dismounted and let his own buckskin loose with the sorrel.

"Where is he?" Mawson wanted to know.

"Close by," Cha answered.

"I know that," Mawson said impatiently. "He won't get out of the mountains without his horse. But where is he, Cha?"

Cha shrugged.

Mawson raised his eyes to the peaks all around. "Go find him. Don't let him see ya. Jus' find out where he is and come back, then we'll trap him 'tween us."

Cha met his eyes. "What will you do while I look?"

"I'll wait here," he said. "If he comes back, I'll be ready."

Cha nodded. "I'll find him," he said.

He searched the meadow where the sorrel grazed, finding in the frozen grass a path where the blades had been bent beneath a man's weight. He followed the trail and saw the bootprints clearly in the sand between the rocks, telling him the man was making no effort to hide. His path led toward the highest peak and Cha wondered if he would find an eagle there, since the man's confidence in his Power was so great that he invited a conference with his predator. Cautiously Cha approached the promontory. When he was still obscured behind the final turn, he raised his rifle, then stepped around the boulders and met the gray eyes watching him.

The man too held his rifle ready to fire, and for a long moment they stood on the peak and met each other's eyes through the sights of their weapons. Then the man smiled. Cha lowered his rifle the barest of increments, and boldly the man swung his aside. Holding it with one hand on the barrel, he leaned it against a rock and let go of it, his eyes not breaking their hold on Cha's. He still wore a sixgun and the knife he was so adept at using, and Cha knew if he fired now, the man would retaliate with death. He lowered his own rifle and set it aside.

The man hunkered down on the rocks warm with the last of the sun and looked up at Cha with an invitation to talk. Cha moved forward and hunkered near him, both of them sitting on their heels, ready to regain their feet at the least hint of provocation.

"Name's Seth Strummar," the man said softly.

"Tcha-nol-haye," he said.

"You're a mighty fine tracker, Tcha-nol-haye."

"My teacher was Geronimo."

"I'm honored."

Cha nodded. "I, also. I saw the man whose throat you cut in El Paso, and the woman whose heart you stopped with one stroke of your blade. Any fighter can learn to use a gun, but the knife is a weapon for true warriors."

"I was taught by an Apache," he said.

Cha smiled. "The young woman who went north with the Mexican is your wife?"

He nodded.

"You were wise to send her away. Like the army, Mawson has no mercy. He shot your friend, the woman of Ramon."

He winced. "Did he kill her?"

"He shot her foot, hoping she would tell where you'd gone. She would have made a good Apache."

The man smiled. "You know why Mawson's tracking me?"

"He says you have killed many white eyes."

"Seems to me," he answered with a soft chuckle, "that should put us on the same side of the field, Tcha-nol-haye."

He studied the gray eyes a long moment. "I met your friend, the Mexican, by the river in El Paso. He told me you were his teacher." A warmth flickered in the eyes watching him, and Cha knew the man had parted from his friend with regret. "He also told me we were brothers," Cha smiled, "but I never learned his name."

"Joaquín Ascarate."

He nodded. "We spoke of mercy and vengeance. Our friend is untested."

"He hasn't yet killed."

"Is that what he sought to learn from you?"

The man winced again, then said, "I tried to learn when not to from him."

Again Cha stared into the gray eyes for a long moment. "Did you learn this?" he finally asked.

The man shook his head.

"Sometimes a lesson is like a seed," Cha said. "It lies in the ground for many years, and then an especially sweet rain comes and it blossoms with fruit."

The gray eyes smiled. "Sometimes a man learns his greatest lessons from his enemy."

"Can my friend's teacher be my enemy?"

"Reckon that depends on what you think of his wisdom."

"I think he is wise in the ways of death."

"Is that enough?"

"Only by staying alive can a man learn the wisdom of life. Mawson seeks your death."

The man nodded. "There's no need for two men to die."

"Or to kill," Cha said.

The man smiled, waiting with a discretion that Cha felt honored them both.

"At first sun of dawn," he finally said, "I pray to Ussen. Neither white eyes nor Apache disturbs my prayers."

"May Ussen spread pollen before the moccasins of your children."

His heart warmed at hearing the ancient blessing. "Walk softly, Man Who Knows Death. Your own is as near as the thunder of your heart." Then quietly he rose and returned down the mountain to the white eyes waiting below.

"What'd ya find?" Mawson demanded.

"We should wait," Cha answered. "He will return for his horse."

"What's he doin' out there without it?"

"Looking for food perhaps."

"Then we'll hear his gun, won't we?"

"Unless he uses his knife."

"He's good with it," Mawson scoffed, "but I ain't never known a man could hunt with a knife."

Cha gave no answer, moving silently to take his bedroll down from his saddle and shake it out. "He won't be back before dawn," he said.

Mawson wondered how he knew that, but Cha was never wrong. He watched the Apache roll himself in his blanket and go to sleep. They'd come a long way tracking Strummar, and if Cha said he wouldn't return before dawn, Mawson figured he might as well get some rest and face him fresh.

When the constellation of Orion dipped its bow beneath the western horizon, Seth rose from where he'd been sleeping and started down the mountain. The other stars were just beginning to dim in the black sky, fading to the barest tinge of gray. Quietly he approached the meadow where his horse grazed with that of his enemy and the mustang of the Apache. He stood by his sorrel, seeing how the Ranger slept near his gear, preventing his escape unless he went without his horse.

As the eastern horizon began to seep the colors of dawn, first a golden glow like a halo above the peaks, then the highest clouds chalky with the soft purple of a martyr's blood, Seth watched Tcha-nol-haye rise from his blanket and walk toward the new day. High into the mountains he walked, carrying his rifle. When he stopped, he raised his arms and stood silhouetted against the sky to greet his god. Silently Seth moved into the camp.

Mawson still slept in the stupor of ignorance as Seth sat down crosslegged directly in front of him. With his rifle beside him and his sixgun still in his holster, he drew his knife and waited for his enemy to wake up.

The Ranger stirred in the deadly dawn. He turned on his back taking in air with a greedy gulp, scratched his groin, then rolled onto his side and looked into the flash of sun on the steel of the knife. His hand gripped his gun beneath the tangle of blankets just as the tip of the blade pressed against his neck.

"Another move will be your last," Seth said.

"What're ya waitin' for?"

"I want to know why you tracked me so hard."

Mawson snorted. "Two dozen corpses on your head oughta be reason enough."

"Not for a man like you."

"I'll give ya the name of one. Jeremiah Strummar."

Seth held back from thrusting the blade deep into the throat speaking the name of his brother against him, held it back just enough that he didn't pierce the artery but blood ran down the Ranger's neck.

"Ya can kill me," Mawson growled. "But ya can't kill the law."

"I don't even want to. I just want it to leave me alone."

"Too late for that. Your fate is writ in the blood ya've shed."

"Doesn't have to be yours."

The Ranger's eyes were calculating. "Ya tellin' me ya'd ride away and let me live?"

"If you go back to Texas and leave me be."

"Go on, get outta here then. I won't stop ya."

"Hand over your gun."

"What for? I said ya could go."

"I don't believe you, Mawson," Seth smiled.

"I'm gonna pull the blanket back so ya can see my gun, then ya can get it yourself."

"All right."

Slowly he tugged the blanket off himself, revealing the pistol at his side. Seth took it, then gained his feet. "Get up," he said. "Move away from the gear."

Mawson obeyed him, and Seth held the Ranger covered as he bent to collect his rifle, bridle, and blanket with his saddle. He managed to do it without putting the knife or pistol down, then hefted his outfit and backed toward his horse, turned it so he could watch Mawson as he smoothed the blanket on, his knife in one hand, the gun in the other.

Mawson's gaze kept flicking to a point behind Seth, and he figured Tcha-nol-haye had returned. Seth remembered how for years he'd told himself that once Pilger was dead he wouldn't care what came after. Joaquín had changed that by resurrecting the love of his brother, and Seth decided maybe Mawson brought justice after all. Not in any way the Ranger imagined but in the person of Tcha-nol-haye, who had made friends with Joaquín one lonely night along the Rio Bravo.

With the knife still in his hand, he tossed the gun onto the grass at his feet then bent to retrieve the cinch from where it dangled beneath his horse's belly. He pulled it through the metal ring, yanked it tight and tied the knot, then swung into the saddle. He had delivered mercy and now the test was his, he had to turn his back to find out if Joaquín's friend would save him.

When he reined his horse toward the peaks and the trail leading down the other side of the mountain, he was facing Tcha-nol-haye. Seth watched for the truth of his influence to be reflected in the Apache's dark eyes. Suddenly Cha raised his chin to point. Seth whirled and impelled his knife across the emptiness into the heart of the Ranger.

Mawson staggered backward from the blow. He fell to his knees, dropping his rifle and clutching his chest with impotent hands. Two pairs of eyes watched his death, then met in unison across the silence of the mountain meadow. Seth smiled at Joaquín's friend, swung down and walked over to retrieve his knife.

Blood oozed across the frozen grass, reminding him of Rosalinda. Neither she nor Mawson would have died if they'd left him alone, and that made him think of Johanna. He had sent her to Texas, the one place he could never go, but he'd sent her with Joaquín. He eased his weapon from the fatal wound, then looked at Tcha-nol-haye watching him, and Seth knew some ties could never be broken.

BACKTRAIL

BY

ELIZABETH FACKLER

1

Joaquín's first thought when he woke up was to wonder what had happened inside Rosalinda's bordello back in El Paso. When they had arrived in Mesilla seeking sanctuary the night before, he had watched Seth slide his arm around Johanna's waist and seen her flinch with fear, and Joaquín had known everything was different.

He dressed quickly and carried his bedroll down the ladder, fed the horses, then shivered in the cold wind as he crossed the courtyard to the latrine. When he came out he looked toward the house, but his suspicions told him not to intrude so he headed back for the stable.

Behind him, the kitchen door opened and he turned to see Seth coming toward him. Joaquín met his friend's eyes and the hurt he saw stopped him from calling a greeting. He wondered again what had happened at Rosalinda's, but Joaquín wouldn't ask.

Seth was tall and well-built, in every way the opposite of Joaquín, who was slight and dark. He was only eighteen while Seth had passed thirty, but Seth was the superior in much more than years. He was experienced in staying alive, effecting his will, achieving things Joaquín could only admire. When Seth laid his arm across his shoulders as they entered the stable, Joaquín felt honored by the gesture of affection.

They walked down the aisle of stalls to where Seth's horse was just finishing its grain, and Joaquín felt a sudden twinge of loss as Seth went into the stall alone and backed his sorrel out. He tried to argue with himself that he hadn't lost anything, but the suspicion wouldn't be denied.

Seth smoothed the blanket on his horse's back without looking at him and said, "I need to ask a favor."

"Anything," Joaquín answered, watching him settle his saddle onto the blanket, then lean beneath the belly for the cinch.

Seth stood up and met his eyes across the back of the horse and Joaquín had never seen such sorrow in his friend, not even on that last day in El Paso when they'd talked of the man who had lynched Seth's brother.

Seth looked down to pull the cinch tight and tie it, then dropped the stirrup and met his eyes again. "I need you to take Johanna to my father in Austin. Can you do that?"

"Sí," he answered hesitantly. "Are you not coming with us?"

Seth threw a lock of his sorrel's red mane across its neck to lie smooth with the rest, then said, "Sharing my company ain't healthy right now, Joaquín. I need to know she's taken care of."

"In such cases," Joaquín conceded, though he felt confused at the sudden change, "it is always best to turn to family."

Seth smiled bitterly. "Why?"

Seeing the mockery in his eyes, Joaquín considered his answer carefully. "A person is stronger with kin. Do you not think this is true?"

"Not always," Seth said, his voice hurt, "but I hope so for her."

Softly, Joaquín asked, "Are you certain you wish to leave her behind?"

"Ain't a question of what I want," Seth replied tersely. "That lawman's right on our tail. He'll follow me and leave you alone."

"You also will be alone," Joaquín said.

Seth slid the bit into his sorrel's mouth, then secured the bridle over its ears. "I can handle it. Can you?"

"Sí," he said again. "But I would rather help you."

"You are helping me. It's what I need you to do." He tied his saddlebags and bedroll on, then faced him. "There're plenty of vermin between here and Austin who could profit with my wife in their hands. You understand what I'm saying?"

"Sí," he said cautiously. "I won't let you down."

"There's only one way you could, and that's to quit and leave her alone. I want your word you'll see her safely to Austin."

"You have it," he said.

Seth smiled and held out his hand. "Been a pleasure, Joaquín."

He was saying goodbye and Joaquín was speechless with the enormity of the change.

"Take care of yourself," Seth said gruffly, letting go of his hand. He led his sorrel out of the stable and across the bright, cold yard to tie it in front of the room where Johanna was.

Joaquín watched as Seth opened the door but didn't go in, merely stood there suspended between his impending departure and the wife he was leaving behind; then he walked across the courtyard and stood beside Esperanza, who had come from the kitchen. Ramon was there too, and the three of them met each other's eyes but said nothing. Joaquín looked at the calico bag Esperanza held, guessing it was food for Seth to take with him. It felt so final, this parting, and Joaquín wasn't prepared for it. He had counted on following Seth's lead, learning to be a man under his guidance. Now he was to take Johanna to Texas while Seth rode into the wilderness alone. Joaquín wanted to go with him but he'd already given his word, and he'd give it again, he'd do anything Seth asked.

Seth spoke with Johanna from where he stood in the door, and Joaquín saw her come and stand before him with pleading eyes. Joaquín looked away to give them privacy, though if he'd wanted privacy Seth would have closed the door. Their love had been a pleasure to watch, and Joaquín wondered what could have happened that Seth wouldn't even be alone with her now.

He turned away from his wife and led his sorrel across the yard to where the three of them stood waiting. He shook hands with Ramon and thanked him for being a good friend. Esperanza held out the bag of supplies and he took them, then leaned down to embrace the short, broad woman and kiss her goodbye.

She held him close a long moment and Joaquín heard her whisper, "Vaya con Díos, Seth."

He laughed, a sound without joy as he met Joaquín's eyes for one painfully brief moment of regret, then he swung onto his sorrel and rode out of the yard, leaving them alone in a silence broken only by the wind.

Joaquín looked at Johanna standing in the door, tears glistening on her face as she watched Ramon closing the gate, then she disappeared inside the room again. He walked across and stood in the door as Seth had. Johanna was only sixteen and looked almost a child in her leather skirt covering the tops of her high boots, her blouse stretched tight over her small breasts, as she settled her black hat on the lustrous brown of her short-cropped hair. "Are you ready to leave?" he asked softly.

She turned and looked at him, her face streaked with tears. "I failed him, Joaquín," she said in a tiny voice, "and he sent me away."

"Because he is thinking of your safety," he argued.

She half-laughed, a pitiful heart rending sound. "He doesn't want me any more."

"If that were true, he wouldn't send you to his father's, but back to El Paso."

"Do you think he'll write?" she asked hopefully.

"Did he say he would?"

"Yes, but . . ." she stopped, then whispered again, "I failed him, Joaquín."

"Seth does not make promises he doesn't keep."

"What did he promise in the marriage vows?"

Joaquín thought back, remembering the ceremony in the church in Zaragoza. "To take care of you always," he answered.

"Does it count if it was in Spanish and neither of us knew what we were promising?"

"It was in the eyes of God. It counts most of all," he said.

She smiled sadly. "Seth doesn't believe in God."

Joaquín shuddered at the loneliness of such a thought, but he said only, "He believes in himself and his word, and he understood what it meant to marry you. By the time we get to Austin you will find a letter waiting."

"Do you think so?"

He nodded. "Pack up quickly. I will get the horse."

2

The winter dusk was threatening snow when they rode their one horse into Tularosa. Joaquín reined up in front of the only tendejón and scanned the village as Johanna slid off over the rump. He swung down and tied the reins to the portal, then pulled his rifle from its scabbard. Still looking around warily, he held her elbow as they walked into the low adobe building.

The smoky room was warm and fragrant with coffee hot on the stove. He chose a corner table, leaned his rifle in the shadow and sat down with his back to the wall. She folded her arms and rested her head on them, her face hidden by her hat. He watched her a moment, then called in Spanish across to the proprietor that they wanted something warm to eat and drink.

He brought two mugs of coffee and set them down, studying Johanna briefly, then meeting Joaquín's eyes. "Hay pollo y arroz, señor," he said. "¿Le quiere usted?"

"Sí, por favor," Joaquín answered, leaning back to tilt his chair against the wall as he surveyed the room. Except for the proprietor he had thought it empty, but now he saw that another man sat in the opposite corner, watching them with more than passing interest. Joaquín nodded as their eyes met, then took off his hat. As he passed it in front of him to lay it on the table, he slipped the keeper strap off his pistol.

When the proprietor brought the plates of chicken and rice, Johanna sat up and wiped her hands on her skirt. Joaquín waited until she'd finished eating, then while she surveyed the room he ate his own supper, a reciprocity of vigilance he had decided they should perform. In the day of riding and listening to Johanna cry, Joaquín had realized the dangers of escorting an outlaw's wife across unknown territory. Besides the lawmen who might track them, there was also the threat of bounty hunters.

When the proprietor brought the coffeepot to refill their cups, Joaquín looked up and asked softly, "Can you tell me, señor, if there is a hotel in this town?"

"Señora Eschevez has rooms to let," he answered. "Her house is half a mile east on the Lincoln road. That'll be four bits for supper."

Joaquín took a silver half-dollar from his pocket and laid it on the table. "Gracias, señor," he said. "It was good."

The man nodded, slid the coin off the table and returned to the stove.

Joaquín whispered to Johanna, "Do you recognize the man in the corner?"

She looked across the room then shook her head.

"He seems to have an interest in us."

She shrugged, ignorant of the danger. "We should buy another horse, Joaquín. We'll do better with two."

"To get a good one will take all our money," he answered, not for the first time.

"Where do you think he went?" she asked forlornly.

"México, maybe."

"We should have gone with him."

"He didn't want us to," he said, also not for the first time.

"We could steal one," she whispered.

He met her eyes, bright blue even in the gloom. "Do you wish to show up at his father's on a stolen horse?"

"I don't want to go there at all," she replied.

"It's what he told you."

"You don't want to go either," she said.

"I promised I would take you."

She leaned closer to whisper, "I promised him I'd never steal again, too, but promises can be broken."

"Do you think it would be easy to find him? It's not like we can just ride into a town and ask if he's been there. That would do more harm than good. We should go to his father's and wait. Didn't he say he'd say he'd write you there?"

"Do you believe he will?"

"When he thinks it is safe."

"It never will be, though, will it?"

Joaquín shrugged.

"It's because I was upset at seeing Rosalinda," she

whispered desperately. "I tried to make it up to him but he didn't believe me after that."

"What did you see?" he asked.

She looked down. "He killed her," she whispered.

Joaquín stared at her. "Why?" he finally managed to ask.

Johanna raised her eyes, shiny with tears in the lamplight. "Do you know who Pilger was?"

"The man who lynched Seth's brother."

Her voice strained against crying as she whispered, "After he left us, he ran into Pilger on the road and killed him. Hung him long and slow, is how he said it." While Pilger was dying, he told Seth that Rosalinda had betrayed him to the Rangers, so he rode back to El Paso and killed her too." She sobbed, looking down again and hiding her face as she struggled to control her tears. "I walked in right after he'd done it. There was blood all over his knife, Joaquín."

Joaquín was struck dumb. He had though he'd convinced Seth to leave Pilger to God, and he understood now why his eyes had been so full of sorrow as he said goodbye. Joaquín felt bitter that his victory had been stolen.

Why hadn't God given Seth time to strengthen his resolve? Why had He put an irresistible temptation directly in front of him at the very moment when he was on the road to a new life? He had been in the act of leaving his past behind, intending to take his wife to California where he could live clean. Joaquín felt a cold rage at God's betrayal after he'd tried so hard to save his friend. He looked across the room and met the eyes of the man watching them.

"Let's go," he said to Johanna. "This is not the place to talk."

She rose obediently as he picked up his rifle and they walked out into the rapidly falling darkness. He let her ride in the saddle now and swung up behind to hold the reins with his arm around her as he turned the horse east into the mountains.

WESTERN ADVENTURE
FROM TOR